The tank rocked and vi... of the chase was upon ... ...ger was forgotten, death was forgotten, the very war was forgotten. They only knew they had to kill . . . The figures in khaki were no longer men, no longer soldiers. They were wild beasts who had to be crushed . . .

They laughed aloud as they crushed their prey beneath them. They shouted in triumph as their victims cowered in holes . . . and then they turned towards them and blasted them out of existence.

By Sven Hassel

The Commissar
OGPU Prison
Court Martial
The Bloody Road to Death
Blitzfreeze
Reign of Hell
SS General
March Battalion
Liquidate Paris
Monte Cassino
Assignment Gestapo
Comrades of War
Wheels of Terror
The Legion of the Damned

MARCH
BATTALION

SVEN HASSEL

Translated from the French by
Jean Ure

CASSELL

Cassell Military Paperbacks

Cassell
Orion House
5 Upper St Martin's Lane
London WC2H 9EA
An Hachette Livre UK company

First published in Great Britain in 1970
by Corgi
This Cassell Military Paperbacks edition 2007

10 9 8 7 6 5 4 3 2 1

British Library Cataloguing-in-Publication Data.
A catalogue record for this book is available
from the British Library.

ISBN 978-0-7528-8228-4

Printed in Great Britain by Clays Ltd, St Ives plc

The Orion Publishing Group's policy is to use papers that
are natural, renewable and recyclable products and made
from wood grown in sustainable forests. The logging and
manufacturing processes are expected to conform to the
environmental regulations of the country of origin.

MARCH BATTALION

EDITOR'S NOTE

The character who in this book is called
'Little John' has appeared in other novels
by Sven Hassel under the name 'Tiny'.

'It was the Spanish Civil War,' said Barcelona Blum, spitting casually through the open side panel of the Russian tank in which we were travelling. 'I started off fighting for one side and ended up fighting for the other. To begin with I was a miliciano in the Servicios Especiales. Then the Nationalists got hold of me, and after I'd managed to convince them I was only an innocent German who'd been pressganged into service by General Miaja, they shoved me into the 2nd Battalion, 3rd Company, and made me fight for them, instead. Though mind you, as far as I was concerned there wasn't any great difference between the two sides in any case .... In the Especiales we used to round up everyone suspected of being a Fascist or a fifth columnist and take them off to the Calle del Ave Maria. In Madrid. We used to line 'em up against the wall of the abattoir. The sand there was so dry the blood used to soak right up in a matter of seconds. No need to bother with cleaning operations ... Mostly we preferred to shoot them standing up, but some of the buggers just curled into a heap and you couldn't budge them for love or money. At the last minute they always used to shout, 'Long live Spain!' ... Of course, when I got nabbed by the Nationalists it was just the same thing in reverse. Only difference was, they made us shoot them sitting down, with their backs turned. But it all came to the same thing in the end. They still used to shout "Long live Spain!" before they died.

'Funny thing, that: they all thought they were patriots. But when it came down to it, there was only one way of showing you were on the right side. You had to denounce someone. It didn't matter who, so long as you denounced them. They never got a chance to speak in their own defence, anyway. They were always told to shut up before they'd even opened their mouths ...

'Come the end of the war, we had a real problem on our hands. There was practically a five-year waiting list of people due to be exterminated. We had to take over the bull rings,

7

Herd them into the arena and mow them down with heavy machine-guns. We had four squadrons of Moors to give us a hand. Villainous bastards THEY were. . . . After a bit, even the police had a go. Everyone wanted to be in on the act . . . And when it came to it, they all died the same way. It didn't make an atom of difference which side you were on.'

There was a moment's pause for reflection, and then Little John spoke. In his usual forthright fashion.

'I'm pissed off with the bleeding Civil War. Didn't they have any birds in Spain, for God's sake?'

Barcelona shrugged his shoulders and wiped the back of his hand across his eyes, as if to suppress the memories of slaughter. He began to speak of other things. Of orange groves and vineyards and people dancing in the street.

Little by little we forgot the burning cold and the icy snows of Russia, and, for a while, we felt only the sun and the sand of Barcelona's far-off Spain.

CHAPTER ONE

Across the vast open spaces of the steppes blew the eternal wind, whipping the snow into eddies and whirlpools. The tanks stretched out nose to tail in a long line. They were stationary now, with their crews huddled together on the leeward side of the vehicles, seeking what little shelter they could.

Little John was lying beneath our Panzer 4. Porta had concocted a nest for himself between the caterpillar tracks, and he sat hunched up like a snow owl, his neck sunk deep into his shoulders. Between his legs crouched the Legionnaire, his teeth chattering and his face mauve.

For the moment, our hectic advance had been called to a halt. None of us knew why, and frankly none of us was very much bothered. War was still war whether the column advanced or whether it stood still. Much we cared.

Julius Heide, who had dug himself into a hole in the snow, suggested a game of pontoon, but our hands were too numb to hold the cards. The Legionnaire, indeed, had serious frostbite on both fingers and ears, and the ointment used for treatment seemed only to aggravate the condition. Porta had jettisoned his supply on the very first day, complaining that it stank of cat shit.

After a bit, Alte appeared, fighting his way towards us against the wind. We looked up at him, questioningly, knowing that he'd come straight from the C.O.

'Well?' said Porta.

The Old Man didn't reply immediately. He tossed his gun to the ground and more cautiously lowered himself on to the snow beside it. The next step was the ritual lighting of the pipe, the famous old pipe with a cover over the bowl, which he had made himself. The Legionnaire handed over his lighter. It was the very best lighter in all the world and had never yet been

9

known to fail. It, too, was home-made, manufactured from an old lead box, a razor blade, a few scraps of rag and a piece of flint.

'Well?' insisted Porta, growing impatient. 'What'd he say?'

Little John, beneath the tank, began beating at his thighs in an effort to restore circulation.

'Christ Jesus, it's perishing!' Gingerly, he rubbed the parchment cheeks of his face. 'Did someone say spring was just around the corner?'

'Like hell, it's bloody Christmas in three weeks!' came the cheerless retort from Porta. 'And I can tell you here and now the only present you're likely to get is one in the head from Ivan.'

The Old Man, with deadened fingers, had pulled a map from his tunic pocket and was carefully spreading it out on the snow.

'Here you are. This is where we're going.'

He pointed to a spot marked on the map. Little John crawled out from his resting place to take a look.

'Kotilnikovo,' said Alte, jabbing a finger on the map. 'Thirty kilometres behind our front line. From Kotilnikovo we take off in the direction of some place called Obilnoje to have a look at the Russian troops. See what they're doing, how many of 'em are doing it . . . In other words, it's a reconnaissance trip. And if by any chance we find ourselves cut off with no means of getting back—' The Old Man smiled, pleasantly – 'our orders are to try and make contact with the 4th Rumanian Army, which is believed to be somewhere south-west of the Volga . . . At the moment, that is. God knows where it'll be when we want to get hold of it. Blown out of existence, probably.'

A moment of silence. A reverberating fart from Porta spoke more or less adequately for the entire group.

'Who's got bats in the brain box, you or the C.O.? Ivan's not bloody blind, you know. He'll spot these tanks a bleeding mile off.'

The Old Man smiled again his pleasant smile.

'There's more to it than that. The best is yet to come. Just wait till you've heard it.'

He removed his pipe from his mouth and thoughtfully scratched his ear lobe with the stem.

'The idea is to dress up in Russian uniforms and move about behind the Russian lines in the two T.34s we captured off them.'

The Legionnaire sat suddenly bolt upright.

'That's the next best thing to suicide.' His tone was accusing. 'They've no right to do it. If Ivan catches us dressed up in his clothes like that, we're done for.'

'It might be a quicker death than slowly freezing at Kolyma,' murmured Alte. 'On the whole, I think I should probably prefer it.'

Without giving us the chance of further comment, he brought us to our feet and we slouched unsoldierly through the snow towards the C.O.'s vehicle.

Captain Lander had not been long with the battalion. He came from Lesvig and he was known to be a fanatical Nazi. Dubious rumours, linking his name with various cases of ill-treatment of children, had reached the ever-receptive ears of the men at the front. Porta, as always, was the one who dug out the truth, via his friend Feders. A story emerged of icy baths in a certain 'place of education' with which it appeared Captain Lander had been connected. We were not particularly surprised. Many of those who joined the battalion had past lives that hardly bore investigation. Men who clapped you on the shoulder and called you friend, men who freely passed round their cigarettes, who received parcels of bacon and ham from Denmark, who boasted of the way they got on with the people of the occupied countries – sooner or later, their past caught up with them, and then it was either Porta or the Legionnaire who was responsible for their future.

Some were knifed between the shoulders blades during the course of a general attack; some were left to die of cold; and some were handed over to Ivan. What he did with them we never knew for certain. Perhaps it was just as well.

Captain Lander was waiting for us, standing with legs apart, gauntleted hands on hips. He was a smallish, plumpish man, about fifty years of age, the former owner of a delicatessen. He was much given to biblical quotations and scriptural-sounding speeches. Whenever he court-martialled a man, it was: 'This hurts me far more than it hurts you, but it is the will of God. His ways are imponderable when he leads the straying sheep back to the path of righteousness.'

Captain Lander prayed a great deal. Before meals, he said a lengthy grace. Before signing execution orders for Russian civilians (taken by him and him alone to be partisans) he invariably invoked the Holy Ghost. The sight of mangled and bullet-ridden bodies merely brought forth the observation that those who lived by the sword should die by the sword.

The day on which he himself executed a young girl produced the following fine turn of phrase: 'You will find a better world than this in the kingdom of the Lord.' He then gently stroked her hair and had to shoot twice before he succeeded in despatching her to the aforesaid kingdom.

In general, there seemed to exist a confusion in his mind between God and Adolf Hitler.

The Captain kept himself always a respectable distance from the actual fighting. His iron cross was, quite simply, the result of a colossal red-tape *faux pas*. When the regiment made an attempt to discover what acts of heroism lay behind the award, Lt.-Col. Hinka received orders direct from those in the highest authority in the Bendlerstrasse to drop all inquiries forthwith.

Alte made his report, and Captain Lander turned a grave face towards us.

'War,' he explained, solemnly, 'demands its victims. It is the will of God. If a war does not kill, then it is no war. The mission on which I am sending you will for most of you no doubt end in death. But it will be the death of a soldier. An honourable death.'

'Fucking hooray,' muttered Little John, very audibly.

The Captain paused. He gave Little John a look that managed to be disapproving without in any way displaying annoyance. He had been well taught in the military school in Dresden: an officer never loses face. As a cadet, Lander had filled twenty-six exercise books with notes on the comportment of officers in all possible circumstances, including a complete section on 'how to behave on a bicycle'. He now, therefore, contented himself with a lofty stare in Little John's direction and continued with his homily.

'Death can be beautiful,' he told us. He lifted up his voice and sang out loud to the falling snowflakes. 'It can even be sweet!' he cried. 'Death can even be sweet . . . It is the bounden duty of a German soldier to fight for the Fatherland. To give up his life if called upon to do so. What more could he ask than to die a hero's death?'

'I could tell you, if you're really interested!'

Little John again. It was obvious from the Captain's twitching lips that he was under a strain. His face, already blue with cold, passed rapidly from purple to scarlet, and then slowly paled.

'I shall be glad, Corporal, if you will kindly remain silent until such time as I choose to speak to you.'

'Yes, sir!' said Little John, smartly. 'Remain silent,' he murmured, as if to lodge the words more securely in his memory. 'Remain silent until Captain chooses to speak to you.'

Porta guffawed, and the Legionnaire drew his features into a hideous grin. Steiner spat lustily upon a nearby corpse half buried in the snow.

Captain Lander gnawed at his lower lip. With his right hand he sought the comfort of his gun belt, fingering the Walther revolver that he carried.

'The mission with which you are to be entrusted is one of vital importance. You should be proud and happy that you have been selected for it. It is evidently the will of God that you men should penetrate beyond the Russian lines.'

'God?' said the voice of Little John, plaintive and puzzled. 'I thought it was the will of our Generals?'

In one instant, twenty-six exercise books with notes on the comportment of officers were swept aside. Lander strode forward to Little John and stood quivering, his head on a level with Little John's chest. As he spoke, a spray of saliva came from his lips.

'Insubordinate sot! It's three days' hard labour for you, my man. Insolence towards officers will not be tolerated in the

13

German Army! One more sound out of you and I'll shoot you on the spot! Repeat what I have just said.'

Little John rolled anguished eyes at the rest of us.

'How can I?' he asked, humbly. 'One more sound and I shall be shot.'

For a moment, it seemed only too probable. Lander's hand hovered above his revolver. The seconds passed.

'Down on your knees!'

Little John stepped back a pace and bent his head for a better view of the Captain.

'Who, me?' he said.

The order came a second time, rapped out falsetto.

'Down on your knees!'

Obediently, Little John plummeted down into the snow, like a sack of potatoes falling from a great height. Lander drew a breath, spat disdainfully, turned back to the rest of us.

'This man is a disgrace to the regiment. He shall be dealt with by a court martial.'

Little John muttered to himself in the snow, but Lander either did not hear or chose to ignore it. Abandoning his more usual biblical turn of phrase, he gave us the details of the glorious mission we were to undertake for the Fatherland. Quite simply, it was intended that we should dress ourselves up in Russian uniforms and set off in two captured T.34s for the enemy lines. It was a clear violation of the Geneva Convention, but Captain Lander dismissed both us and the Convention with a wave of the hand. It was plain that as far as he was concerned we were already to be regarded as 'missing, believed dead'.

The first difficulty that we encountered was finding a uniform large enough to cover the bulk of Little John's elephantine frame. He himself declared that it was not so much a question of violating the Geneva Convention as of violating the basic rights of man to make a person put on such a uniform. Only minutes before our departure we were still fighting to squeeze him into a pair of Russian trousers designed for a man of far more modest proportions.

There were no fanfares as our section took its leave of the rest of the regiment. Our tanks moved off across the steppes and were soon lost to sight behind a curtain of snow.

'And that's the last we'll see of them,' seemed to be the general feeling of those who watched us go.

The tank hauled itself, groaning, up the side of a steep incline. A burst of blue flames came from the exhaust pipe, and the sound of the motor rolled and reverberated in the mountain valleys. The adjutant, Blom – Barcelona Blom, who dreamt of Spanish sunshine and orange groves – opened one of the side panels and peered out into the night.

'Mountains,' he said, in tones of disgust. 'Nothing but bloody great snowy mountains.'

'And Ruskies,' added Alte, dispassionately. 'You can bet your sweet life those hills are crawling with 'em.'

'Do you reckon we're behind their lines yet?'

'Hours ago.'

Alte had his forehead pressed hard against the rubber surround of the turret window. For some time he had been unsuccessfully attempting to see out, but the snow was too thick and visibility was down to nil.

'I just hope to heaven we don't run slap bang into a minefield,' he muttered.

Little John gave a sour snicker and crammed his old grey bowler more firmly on to his head. Little John's bowler was the pride and joy of the battalion – though there were those who said it had been responsible for more than one officer throwing a fit of apoplexy – and he refused to be parted from it for so much as a minute.

'Here—' He turned hopefully to the Legionnaire. 'What's the chance of me getting into this Garden of Allah you're always on about?'

'Not very good,' said the Legionnaire. 'On the other hand, if you could only manage to stop sinning and start praying I don't doubt Allah would manage to find a place for you.'

Porta made a vulgar noise with his lips.

'Allah wouldn't want scum like him mucking up his garden!'

'Besides,' added Heide, gravely, 'if he let Little John in there just think of all the trash that would follow. Before you knew where you were it wouldn't be a garden any more, it'd just be a bloody great rubbish dump.'

'You shut your mouth,' warned the Legionnaire, who was touchy on the subject. 'Allah knows what he's up to without any help from the likes of you.'

A stifled cry from Alte brought us all back to earth. Once again we were soldiers, professional killers. We had run into the rear end of a regiment of Russian infantry, and Porta jammed on the brakes with only seconds to spare. The Russians were waving at us, shouting to us, but the sound of the motors drowned their voices and they were quickly lost to sight once again in the blinding snow. To our relief, our sister tank presently appeared, a massive black shadow in the white world. There had been no signs of alarm amongst the Russians: evidently there was nothing amiss with our T.34s adorned with the red star of the Soviets. Alte spoke on the radio:

'Distance between vehicles.'

The other tank slowed down, the shadow faded, and we were aware of her presence only by the grinding of her caterpillar tracks coming over the radio.

'Dora here, Dora here,' droned Alte. 'Direction 216, speed 30. Over and out.'

The sounds of the other tank were abruptly cut off and again there was silence.

'God, it's bloody freezing,' I said.

As if anyone cared.

'Get out and run along behind us shouting "Heil Hitler",' suggested Porta. 'You won't be freezing for long. Not if those Russians are still within earshot.'

'It's all very well,' I said, 'but it's not much fun moving along cheek by jowl with enemy troops. If they get the least idea that we're not what we seem to be—'

'Then it's curtains for us,' said Alte, shortly. 'And who could blame them? We're violating all the rules of the game.'

'So why are we doing it?' demanded Little John.

'Because it's bloody orders!' snapped Heide. 'And orders is orders, you ought to know that by now.'

We continued throughout the night, quarrelsome and companionable by turns. We were in the midst of one of our interminable slanging matches when Alte suddenly let out a small, high-pitched bark of terror. The slanging stopped instantly.

'What is it?'

'Prepare for combat.'

No one spoke. The Legionnaire picked up his gun, I groped silently for a grenade, Barcelona glued his eye to the observation panel. A harsh voice suddenly yelled something in Russian, and Alte replied in a Baltic dialect. The other T.34 close behind us, saw us too late to pull up in time and crashed into our rear. The Russian voice cursed it fluently with all the remarkable variety of obscenities available in that language. The owner of the voice then jumped on to our vehicle and bellowed out an order.

'Follow that column of tanks away to your right!'

It was an officer, wearing a cap with the green cross of the N.K.V.D. The sight of him was enough to paralyse us with sheer terror. Little John opened his mouth to yell, but fortunately no sound came out. Alone amongst us, Alte retained his presence of mind.

'Where do you come from? The Baltic?' demanded the Russian.

'Da.'

'I gathered as much from the disgusting dialect you speak. Try to learn some good Russian after we've won the war ... and get this bloody tank moving.'

'Dawai, dawai (quickly) you idle load of sods!' shouted Alte, in our direction, and he added the obligatory string of oaths.

Meekly we took our place at the end of a long column of tanks. The police of the N.K.V.D. were all over the place, shouting, stamping, gesticulating, trying to keep some sort of order and creating only chaos.

'Where the hell have you lot come from?' asked the officer, offering the Old Man a machorka.

Alte babbled something incoherent about a special mission, but the officer seemed not particularly interested and in any case his attention was diverted by a sudden bottleneck that brought the entire line of tanks to a halt. We heard him disputing vigorously with one of the policemen, demanding that a passage be cleared for our two tanks – it seemed that he himself was in a great hurry to arrive somewhere, and after a few sharp exchanges, in which the word Siberia occurred with horrid frequency, the police moved back and waved us forward.

'Step on it!' snapped the officer.

Porta only too willingly did so, his performance with the heavy tank bringing forth words of grudging praise and the request that Alte should speak to the C.O. as to the possibility of Porta being seconded to the personal service of the Russian. Alte gravely promised to give the matter his urgent attention.

After some fifteen minutes the officer abandoned his exposed position on the outside of the vehicle and came to join the common rabble inside. Alte silently gestured a warning to the rest of us as two booted feet swung into view. A second later, the officer appeared in his entirety. He stamped his feet loudly on the metal floor of the tank, in an effort to restore his circulation.

'This place stinks like a brothel.' He looked round at us, studying each in turn and dwelling for some while on Little John and his grey bowler. 'Where's the vodka?' he demanded, at last.

Alte handed over a jar, and we watched in silence as he poured the contents straight down his throat.

We came at length to a check point, when an N.K.V.D. sergeant demanded the password.

'Papliji tumani nad rjegoj,' replied our officer.

'Do these tanks belong to the 67th?' the sergeant wanted to know.

'Niet. They're on a special mission.'

The sergeant told us to wait while he consulted his superiors.

'Hell and damnation!' The Russian hoisted himself out of the tank and jumped to the ground. 'I can't hang around here all day. Time's precious, I'm in a hurry.'

Muttering and cursing beneath his breath, he followed the sergeant. We watched as they approached a major, who was sitting on a canvas stool beneath a tree and was surrounded by a swarm of N.K.V.D. men. We saw the officer waving a handful of papers, saw the major leafing through them; saw him finally look across at our tank and laugh, then point towards another vehicle standing nearby. Our officer also looked and also laughed. Plainly he was being offered a more comfortable means of transport than a T.34.

After a bit, the sergeant came across to us and handed over several sheets of paper.

'Here you are. New password. You can forget the other.'

'How come?' inquired Alte, very casual and offhand.

'There's a rumour that a bunch of Krauts are junketing about behind our lines in a couple of our own tanks, but we'll soon get our hands on them. Just to be on the safe side, we've changed all the passwords . . . Where's the vodka?'

Alte passed up Little John's own personal supply, and once again we watched spellbound as it disappeared rapidly down an avid Russian throat. The bottle was tossed into the snow and the sergeant broke wind very loudly at either end of himself.

'That's better . . . O.K. The new password. You'd best take careful note of it. It's been specially chosen so that any stray Krauts that might be in the area couldn't pronounce it even if they knew what it was – not that you'll be in much better case with your lousy Baltic accents, but still, I can't teach you good Russian all in five minutes . . . Now try to get it into your thick skulls. "Raswjetili jablonski i gruschi". Panjemajo? (Got it?) The reply is "Schaumjana uliza". And if anyone says otherwise, shoot first and ask questions afterwards. Schaumjana uliza. Headquarters of the N.K.V.D. in Tomsk, in case your ignorance is even greater than I imagined. Now, then—' He climbed up on to the tank and leaned forward towards Alte. 'This is your new itinerary. Take the road for Sadovoje, but don't go through the town, it's already crowded out with the whole of the 14th Division. Take the road to the south, to Krasnoje. They'll give you a new password there. Panjemajo, Gospodin?'

'Da,' said Alte.

'O.K., then.'

The sergeant raised his hand in a farewell salute and jumped off the tank. We were free to go our own way once more – only this time we had the blessing of the Russians to go with us!

For some hours we drove eastwards, giving a wide berth to any villages en route. Several times we passed groups of Russian soldiers, but only once was the password demanded of us.

In the late evening we reached the mountains and called a temporary halt in a wood, where the tanks were well hidden from any prying Russian eyes. Alte called up headquarters for new directions, and the order came through at once: proceed towards Tuapse.

We set off again, in a south-westerly direction, and proceeded for some miles in comparative silence, which was ultimately broken by the voice of doom coming from Porta:

'We'll be out of gas pretty soon.'

No reaction from any of us save Little John, who wished to know how we were to continue without petrol, and warned the world in general that with (a) his corns and (b) his piles it was no earthly use expecting him to walk half way across Russia. No one deigned to reply.

As we pressed on, the storm clouds gathered above us and on either side the mountains closed in. The country grew ever more wild, ever more bleak. It breathed hostility in every breath. The road we were following was shown on the map to be broad and straight, but it grew narrower and steeper mile by mile. The heavy tanks tended to skid on the glassy surface and it required great skill on the part of the drivers to keep them under control. The observation panel was a solid block of ice, totally useless. We had to keep the side panels open, with the result that the wind blew the snow in upon us in cold gusts.

Quite suddenly, our sister tank, driven by Steiner, skidded on a patch of ice and slewed round in a semi-circle, and we were forced to call a halt and go to her assistance. We broke two steel hawsers trying to drag her back on to the road facing in the right direction. They simply snapped in half as if they had been pieces of cotton. Next we tried it with the heavy, linked-chain towline. That got her moving all right, but she skidded once more on the same patch of ice and this time she came to rest on the extreme edge of the road, her front half overhanging the abyss. General consternation. Then Porta put his foot down hard on the accelerator, the towline straightened

20

and held, the tank began slowly edging back on to the road. Just as we were all starting to let out breaths of relief, the towline parted company from the tank, which went crashing down into the depths, and somehow managed to take little Müller down with her. God knows how it happened. For a few moments we remained silent and stunned, and as usual it was Alte who was the first to pull himself together.

'How much petrol have we?'

Porta considered the matter.

'Just about enough to clean Little John's trousers.'

'That's O.K., then,' said Heide, cheerfully. 'That should mean there's enough to take us all the way to Siberia and back.'

Alte rounded on him.

'Do you mind? This is no laughing matter. I want to know exactly how much farther we can hope to get.'

'According to the petrol gauge, no farther at all,' admitted Porta.

'Right. In that case we'll send her over the top with the other. We'll strip her of arms and ammunition, anything that might come in handy – and just remember that the machine guns are of more use than the vodka. There's another 600 kilometres between us and the German lines.'

'Nothing I like more than a nice stroll in the country,' said Porta, beaming round at us.

'What about my corns?' hissed Little John.

'I don't give a monkey's cuss for your corns!' snapped Alte, exasperated. 'If you don't want to walk you can stay here and rot.'

Heide shrugged a shoulder.

'As far as those other bastards are concerned, we were goners from the moment we set out.'

We unloaded the tank, Porta set the motor running, turned her towards the edge of the road and jumped out. We watched with a certain satisfaction as the heavy grey mass moved slowly into space.

'That's that,' said Steiner, hoisting one of the machine guns over his shoulder. 'Come on, you band of bleeding heroes ... get walking!'

'I don't feel at home in all this snow,' complained Little John. 'It's not a bit like the Reeperbahn . . . number 26.'

'What's so different about that?'

Little John's eyes clouded over and an expression of dreamy imbecility spread across his face.

'It's a whorehouse,' he said, blissfully.

We walked on throughout the night and the following morning, not calling a halt until late in the afternoon. Little John produced a packet of machorkas, of the kind doled out to the Soviet troops, and we sat about in the snow smoking them, hungrily drawing the raw smoke into our lungs, exhaling on long sighs of satisfaction. Our rumbling bellies, our aching feet, our frostbitten hands and faces and our desperate position were all temporarily forgotten in the earthly joys of the vodka bottle and a packet of fags.

On the sixth day we emerged from the mountains and were once more in the plains. Alte, Steiner and Barcelona trekked doggedly on, while the rest of us, Porta and Little John, the Legionnaire, the Professor and myself, took momentary shelter behind a jagged line of rocks and shared out, with scrupulous care, our last hunks of bread. Sheer fatigue had robbed us all of our former alert watchfulness. When the harsh cry of 'Stoj kto!' (halt) came ringing across the plain towards us we were scarcely able to believe our ears. Or, seconds later, our eyes, when we turned in the direction of the sound and found a dog sledge moving towards us across the snow. It had come up unexpectedly, previously hidden by a fold in the ground, and it was on us before we had the wit to prepare ourselves.

The sledge drew to a flying halt a few feet away from Alte and the other two. Its only occupants were a couple of soldiers, short and stocky, wearing the green cross of the N.K.V.D. They both had skis on their feet and they both carried guns. As the sledge drew up, one of the soldiers stepped off into the snow and went towards Alte, holding out his hand imperatively while the other stood covering him. It was plain to the rest of us, now crouched down behind the rocks and furtively watching every move, that they were asking for papers. The imperious gesture was unmistakable, even on the wind-swept wastes of the Caucasus.

There seemed little we could do to help the situation. Our own comrades stood between us and the two Russians, directly in the line of fire. Impossible to shoot without hitting them. The Legionnaire, hardened by long years of fighting in the mountains and the deserts of Africa, was the only one of us capable of dealing with such a situation. Inch by painful inch, he left the cover of the rocks and dragged himself on his belly through the snow. Alte and the others were fortunately standing in a close group, the snow blanketed all sound, and the Legionnaire was able to move right up behind them before anyone was aware of his presence. At the last moment he rose up like an avenging ghost and opened fire without giving the Russians a chance to defend themselves. One, indeed, managed to turn tail and run, but Little John's knife was between his shoulders before he had gone more than a few yards.

The dog team had bounced forward at the sound of the shots. Alte fortunately managed to head them off, and caught hold of the leader's harness. The dog growled, menacingly, attempted to sink its teeth into the nearest portion of human flesh, but the Old Man clenched a firm hand round its muzzle and spoke soothingly to it.

Piled high into the sledge were spare skis and a supply of both food and arms, not to mention two kegs full of vodka. In five minutes flat we were ourselves full of vodka, and the Russian soldiers had been stripped naked, even down to their identity discs. We left them lying in the snow and set off once more on our interrupted journey, making use of both sledge and skis. Before we left the spot, the two naked bodies were already frozen solid.

*We called him 'the Professor'. He was Norwegian, and at the
outbreak of war had been a student. He had voluntarily en-
rolled in the S.S. No one was quite able to make him out. Porta
said he was a traitor and would be hanged in the Gudbrandsdal
if ever he went back to Norway. Alte attempted to defend him,
by pointing out that we did not know precisely what had led
him to join up, but Porta maintained that if he were not guilty
of treachery he was guilty of stupidity, and stupidity in itself
deserved punishment.*

*He was certainly naïve. Having made the initial mistake of
joining forces with Hitler, he then discovered to his amazement
and dismay that he was by no means in agreement with certain
of the methods of the S.S. — and was foolish enough to imagine
that he could voice his opinion on the subject and get away
unscathed. He was naturally transferred immediately to Camp
KZ and from there to the front line, to a disciplinary regiment.
Our regiment.*

CHAPTER TWO

EVERY now and again, Little John would trip over his skis and fall flat on his face in the snow. And every time Little John fell flat on his face, the steppes rang from one corner to another with vicious oaths. The Professor stumbled along behind, no more skilled in the art of skiing than Little John and even less able to cope. His spectacles were iced over and he sobbed convulsively, without, I think, being aware of the fact.

'Bloody S.S. man!' jeered Porta. 'That's what you get for volunteering!'

The Professor caught his skis together and lurched forward. His spectacles fell into the snow.

Julius Heide was running alongside the dog team, encouraging them with a flow of abuse.

'Come on, you bastards! Get a flaming move on, can't you?'

The leader of the team raced neck and neck with him, curling its lips back over its teeth and from time to time, when man and dog converged upon each other, taking quick, hopeful bites in Heide's direction. Heide would then roar with rage and shake a fist.

'Lousy stinking dog! Tschorny! (Pig!) Bite me again and I'll punch you in the throat, you mangy yellow cur! If I hate one thing more than Jews, it's dogs . . . And if I hate one thing more than dogs, it's snow . . .'

Heide made an effort and for a moment outpaced the team. Then the leader bounded forward and overtook him, the other dogs straining forward in its wake, and as the sledge passed by Heide tripped and fell headlong.

'Hoha! Hoha!' bellowed Alte, cracking his long whip above the heads of the team.

The sledge moved on, swift and silent. Heide picked himself up, shook an angry fist in its wake and stepped out again with his long, rangy strides.

'I've had just about as much of this as I can take,' I confided to Porta.

'Then drop out and die,' came the unfeeling response.

I began counting every step I took. One step must be about a metre. More or less. Perhaps a bit more . . . No. One step was a metre. Therefore a thousand steps were a kilometre. We covered one kilometre in three minutes. For twelve hours – twenty-four hours – forty-eight hours – I continued counting steps. I fell down, I stood up, I closed my eyes, my legs moved automatically, I lost count, I started again, I fell into reveries in the middle of it all. But I calculated that in fourteen days we should reach the German lines. Always assuming that there were still any lines to reach.

Frequently, Alte checked the direction with his compass. Far, far away to the north-west there was the Baltic, and on the far side of the Baltic were Sweden and Denmark.

I was dreaming of Sweden and Denmark when the Professor – it had to be him – gave a pitiful wail of despair and announced that one of his skis had broken. The news brought us to an immediate standstill. Alte called the dog team to a halt, slowly stepped off the sledge into the snow and pulled out his pipe. Little John sank to the ground and lay sprawling with legs falling apart. Within seconds he was covered by a thick layer of snow. He looked quite ridiculous. Porta sat propped up against the runners of the sledge, Heide lay down full length on his stomach. The rest of us flopped about in various positions. We were all too weary to talk, or even to think. The dogs had also settled down. They huddled together, nose to tail, huge furry snowballs. We stared at them, unseeing, until at length Alte removed his pipe from his mouth and shook us out of our lethargy.

'Can't stay here like this, not moving. Let's call it a day and get dug in.'

Mechanically, we began scraping up the snow with our hands, crawling on all fours like children, fashioning solid blocks of snow for our nightly igloo. Little John worked with a fury that put the rest of us to shame, producing four blocks for every one of ours. In his haste and enthusiasm he occasionally dropped and broke one of his freshly-made blocks. He then expended yet more energy in trampling it underfoot with a volley of curses directed partly at the weather, partly at 'those bleeding Russians'.

'Pat-a-cake, pat-a-cake, baker's man,' chanted Porta, lovingly kneading the crisp snow into shape. 'Has it ever occurred to you lot that the upper classes spent hundreds going winter sporting every season? And here are we, getting it all for nothing—'

'Oh, put a sock in it!' growled Heide.

'You don't know when you're well off, that's your trouble—'

'Be quiet!' The Legionnaire suddenly sat up straight, his head on one side. 'I can hear something.'

We all listened.

'Balls!' said Porta, succinctly. 'As I was saying—'

'They've heard it, too.'

The Legionnaire nodded towards the dogs. Their ears were pricked up, their hackles raised. We all listened once again, but there was no sound anywhere on the silent steppes.

'You're dreaming,' said Barcelona.

'Oh? And what about the dogs?'

'They've caught it from you. You think there's something out there, so it makes them think there's something out there. Snow madness, like water in the desert.'

The Legionnaire merely pursed his lips, picked up his gun and held it at the ready, as if he were expecting someone or something suddenly to surge up out of the whiteness. And then, disconcertingly, the dogs began to whine. They sat up, stiff and straight, their heads turned towards the west. We all stared in the same direction. The Professor frantically wiped the snow from his glasses and screwed up his short-sighted eyes.

'I can't see a thing,' he complained.

And then Alte pointed sharply ahead.

'Dogs! Get down, all of you ... Professor, stay with our team, and God help you if any of them start barking. Porta and Heide, over there with the heavy guns. Sven, you and Barcelona over on the left with the flame throwers. The rest of you, space yourselves out. Fifty metres between each man.'

We had carried out his orders almost before he had finished speaking, digging ourselves into the ground with weapons at the ready. The snow quickly camouflaged us.

We could all hear the approaching dogs now, although we could not yet see them. They burst suddenly into view: two long sledges, with three soldiers of the N.K.V.D. on each. They were passing within forty metres of us, going south at a spanking pace, drawn by two teams of three dogs. We heard the crack of a whip and the encouraging shouts, 'Ho aho! Ho aho!' and we lay trembling in our dug-outs praying that our own dogs would not respond to the call.

A miracle: nothing happened. We held our breath to bursting point, unable to believe our luck. The two sledges passed us by, were soon out of sight and sound, and still we remained frozen in place.

'Jee-sus!' breathed Heide, at last. 'That was a close shave.'

'We could have coped with 'em,' declared Little John, roundly. 'What's six Russians more or less?'

'We should have shot them,' said Barcelona. He appealed to Alte. 'We ought to have shot them. One N.K.V.D. type in the bag is worth half a dozen of any other sort.'

Alte shrugged his shoulders and squinted up at the sky. The weather seemed to be growing worse, if that were possible. The sky was entirely hidden by the snow and the Russian wind was howling as if in sympathy with its six compatriots who had passed within so short a distance of the enemy without ever seeing them. The whole country seemed to be against us, screaming out its hatred of all invaders.

With a sudden violent burst, the wind excelled itself. We saw our equipment hurled in all directions, flung wildly about by the tempest, and with shouts of rage and despair we hurled ourselves after it, staggering in the face of the gale.

'Sodding awful country!' screamed Heide.

The Professor came stumbling back with his arms full of equipment. Tears were running down his face.

'I'm so tired. I'm so tired. I'm so—'

'Flaming shut up!' shouted Porta. 'If you'd have had any sense you'd have stayed nice and safe at home in Norway. You got yourself into this mess, didn't you? You wanted to be a hero, didn't you? Gallant little Norwegian fighting the good fight against the nasty wicked Bolsheviks? My God, old Quisling must have been proud of you!' He turned and spat into the face of the wind. 'You wait till you get back home again, that's all I say.'

The Professor wiped his nose on his sleeve.

'I shan't ever get back home again.'

'No?' said Porta. 'Well, in that case it's the Ruskies that'll get you. You listened to Moscow radio recently?'

'Of course not. It's forbidden to tune into foreign stations.'

Little John smote his fist hard against his forehead.

'Holy cow, just listen to him! You still think the great German Army's going to win this war?'

The Norwegian doubtfully shook his head.

'You think we're going to lose?' he asked.

'Let me tell you something.' Little John took the Professor's arm, turned him round and pointed in a vague, northerly direction. 'Over there, they've got enough cannons to blow the whole of the Sixth Army sky high. And all the rest of the bunch, too, right down to the last soldier.' He paused. 'You know who that's going to be?' he demanded.

The Professor blinked myopically.

'None other than yours truly!' declared Little John, puffing his chest out. 'And when the Chancellery of the Reich is nothing but a heap of rubble, it's going to be me that stands amongst the ruins and spits on it all. And on all the bones of our glorious dead heroes.'

'That wouldn't surprise me in the slightest,' murmured Alte.

Little John kicked angrily at the snow, and then gave a shout of surprise and fell on his knees and began digging. Suddenly, a hand appeared, like a plant growing out of the earth. Shortly afterwards Little John uncovered a face, hideous to look upon, blue, shrunken, lips drawn back over the teeth, eyes sunk deep into their sockets. After a moment's shock, we all fell to scrap-

29

ing away the snow like a pack of terriers. There were two bodies in the shallow grave. Two German infantrymen. The arm of one was still held upright, finger crooked, frozen into position, as if beckoning us to join him. Little John prodded it with his toe and turned away in disgust.

'I never accept invitations from strange men,' he said.

'Have a look in his pockets,' urged Barcelona.

'Have a look yourself,' retorted Little John. 'I don't care for corpses.'

Barcelona hesitated.

'Well, go on, if you're so interested!'

It was the Legionnaire who stepped forward. With a swift movement he took out his knife, bent over one of the bodies and slashed off a flask that was attached to the belt of the uniform. He tossed it towards Heide, who caught it awkwardly and stood for a moment with his mouth open, looking at it. Eventually he unscrewed the lid and held the flask beneath his nose. He twitched his nostrils delicately.

'Smells like vodka.'

He held it out to Barcelona, but Barcelona shook his head. Little John also declined the offer. It seemed suddenly that the whole group had turned teetotal.

'Bloody idiots.'

The Legionnaire stepped forward and snatched at the flask. We watched apprehensively as he raised it to his lips. We watched his Adam's apple rise and fall. Then we waited, expecting God knows what to happen. The Legionnaire wiped the back of his hand across his mouth.

'Not bad,' he said. 'It's not vodka, but it's certainly alcohol.'

At that, we reverted instantly to type. Porta and Little John soon had possession of the second flask, and amongst us we finished off both of them within a matter of seconds. Steiner thoughtfully removed the personal papers and identity discs from the two corpses, and we then retired into our roughly-built igloo, hudded together in a tight circle. Ignoring Alte's protestations, we were firmly bedded down for the night and had every intention of falling asleep on the spot. No one was anxious to stand guard duty. As Little John remarked shortly before I sank into unconsciousness, we had twelve able-bodied dogs to keep a watch-out for us.

The Legionnaire mocked at everything, had pity for no one. There were but two subjects on which he felt deeply: one was his religion (he was a fanatical Muslim) and the other was France. He himself, of course, was a German, but many years spent in the Foreign Legion had made a Frenchman of him.

Beneath the black uniform of the tank regiment he wore the Tricolor, wrapped round him like a scarf. In his breast pocket, with his military papers, he carried a small yellowing photograph of the man he persisted in calling 'mon Général'. Lt. Ohlsen told us one day that it was a photograph of a Frenchman, Charles de Gaulle, who was fighting with the Free French in Africa.

Heide stored up this piece of information and made use of it at a later date, during the course of a violent disagreement with the Legionnaire, when he gratuitously referred to 'mon Général' as 'a shit of the desert'. Before any of us could move, the Legionnaire had whipped out his knife and scored a deep cross on Heide's cheek. The wound had needed several stitches and even now, whenever Heide grew angry, the shape of a cross appeared lividly on his face. The rest of us found it highly amusing, but both Heide and the Legionnaire took the affair very much to heart.

'Say what you like about anyone else,' said the Legionnaire, 'but if I hear another word against mon Général somebody's going to get this knife right between his ribs. I'm telling you.'

We took note of his warning, even though we laughed. No one ever insulted mon Général again – at least, not in the Legionnaire's presence.

CHAPTER THREE

'O.K., take it easy. We'll break for half an hour.'

Alte called the team to a halt. The rest of us thankfully unstrapped our skis and flopped down into the snow. The dogs lay panting, their breath forming clouds in the frosty air. Alte lit up a pipe, Barcelona gnawed on a frozen crust of bread. There was silence, comparative peace. And suddenly into this silence, Heide began to pour out the story of his life.

The words flowed out of him, and to begin with we none of us paid any attention. It was not unusual for one of us to start talking, aimlessly, about nothing at all, without expecting or ever wishing anyone to take note of his words. It was a consequence of the life we were leading, the snow, the cold, the constant fear and the nearness of death. We slept together and we ate together, we were never apart from each other and yet there was this sense of individual isolation, a desperate aloneness, that led us from time to time to hold long conversations with ourselves as if there were no one else for miles around.

And so it was that Heide began speaking. The words flowed from him in a compulsive stream. He spoke not to us but to the steppes, to the dogs, to the snow and the wind. We, if we listened at all, were mere eavesdroppers.

'My old man was a drunk,' he said, and he spat contemptuously into the wind, which threw it straight back at him. 'Drank like a fish, he did. You know that? He drank like a ruddy fish. . . . And Christ almighty, the stuff that bloke could get through! I'm not kidding you, six bottles were nothing to my old man. Nothing at all. You think you can drink?' He laughed scornfully at the listening dogs. 'He'd have had you under the table any day of the week . . . Not that he remained sober, I'm not saying that. Matter of fact, I hardly ever remember seeing him sober.' Heide frowned. 'He never was sober, that's the simple truth of it. Never sober, always pissed . . . And whenever he was pissed, he used to beat us kids black and blue with a whacking great leather belt he wore. Almost every day he used to beat us. We just accepted it, in the end, but my old lady, she used to pray all the time. I never knew what she was praying for, she just used to mutter to herself in a corner. Dear God, please do this, dear God, please do that . . .'

Heide stared past us towards the west, his eyes extraordinarily clear and blue, presumably seeing not the everlasting carpet of snow and the tall pine trees but the town in Westphalia and the hovel where he was born.

'Know what my old man used to say when he beat us? "It's not because I'm drunk", he used to say. "I'm not doing it because I'm drunk, you mustn't think that. I'm doing it for Germany. It's all for Germany. The sinful flesh must be mortified." That's what he used to say. The sinful flesh must be mortified . . . He used to mortify his sinful flesh, all right. In bed, with the old woman . . . Sometimes we used to lie there listening to them, other times they'd send us out to the park for half an hour. We used to sit and look at a statue of the Kaiser sitting on a horse. Just sit and look at it until we thought we could go back in again. I even had to take my kid sister with me, I had to carry her everywhere, she hadn't learnt to walk yet . . . I had another sister once. Bertha. She was the oldest, but she died. They gave me her scarf. I remember I went to church and said thank you for letting me have Bertha's scarf, on account of it was so cold that winter and I didn't have any overcoat . . . I never did have an overcoat. Except once, I half inched one, only they found out before I had a chance to wear it. I had to go and talk to the priest about it. He hit me so hard I fell down and knocked his china cabinet over. Then he hit me again, harder than ever. Almost as hard as my old man used to wallop us. He was more mad about the china being broken than me nicking an overcoat . . .

One of my brothers, he got out and joined the army. He wrote us a letter, with a photograph, showing what he looked like in uniform, but we never heard from him again. He called himself a Communist. Probably ended up in a concentration camp. He asked for trouble, that one. Never knew when to hold

his tongue. Always screaming about the victory of the proletariat.'

Heide laughed, cynically, at his brother's innocence.

'Then there was Wilhelm. He was another of my brothers.
He was the one that taught me to jump on trams when the
conductor wasn't looking, and when he came up and asked for
the fare we used to jump off again shouting all the rude words
we knew. And we knew some, I can tell you ... We thought
that was fun, shouting words at him when we could get off and
run and he had to go on standing there and couldn't do a thing
about it. Only one day he did it and Wilhelm fell under the
tram and got crushed.'

Heide shook his head.

'They blamed me for that. They said I'd led him into
trouble, but it wasn't true, I was younger than he was. It wasn't
my fault he died ... I wanted to have his shoes, only they
wouldn't fit me. I was bigger than Wilhelm. Younger but
bigger, see? Wilhelm was always a skinny little bugger. So they
gave his shoes to Ruth, but that was just a waste. She didn't
need them for long on account of she was bought by some rich
people in Linz – well, THEY called it adoption, only my old
man got money for it so what I call it is selling her. She didn't
half cry when she knew she'd got to go. The old man beat her
black and blue until she stopped ... He got fifty marks for
Ruth. It mightn't sound much to you, but it was a fortune to us,
I can tell you. Kept the old man in booze for a few days, any
rate ... He'd have sold the whole lot of us, if anyone'd been
willing to buy, but no one wanted a couple of snotty-nosed
brats. That's what he said. He went out and got plastered that
night and when he came back we hid under the roof and didn't
come down till he'd passed out, but anyway he beat us just the
same in the morning ... It wasn't long after that when I came
home from school one day and found the old lady sitting on the
bed, weeping. I remember that day. I shall always remember
that day.'

Heide glanced up at the falling snow, then held out his hand
to his hated enemy, the leader of the dog team, the mangy
yellow cur he was always threatening to punch in the throat. To
our amazement, the dog crawled up on its belly and began

35

earnestly licking Heide's face, while Heide thoughtfully scratched behind its ear. By this time, we were all listening to his story.

'I never knew why she was weeping,' he said. 'But I sat down on the bed with her and I started weeping, too, and we just wept together until I fell asleep. The other kids weren't there, I don't know where they'd gone. Playing in the streets, I expect. Anyway, it was dark when I woke up. I knew something was wrong – you know how you do? I could feel the old lady still lying there, but it was like being alone, all by myself. I couldn't hear her breathing or anything. I was so scared I couldn't move ... After a bit, I lit the candles and she was just lying there, staring up at the ceiling with her eyes wide open. I knew at once she was dead. I was only ten – nine and a half – but even at that age you know when someone's dead.'

Heide suddenly looked directly at us, and his hard blue eyes were full of tears.

'My mother,' he said, very earnestly, 'was a good woman. She came from a good family. Respectable and hard working. She never used to beat us or swear at us. And you can believe this or not, but I'm telling you it's the truth, my mother never once got drunk in all her life. The old man tried to make her, once. Him and one of our neighbours. They tried to force a bottle of booze down her. But she wasn't having any of it. You know what she did? She got hold of the bottle and she bashed the old man over the head with it. And when he got mad at her, she simply picked up the breadknife and stuck it into him.' Heide chuckled, reflectively. 'That put a stop to it, I can tell you! He had to have a couple of stitches put in his leg ... Of course, he beat the hell out of her afterwards. That was only to be expected. But he couldn't force her to do anything she thought was wrong.'

'What happened that time you were talking about?' demanded Little John, suddenly breaking in on the monologue. 'When you woke up and found her?'

Heide scratched at his frostbitten face, removed a scab and handed it to the dog. The dog sniffed at it suspiciously, then ate it. Heide frowned.

'The old man came in. Pissed as a newt, as usual. Just roaring for a fight with someone. He brought one of his pals with him. A fellow called Schmidt. A real bum.'

Heide's frown intensified. His eyes were dry again, very hard and bright, and his mouth took on the thin, bitter line that we knew so well of old, lips pulled together as if he were sucking a lemon.

'One of these days, I'm going to get that bastard Schmidt,' he said.

'Why?' demanded Little John, at once interested. 'What's he done to you?'

'He's a shit,' said Heide, as if that in itself were sufficient reason. 'He used to work down the mines with my old man, then they threw him out of there and he went to the local loony bin and called himself a male nurse. Nurse! From all accounts he used to bash the patients about something terrible. He must be having the time of his life right now. He's in charge of the crematorium, and believe me there are plenty of bodies waiting to be burnt. They're being killed off like flies down there. It's supposed to be a government secret, but everyone knows about it.'

'Why?' demanded Little John, again. 'Why's it supposed to be a secret if the nuts die, when it's not secret if you or me die?'

'It's different,' said Heide, irritably. 'In the bin, they inject them with things and call it euthanasia.'

'What for?'

'How the hell do I know what for? Because they aren't any use to anyone, I suppose. It's the doctors that do it, it's all quite legal, it's just top secret.'

There was a pause, while we considered the question of the nuts being put out of the way because they weren't any use to anyone. You could see the logic of it, but somehow it still left a bad taste in your mouth.

'What about this Schmidt fellow?' asked Porta. 'This pal of your old man. You haven't told us what he was supposed to have done.'

'What he did do,' corrected Heide. 'What he did and what he said ... When they came in, the pair of them, roaring and cursing and yelling at the old lady to get up and get their food for them ... I told them she was dead, but they wouldn't believe me. Schmidt just laughed and said she was putting it on. He said the mad old bags in the bin did that sort of thing. He knew how to deal with them. He said, why don't you try beating a bit of life into her? I reckon that'll make her drop her drawers and give us a little bit of something ... Those were the words he used.'

Heide looked round at us.

'I swore then I was going to get him one of these days.'

'How?' asked the Legionnaire, practically.

There followed a lurid discussion on the best way of dealing with a person like Schmidt. Heide listened, but did not join in.

'I'll get the bastard,' he told us. 'I'll get him, don't you worry.'

He gave us one of his diabolical smiles.

'They beat the old lady practically to a pulp before they admitted she was dead. Then they broke my arm and kicked me round the floor and went back to their drinking. I went and got the police. I said I didn't remember anything, and they arrested the pair of them on a charge of murder. They kept them in jug for six weeks before I decided to talk. When they came out the old man was so furious he half killed me ... So after I left hospital, I just packed my bags and went off on my own. And it's been that way ever since.'

There was another silence. Many of us in the disciplinary regiments had pretty hard stories to tell, but I think Heide's was one of the hardest I'd heard. You couldn't like the man, but at least, now, you could understand him. If there'd been room in our hearts for sentiment, we might even have pitied him.

'This Schmidt,' said Porta, eventually. 'You've left it a bit late, haven't you? I mean, you were just a kid—'

'Seventeen years ago,' said Heide. He cuffed the dog away from him and stood up. 'Don't you worry, I haven't forgotten. I know where he is, and I'm going to get that bastard one of these fine days.'

We believed him. It was one of those subjects, like the Legionnaire and mon Général, that you just didn't joke about. Most of us had our weak point, some obsession dear to our hearts, and men learnt not to talk lightly of these things.

'I tell you,' repeated Heide, 'that bastard's got it coming to him.'

'You bet!' said Porta, clapping him on the shoulder. 'You'll get him all right, don't you worry.'

Turkey! We could hardly believe our luck when we learnt that we were within easy reach of the border. It seemed too good to be true. Within seconds of hearing the news we were indulging in our usual wild flights of sexual fancy. We dreamt of brothels and harems, of belly-dancing and of exotic women.

Within easy reach of the border! So near, and yet so very far. . . . It seemed too good to be true: it was good to be true. Our fantasies were short-lived. There was no way of crossing the frontier . . .

We left the village as we had entered it, Alte driving the dog team, the rest of us on skis, Heide cursing the mangy yellow cur. The only difference was that now we had a prisoner to accompany us on our long trek.

CHAPTER FOUR

THE dogs were exhausted. They stretched out, panting, in the snow, their flanks heaving, their tongues lolling. It was plain for all to see that we were an inexperienced crew when it came to handling dog teams. Even Alte, the all-wise, was by no means an expert. He was a miller by profession, and doubtless a most excellent one. He was a soldier by necessity. A first-class soldier. He loved the former and he loathed the latter. As for the dog team, he did his best and certainly he handled them better than the rest of us could have done, but the fact remained, the dogs were exhausted.

We ourselves were in no better state. The country was hostile. It breathed hostility in every fresh gust of wind. We felt it every minute of the day, and we felt that it was slowly destroying us. We fought and bickered amongst ourselves, we moaned ceaselessly, spirits were low and tempers generally were at breaking point. That very morning Little John and Heide had fought each other with bare fists and in bitter silence for more than twenty minutes. Heides nose was battered to a raw bleeding pulp. It had been left to Alte to end the fight by threatening the two combatants with his revolver. There was never any question of his using it, and both Little John and Heide were well aware of the fact, but there was more authority in Alte's quiet voice than in a whole regiment of sergeant majors. The fighting ceased, although the abuse continued. They threatened each other with death, and they seemed to mean it.

One of the dogs was limping badly and in obvious pain. It was decided to put an end to its misery, and Little John offered to do the job. He slit the creature's throat from ear to ear, grinning all the while like a maniac. When we protested, he rounded furiously upon us.

'Why shouldn't I enjoy it? It wasn't the dog I was killing, it was Julius Heide and his insane prejudices!'

We pushed on with the rest of the team. Quite suddenly, for no apparent reason, Alte pulled to a halt at the top of a small slope. We hurried up to him and stared ahead in amazement.

'Allah!' said the Legionnaire, wonderingly. 'It looks like the sea.'

'That's impossible.'

'What is it, then?'

We checked the map, we checked the compass, and when we looked again the sea was still there, in all its miraculous impossibility. Alte shook his head. He had not mistaken the route we were taking, and the sea was hundreds of miles away. Or should have been.

'Strange,' said Porta. 'I'd have sworn it was only about thirty metres ahead of us.'

'It is.'

'What the hell is it, then?'

'A lake?'

'Which lake?' said the Legionnaire.

We turned back to the map. No lake was indicated.

'I don't understand it,' confessed Alte.

We stood in a line, silently contemplating the vast expanse of frozen water.

'A marsh?' suggested the Professor, squinting through the one remaining lens of his spectacles: the other had been broken days before in one of his frequent falls. 'It obviously can't be the sea. The sea doesn't freeze.'

'Well, it's not a marsh. I never saw a marsh look like that.'

'All right, what is it, then?'

The moon was rising, and by its light we thought we could dimly make out a far shore, perhaps two or three kilometres distant.

'That settles it,' said Steiner. 'It's a river.'

Again we studied the map. Fervently the Legionnaire regarded the night sky, measured distances with the compasses, looked again at the sky – then shrugged his shoulders and gave up the riddle. No sea, no lake, no river were to be found.

'The compass can't be at fault. We've got to keep going west. There's nothing for it but to cross the ice.'

'I suppose so.' Alte leaned against the sledge, looking worried. 'I just hope to God it is the right direction. We're running short of food as it is, we can't afford any mistakes.'

The first to venture out on the ice was Porta. He wriggled across on his stomach, and the rest of us followed, full of apprehension. The vast sheet of ice turned us all into quivering cowards. God knew how deep was the frozen water beneath, but a ducking at that temperature would mean almost certain death. The Legionnaire, more practical than the rest of us, finally attempted to bore through the top layer with his knife. He succeeded at last, and withdrew the knife with a nod of satisfaction. The ice was sufficiently thick to carry us. This discovery threw us all into a state of childlike joy. Little John and Porta rushed about in ecstasy, slipping and sliding, with wild whoops of delight.

'You never cease to amaze me,' remarked Alte. 'Have you by any chance forgotten that we're about 1,500 kilometres behind the Russian lines?'

'The Russians can go and get stuffed!' yelled Little John, jubilantly.

He spun in a circle. There was a loud ominous cracking from the ice and we all stiffened in our tracks and stared round with eyes that bulged with terror.

'Let's get on,' said Alte, tersely.

Once again, we began to treat the ice with respect, creeping slowly forward, trying to make ourselves as light as possible. Every creak, every groan from the frozen mass brought its equivalent creak and groan from us. Every minute brought fresh fears, and it took us several hours to cross to the far shore.

Once there, we found ourselves amongst birch trees, and our tension disappeared as quickly as it had come. It was the work of a moment to hack off enough branches to start a fire, and we threw ourselves wholeheartedly into the task.

'This is madness,' said Alte, as the flames began licking up into the frosty air. 'I must be losing my grip. This lot can be seen for miles around.'

'So what?' Little John defiantly threw on another branch. 'If any Russian dares to show his face here he'll be clubbed on the head and dumped straight into the nearest stew pot – who knows? Even a lousy Russian might taste good if you're starving. What about the cats of the Dibuvilla barracks? A nice fat Rusky would be more tasty than a mangy cat.'

'So we're cannibals, now?' sneered Heide. 'I wouldn't put it past you. I wouldn't put anything past you.'

Little John leaned forward.

'I'll tell you what I'll do, Julius: I'll reserve the rump specially for you, even though it is the best cut.'

'Douse this fire!' snapped Alte.

We did our best with handfuls of snow, but in some strange way it seemed almost to add encouragement to the flames. The embers were still glowing red in the night when we finally turned in.

A piercing cry awoke us. Instantly we were on our feet, snatching up our firearms, straining our eyes in an effort to see through the darkness. The cry came again, long and plaintive and blood-curdling.

'God in heaven, what is it?' demanded Barcelona.

By now the fire was almost out. A few cinders gleamed fitfully here and there, but it gave very little light. But as our eyes grew accustomed to the dark, we made out the vast shape of a monster lurking in the trees. Porta gave a scream of terror and flung himself behind Little John. The Professor sank whimpering to the ground. Another wailing cry split the night in two. And then the Legionnaire began to laugh. A laugh of pure joy. I thought personally that his mind had suddenly gone.

'By Allah!' He controlled himself at last and turned to the rest of us, trembling in our boots. 'It's a camel, you fools! A wild camel. His mates are probably somewhere round about as well.'

Cautiously, still very much inclined to doubt his sanity, I stole forward with the others, gun at the ready. And there it was, before us. Unmistakably, and very disdainfully, a camel. As we watched, it was joined by two others and they stood shoulder to shoulder in the icy wind, regarding us with expressions of dislike.

'My God!' exclaimed Steiner, taking a few brave steps forward. 'There are hundreds of the brutes out there.'

'A herd of bleeding camels,' muttered Porta.

'Dromedaries,' said Heide, in his usual self-opinionated way. 'They've got two humps.'

'That's what camels have,' said Porta.

'Dromedaries.'

'Camels.'

'Dromedaries, I tell you.'

'Oh, shut up!' yelled Porta, exasperated. 'Who the hell cares what the things are, anyway? What I want to know is, can you ride them?'

'Of course,' said the Legionnaire, casually stroking the muzzle of the nearest creature. 'Didn't you ever ride on camels at the zoo?'

'Dromedaries,' murmured Heide.

'Camels,' said the Legionnaire. 'They come in both varieties. One-humped and two.'

'And they live in Africa,' added Little John, wisely. 'Take a good look fellers – that out there, all froze over, is the Mediterranean!'

The Legionnaire shook his head.

'No such luck! You can find camels in other places besides Africa. You get them as far afield as China. This must be one area of the Caucasus where they breed. You know the Russians have whole divisions mounted on camels—'

He broke off as a new and more alarming sight caught our eyes: three men, curiously dressed in a shabby assortment of kaftans and animal skins, were coming through the trees towards us. They stopped and smiled, then pointed to the west and began speaking in a language that appeared to have little in common with Russian. Heide reached automatically for his revolver, but the Legionnaire jerked it away from him.

'Don't be a damned idiot! They're probably friendly. They might be able to help us.'

Alte turned to the oldest of the three men.

'Nzementz?' he asked.

The reply was totally incomprehensible. Alte shook his shoulders and pulled a face.

'Nix panjemajo.'

'Germanski?'

We hesitated, unnerved by the realization that they had somehow recognized us for what we were. Was it in their minds to hand us over to the Russians? Dressed as we were, we faced certain death if captured. The strangers laughed amongst themselves. They seemed quite disposed to be pleasant, although it was plain that Little John, twice as tall as any of them, with his battered face and broken nose, put the fear of God into them.

They offered us some bread and goat's milk, and we in exchange handed over a packet of machorkas. They continued laughing happily. We laughed, too, for no reason at all save that such continuing merriment was catching. After a bit their leader made the discreet sign-language suggestion that we might have some spare vodka, and Alte obligingly handed over his own flask. The contents disappeared with the usual rapidity, and, obviously warming to us, the three men took Alte to one side and began gesturing energetically and speaking what seemed to be a pidgin version of their own language. They drew something indecipherable in the snow, pointing all the while to the west. Alte stared dubiously. Then one of them began running in circles, shouting 'Boum boum!' as he did so, and suddenly dropped down as if dead. Alte watched this performance two or three times, then obligingly nodded his head. The three men began laughing again. They certainly seemed to have a ready sense of humour, though what it was they found so perpetually amusing was and always remained a mystery to me.

Two days later we entered a village in company with the three of them. None of us was too happy about it. A village meant people, and where there were people there were also, in our experience, N.K.V.D. men. Our three companions seemed to guess how we were feeling, but it merely increased their general hilarity.

'Njet politruk!' cried one of them, gaily.

Our arrival in the village aroused no particular interest in any quarter. Fjodor, the leader of the camel drivers, pointed out a row of huts and beckoned to Alte to follow him. Not unreasonably, Alte hesitated.

'Njet politruk!' insisted Fjodor, laughing merrily.

The Legionnaire shouldered his rifle and offered to accompany the Old Man.

'O.K.' Alte turned to the rest of us. 'If we're not back in half an hour, you'd better come looking for us.'

We were not left kicking our heels for very long. We installed ourselves in the hut that passed for the local bar, and before we had time to grow really anxious Alte and the Legionnaire returned, pushing before them a young boy, not more than eighteen years old, in the uniform of a German artilleryman.

'Look what Fjodor's given us!'

We looked, and were astonished.

'He's been here three months. He was shot by a Russian firing squad and they've been hiding him in the village ever since.'

The boy regarded us with enormous, frightened eyes, as if we, too, were likely to put him before a firing squad. Doubtless he found it difficult to believe that we were, in spite of our uniforms, fellow countrymen.

'Paul Thomas,' he said, suddenly, 'Gunner, 209th Artillery Regiment.'

Alte picked up a bottle and held it out to him.

'Have a drink. You're amongst friends here.'

'I can't drink.'

'Can't drink?' Porta leaned forward, very much interested. 'Why not?'

'It makes me feel bad.'

The boy turned his head, and we saw a vivid red gash running from the crown to the nape of the neck.

'I'm not in the least surprised,' muttered Barcelona. The wound was still raw and suppurating. 'It makes me feel bad just looking at it. What happened?'

'They took us one evening. The whole section. It was the first time we'd seen any action, most of us.'

He shrugged his shoulders, as if that were all he had the

energy to say. Fjodor, who had been hovering amicably on the edge of the group, held out a bowl of milk. The boy snatched at it avidly and drank it in quick gulps. He smiled at Fjodor.

'Spassibo tovaritch,' he said, fervently.

Fjodor patted him on the cheek, murmuring things in his own language.

'So what happened?' repeated Porta, after a while.

The boy licked his lips, nervously.

'Well . . . Well, Tauber – he was the sergeant in charge of us – he wanted to surrender. Some of the others wanted to go on fighting. Tauber said it was suicide. They outnumbered us by about a hundred to one. Tauber said if we gave ourselves up we'd be treated as prisoners of war. Some of the boys said they'd heard how the Russians treated their prisoners, and anyway we could hold out for another half hour and anything could happen in that time. Well, the Russians kept yelling at us to give ourselves up. They promised we'd be treated O.K. And then Tauber, he said he wasn't going to die just yet and he was a sergeant and we were just privates and we'd got to do what he said. So we gave ourselves up,' concluded the boy, simply.

We stared at him in renewed astonishment.

'Where was the rest of the regiment?' demanded Barcelona, at last.

'They'd already retreated. We were left to guard the rear.'

'And what happened when you threw in the sponge?'

'Well, it was O.K. at first. They gave us schnapps, and some of their fags, see, and one of their N.C.O.s swapped a loaf of bread for Tauber's iron cross Then they started interrogating us, just like we do with our prisoners. They asked us if we was members of the Hitler Youth. Like we always ask them if they're Komsomols.'

'You denied it, of course?'

'Yeah, but they found out we was lying. Well, one idiot, he was carrying round papers that proved it wasn't true, so they started yelling at us then and got really mad. They accused us of torturing people and God knows what . . . They took us to some village called Daskjove. Something like that. I'm not sure even where it was. They didn't treat us rough or anything.

48

They just stripped us of all we had – watches, rings, money, the lot.'

The boy hesitated, looking round fearfully at us as if we might still be hostile towards him.

'Go on,' said Alte, gently. 'What then?'

'Well, they shot us, didn't they? One after another. We had to get in a line and step forward one at a time. I was the last one, 'cos I was the youngest and they said as how I had the right to live longer'n the others. When my turn come they pulled me out front and made me kneel down, and the one that was doing all the shooting, he said I was holding my head on one side, and he made me keep it straight. I could feel the muzzle of his gun in the back of my neck. All cold it was ... And then there was this explosion, see, and it felt like the whole of my head was bursting open.' He looked round at us and directed a hopeful smile at Alte. 'I didn't know nothing more till I woke up and found all the Russians had gone and I was the only one left alive. The others were lying on the ground nearby. Tauber and Willy and all the others. They was dead. And I wanted to be dead, too,' he told us, earnestly. 'I was that scared, just lying there all alone.'

'What did you do?'

'I got out as fast as I could, mate! I couldn't stand upright, I was too dizzy. I had to crawl, and I couldn't hardly do that I felt so weak. And then Fjodor found me, only I don't think he knew what I was at first. I was covered in blood, I don't suppose I looked much like a human being. He brought me back here and they've looked after me ever since.'

'What about your head?' demanded Porta. 'What have they done about that?'

'They sent their doctor to me. I suppose he was a doctor, I dunno. He tied me down to a table and fished about inside my head with a pair of scissors until he found the bullet.'

'Scissors?' said the Professor, horrified. 'Do you mean forceps?'

'No, scissors. Ordinary scissors like you use for cutting things.'

'And no anaesthetic?'

'No.' The boy shook his head, as if apologizing for the

49

doctor's primitive methods of surgery. 'I don't think they have things like that here. Anyway, I passed out long before he'd finished the job.'

We granted him a few moments' respectful silence, broken eventually by Heide.

'What's this crazy language they all talk here?' he demanded.

'It's Turkish,' said Paul. 'I've picked up quite a bit of it.'

'Turkish?' We all stared at him. 'Where are we, then?'

'Not far from the Turkish border.'

'Would you believe that?' said Little John, in amazement. 'How we do get about! One minute we're in the Caucasus, the next we're on the shores of the Mediterranean, then we come across herds of wild camels in China and now we're only a stone's throw from Turkey!' He turned eagerly on the boy. 'Tell me, sonny, what time's the next train due to leave? Once I'm shot of all this lot, old Uncle Adolf can go and get knotted for all I care!'

'There aren't no trains from here,' said Paul, seriously. 'We're stuck for the duration. There's no means of getting away.'

His words had no effect whatsoever upon our suddenly jubilant spirits. In mind, if not yet in body, we were already safe in Turkey. Porta at once gave himself up to his favourite dream: the brothel de luxe and a mad riot of sexual perversities. He enlarged upon the theme from every titillating angle and carried us along with him. Barcelona drew a map on the dusty floor to show Little John exactly where Turkey lay in relation to our present probable whereabouts, and Little John, in his eagerness to set off straight away, promptly jumped all over the map and trampled it back into obscurity. The Legionnaire remembered that he had a friend in Ankara, and together we speculated on ways and means of crossing the frontier.

'Just how far away is it?' Alte wanted to know.

'About fifty kilometres,' said Paul. 'But then there's a sort of no man's land that's heavily mined and swarming with the N.K.V.D. No one's ever yet managed to get through and live to tell the tale. Leastways, that's what Fjodor told me.'

His words fell on deaf ears. The thought of a neutral country so very nearly within our grasp had temporarily unbalanced even the most placid amongst us.

It was some days before the undoubted truth of Paul's words really sank in: it simply was not possible to cross the Russian frontier into Turkey. Fortunately, it was at the peak of our disillusionment that Little John discovered the hidden store of alcohol. Several crates of it, all marked with the red star of the Soviet Army. The fact that it was enemy property merely served to whet our appetites. We drank long and gloriously, and one by one the villagers crept from their huts and hovels and joined in the fun. Someone discovered an old barrel organ and we danced ecstatically in the snowy streets. Very soon there was not a man or a woman, or probably even a child, who remained sober. The entire village was *en fête*. Nevertheless, when Alte suddenly held up a warning hand the whole crowd became hushed and silent, instinctively apprehensive and on the alert for danger.

From the far end of the street came the sound of a man singing. The sound came nearer, and then the man himself came into view. He was a stranger, not one of the villagers. He carried a light machine gun slung over his shoulder, and the song he was singing, in a deep bass voice, was sad and sombre. We stood transfixed as he approached us. He paused a few yards away from the edge of the crowd. His gaze swept over us and finally came to rest on one of the barrels of alcohol. He picked it up, suspiciously sniffed at it, then gave a satisfied grin, tipped back his head and drank deeply. He belched, spat, and drank again.

'Tovaritch,' he said to Porta, who happened to be the nearest to him, 'you are a drunken pig. I salute you.'

With these words he flung the empty barrel over his shoulder, pulled off his fur cap and tossed it into the air with a raucous cry. For the first time, we saw the green cross of the N.K.V.D. You could almost feel the individual hearts of the crowd falter and miss a beat. Suddenly, to everyone's stupefaction, the man dropped his gun into a heap of snow, folded his arms across his chest, squatted down on his heels and began to dance, flinging his legs out in all directions and exultantly banging his heels together.

Quick as a flash, Little John had his revolver in his hand. He levelled it, took aim – and then burst into drunken peals of laughter. His finger inadvertently pressed the trigger and bullets began to spray the air. Those within range fell flat on their faces in the snow, but the Russian continued imperturbably with his mad cavorting. Fortunately for us, he had evidently drunk his fill long before his arrival in the village. Little John stopped laughing. He reloaded the revolver and began to fire into the ground on either side of the man.

At last the dance came to an end. The Russian leapt up, grinning. He seized another barrel of drink and laughed in Little John's face.

'You think that's clever? Well, it doesn't impress me! Here, have a swig.'

While Little John was thus engaged, being congenitally incapable of ever refusing the offer of alcohol, the Russian picked up his machine gun and deliberately sent a stream of bullets thudding round his feet. Little John roared and jumped backwards.

'What the hell are you playing at? You know who I am, Russki? Germanski soldier, that's me! Tankist! Boum boum! And I don't give a shit for you or for Stalin or for any other of your damned countrymen!'

'And now you know that,' said Porta, going up to the Russian and gripping him firmly by the lapels, 'you might as well know the rest ... You Russki, me Germanski, us enemies ... Savvy? Me, corporal, backbone of the German Army. Him—' He waved a hand towards the Legionnaire – 'him not Russki, him not Germanski. Him Franzouski.'

The Russian smiled amiably at Porta, nodded towards the Legionnaire, shook his fist at Little John. Evidently he had not quite grasped the essentials of what had been said to him.

'Look,' said Porta, exasperated. He pulled out his knife and held it to the man's throat. 'I'm warning you, Russki, this blade is sharp. Any trouble, and you're for the chopping block, mate!'

At this moment, in a sudden burst of drunken zeal, Heide sprang into action. He came running from the opposite end of the street, bursting through the crowd with a hand grenade clutched in either fist. I saw Alte try to bar his way, but Heide merely brushed him to one side and continued on his charge. And now the Russian was no longer a drunk and genial soldier but a member of perhaps the most dreaded police force in the whole world. He stiffened, his eyes narrowed, he raised his machine gun. Bullets splattered into the snow on either side of Heide. The warning was ignored.

By now the situation was not even faintly amusing but deadly serious. The Russian levelled his gun and took aim. Alte raised his revolver and also took aim. At the Russian. The Russian saw it out of the corner of his eye. For a second he wavered, and in that second Heide tripped and fell, his head butting hard into the Russian's abdomen. The hand grenades rolled away into the snow and were rescued by the Professor. The machine gun jerked upwards and the Legionnaire lost no time in grabbing at it. Meanwhile, Heide and the Russian had merged into a whirling mass of arms and legs, and Alte lowered his revolver with a shake of the head. With a supreme effort, the Russian managed to free himself from Heide's frenzied grasp. He stepped back a pace, grunting, shook his fist at the whole lot of us, and then informed us in loud and arrogant tones that he, Piotr Yanow, would personally see to it that Heide received the ultimate penalty for daring to lift a finger against a member of the N.K.V.D. He, Piotr Yanow, did not take insults of that nature lying down. At this, Heide gave a maniacal screech of laughter and informed the Russian that he, Julius Heide, had a mind to slit his throat for him.

A stunned silence on the part of the crowd. And on the part of the Russian, who finally fell back on the usual irascible demand for papers.

'Get stuffed!' shouted Heide. 'You can keep that sort of rubbish for p.o.w.'s. It won't wash with us. The German Army doesn't take shit from anyone!'

Slowly, the Russian surveyed each one of us, taking in the details of our uniforms. When he spoke, there was a note almost of supplication in his voice.

'Njet Russki?' he whispered.

Alte took a step forward, his revolver at the ready. The crowd closed in all round us, suddenly given new courage by the sight of their dreaded enemy humbled and at a loss for words. Somewhere a woman cackled with malicious mirth. Little John picked up one of the barrels of alcohol and held it out to the Russian.

'Drink a toast,' he commanded. 'Here's to us and the downfall of our enemies! Confusion to the Russians! Heil Hitler!'

The man drank. He seemed dazed to the point of total non-comprehension. We could understand how he was feeling. The presence of German soldiers so far behind the Russian lines – German soldiers, moreover, wearing the uniforms of a Russian tank regiment – must have seemed a nightmare impossibility. And yet there we were, standing foursquare and insolent before him.

At that moment we felt no particular animosity towards the man. Somewhere in the village they had found and roasted a whole side of pork, and we now invited our tame Russian to join us in a victory meal. He protested faintly that the pork was Soviet property and we had no right to be eating it, but I think even he realized the futility of his words.

We sat him down amongst us in the village street and tore at strips of the roast meat with our bare hands. The barrels of liquor were passed round freely. All differences were soon forgotten. Barcelona fetched the Russian an affectionate blow on the shoulder with the butt of his revolver and shouted 'Vive Moscow!' The Russian belched and shouted encouragement to Little John, who was doing his drunken best to violate a fat, trousered lady of the village.

'Vive Stalin!' cried Barcelona.

'Vive Stalin!' echoed the Russian. 'Long life to Lenin, protector of the proletariat!'

He lost his balance and fell on his side in the snow, and the Legionnaire pulled him upright again. The Russian pointed a finger at him.

'You're under arrest,' he told him. 'All of you, under arrest. I've had my eye on you for some time . . . filthy Trotskyists!'

He cleared his throat, spat over his shoulder, informed the Legionnaire that Karl Marx was a habitual drunkard, fell over again and clutched amorously at Porta. Then he looked all round him, as if to ensure himself of a degree of privacy, leaned forward and whispered hoarsely.

'Tovaritch, tell me one thing: where did you learn to speak Russian?'

'Why, at home,' hissed Porta, with an equal air of secrecy.

There was a pause, then the Russian rocked with loud laughter.

'You must teach me some day!'

'Gladly,' said Porta. 'Or perhaps you'd rather learn German?'

The Russian became suddenly sullen once again.

'Where are your papers?' he demanded. 'I haven't seen your papers . . . Do you have any papers?'

'Naturally,' said Porta. 'But it's not worth the bother of showing them to you. They're all forgeries.'

In the midst of the general mirth, the joke seeming to be much appreciated by our friend Piotr, Fjodor shuffled up to Alte and muttered urgently in his ear. By a mixture of sign language and pidgin Russian the old man was able, in a limited way, to converse with us, and I knew at once from the expression on Alte's face as he turned towards me that the time had come to cease merrymaking and return once again to the sordid business of war.

'Sven! On your feet, and make it snappy! According to Fjodor there's an N.K.V.D. patrol on its way here.'

'Right! I'll get the sledge ready straight away.'

Already the news had communicated itself to the villagers. They were as anxious to be rid of us as we were to be gone, eager to eliminate all traces of our presence. Alte dragged Little John away from his lady friend, shook the Professor out of a drunken trance, picked Heide bodily off the ground and prepared ourselves for a hasty departure. The Russian sat watching us, cradling an empty barrel of alcohol on his lap, obviously at a loss to understand the sudden breaking up of the party.

'What about him?' demanded Porta, jerking his thumb towards him.

Heide would have disposed of him there and then, but Fjodor showed signs of such agitation at the thought of a dead

55

Russian left behind in the village that we had no alternative but to take him with us.

'You shoot later,' begged Fjodor. 'Much later. But you shoot all right. You cut throat, maybe. Bury in snow.'

'With the greatest of pleasure,' said Heide. 'I'll take care of him.' He seized the Russian by the shoulder. 'Come on, you! Time to be off.'

Apathetically, the Russian strapped on his skis and reached out for his abandoned machine gun. Heide promptly took it from him.

'Voina plenny (prisoner-of-war)', he told him. 'No need for guns any more. You do what you're told from now on.'

The dog team was harnessed, Paul was made comfortable on the sledge, the whole village assembled to wave us farewell. With a crack of the whip and a cry of 'Ohaï!' from Alte, we were off. The leader of the team bounded forward, the sledge moved away. The village was left behind and the usual combination of snow and wind quickly dissipated the remaining effects of the drink and the roast pork that had warmed our bellies and raised our spirits. Once more we were alone in a hostile country, trekking along a familiar road in hell.

For three days our prisoner-of-war maintained a continuous and sullen silence. The first words he spoke were to Alte.

'There's going to be a storm,' he told him. 'You'd better get the tent up immediately, unless you want us all to die of exposure.'

Alte stuck his pipe between his teeth and looked up at the low, racing clouds on the horizon.

'All right,' he said, at last. 'If that's your advice we'd be wise to take it. You know your own country better than we do.'

The Old Man's calm seemed to agitate the Russian.

'When I say immediately, I mean immediately! The storm's going to be right overhead in less than an hour's time, and if that tent's not up we'll be dead within minutes. The temperature's going to drop right down. At least 48 degrees below freezing.'

'He's right,' declared the Legionnaire. I've seen plenty of sandstorms in the Sahara and I don't fancy a snowstorm in the middle of Russia, I can tell you.'

Porta looked aghast.

'You're not going to go by what this slob says?' he demanded.

'Why not? He knows the country, doesn't he?'

'You're bloody mad,' began Porta, heatedly, but Alte intervened.

'Shut up and get cracking with that tent.'

Slowly, and with rather bad grace, we began to unload the sledge, Porta muttering mutinously to himself and Heide mouthing the usual obscenities towards the dog team, as if they personally were responsible for the weather. Quite suddenly, as if from nowhere, a tremendous blast of wind with an icy cutting edge like the blade of a knife hurled itself furiously upon us, overturning the sledge and us with it.

'Now perhaps you'll get a move on!' screamed the Legionnaire.

Working as fast as our numbed fingers and the continuing wind would allow us, we set up the frozen canvas of the tent, stiff as a board already and almost impossible to handle, and at the Russian's suggestion began hacking out blocks of ice and snow to form a protective rampart against the coming storm.

By the time the work was done we were all exhausted. We fell asleep huddled shoulder to shoulder, leaving the Professor to keep watch over us and our prisoner. Somehow it always seemed to be the Professor's turn to keep watch.

We were woken by the storm. It was a storm such as none of us had ever seen before, and it could surely only have happened in Russia or the North Pole. For four or five hours it required our combined efforts to keep the tent upright. At last the wind dropped to a more normal pitch, and the Russian relaxed and nodded to the rest of us.

'O.K. We can sleep now.'

'Sleep?' said Alte. 'It must be nearly daybreak. We've got to push on.'

The Russian smiled, pityingly.

'Why don't you try? Take a step outside and see how far you get.'

Little John, of course, had to make the attempt. Uttering words of scorn and bravado, he stepped outside the tent, fell into a snowdrift several feet high, staggered upright again, was promptly knocked over by the wind and rolled head over heels back into the tent, completely covered in snow.

'Fancy a big strong chap like you being bowled over by a little gentle breeze!' jeered Porta.

'How long is this lot likely to last?' demanded Alte.

The Russian shrugged uncaring shoulders.

'Three days, if you're lucky. A week if you're not.'

His estimate was correct. For three days the storm buffeted the snow across the plains. Conversation was almost impossible and our voices became hoarse through constant shouting. From time to time we staggered outside into the freezing white world and saw the dogs curled up nose to tail in the lee of the tent, almost invisible beneath a thick covering of snow. Inside, we fought and quarrelled and slept and woke and fought and quarrelled as the monotonous hours dragged on. Little John and Steiner battered each other almost raw; Steiner then picked on the Professor and half killed him; Heide came to the Professor's rescue and was straightway accused by Porta of supporting the S.S.; in a fury, he then knocked the Professor stone cold and turned to vent the rest of his spleen on his old enemy Little John. Finally, we all banded together against the Russian, sitting silent and morose in a corner, and found ourselves for once in accord in our general decision that he was to blame for the entire war.

On the fourth morning we awoke to an uncannily silent world. The snow was falling heavily from the leaden sky, but the wind had dropped. Drifts were piled as high as mountains, and we played in the snow like children, rolling in it, jumping in it, scooping up great handfuls and hurling it at each other.

Two weeks later we were at last approaching the German front lines. We had exhausted our stocks of food and were all half dead with fatigue. For three days we had been without the dogs. They had been in no condition to continue, and we had simply let them loose to fend for themselves. The sledge had been disposed of and lay at the bottom of a ravine. Our prisoner-of-war was growing increasingly ill at ease. His former arrogance had vanished, and it was plain that all his thoughts were turned to the possibility of escape. Which of us would not have been the same, in his position?

During all this time, we had encountered no one on our march across the steppes, but there came a day when the luck had to break. We were approaching a wood and were about half a kilometre away when suddenly, echoing across the plain, the dreaded cry resounded.

'Stoï!'

Porta and the Legionnaire turned in an instant and sent a volley of shots in the direction from which it came.

'Under cover!' shouted Alte. 'Make for the trees!'

Heide and the Professor threw themselves face downwards behind a ridge of snow to cover our hasty retreat. It was the occasion for which the Russian had been waiting. He began running across the open country towards his compatriots, waving his hands in the air and shouting 'Uhrae Stalino!' at the top of his voice. It was the moment, also, for which Heide had been waiting. He had promised Fjodor, back at the village, that he would personally eliminate the Russian, and at last he could legitimately do so. There was a burst of machine gun fire. From the shelter of the trees we saw the Russian suddenly jerk backwards, as if pulled by an invisible string. He turned a full circle, then slowly crumpled up in the snow and lay still. Heide's gun rattled off another hail of bullets. By now, we had the heavy artillery bombarding the enemy from the shelter of the woods. Heide stood up, defiantly hurled three hand grenades one after another before running for cover in the wake of the Professor. The grenades exploded in a welter of snow and human débris. Heide sang triumphantly as he joined the rest of us.

He was a born killer, was Julius Heide. In peacetime he would doubtless have been locked away as a dangerous psychopath, but this was wartime and Heide passed as an excellent soldier, fearless, unimaginative, always in the thick of every fight and ready at a moment's notice to shoot anything that moved. They decorated him for his courage and rewarded him for his aggression. If he survived the war – and of course he was the type who would – he would become an instructor in a military school. Society can always turn the instincts of a Julius

Heide to its advantage if it only recognizes them in time. Nevertheless, he was not a man you really enjoyed having around.

Panting and exuberant, he dropped down behind the heavy machine gun manned by Porta and the Legionnaire.

'I got at least twenty of 'em!'

'That must have given them something to think about ... being fired on by their own troops.'

'They probably think we're Brandenbergers.'

'Then God help us if they ever get their hands on us.'

'They strangle them with barbed wire,' said Steiner. 'I once saw a couple of Brandenbergers they'd captured. They'd strangled one with barbed wire and they'd roasted the other alive over a spit.'

'Charming,' said Porta. 'And here's me who can't stand the heat.'

'In any case,' gloated Heide, 'I shouldn't imagine there are any of that little bunch left alive to recognize us again.'

We pushed on through the trees but had scarcely covered more than a few metres when we heard the unmistakable sound of tanks not far ahead. With one accord we bounded off the road and dived into the undergrowth as the first T.34 came into view. A grenade whistled past us and we flung ourselves flat on the ground. Porta went racing off down a narrow pathway and crashed headlong into a Russian sergeant, who naturally took him to be friend rather than enemy. He did not live long enough to discover his mistake: Porta emptied his revolver into him at point blank range and seized upon the flame thrower that the man had been carrying.

'Now we'll show the bastards!' he yelled.

He positioned himself straight in the path of the oncoming tanks and knelt on one knee, calmly waiting, as if it were no more than a routine exercise. The rest of us crouched in the undergrowth, biting our nails with anticipation.

'Fire, for God's sake,' muttered Alte.

Little John was unable to contain himself.

'For Christ's sake FIRE!' he shouted to Porta.

All hell was promptly let loose about our ears, but in that instant Porta fired and a long flame snaked out towards the nearest T.34. The tank seemed to rear up in an effort to avoid it. It moved forward a short way, then stopped. An answering flame shot skywards from the turret. A man appeared in the opening. He pulled himself half out into the open air and then fell back again, with blue flames licking greedily at his body. His long cry of agony was enough to curdle anyone's blood. Except, perhaps, Heide's. He probably enjoyed it. The revolting smell of burning flesh filled our nostrils. The two remaining tanks made a half turn and crashed away through the undergrowth in a panic. They had obviously taken the flamethrower for an anti-tank gun and had no intention of remaining behind to be slaughtered.

As for us, we also took to our heels. We ran until we were free of the woods, emerging breathless and exhausted into the open, where we fell to licking the snow like so many animals to soothe our parched throats. All round us it was still and silent, but far away, in the distance, we could hear the whine of shells and the heavy groaning of artillery.

'There it is,' said Steiner, pointing to the north west. 'The front.'

'God, how I hate it all.'

The Professor suddenly flung himself down in the snow, and after a moment's hesitation the rest of us followed suit. We needed a short period of relaxation before facing the next load of problems.

'What do you hate especially?' asked Porta, lying on his back and staring up at the trees.

The Professor made an impatient movement with his hand.

'Everything. All the lies and the cheating and the senseless slaughter. They made it sound so different when we first joined up, back in Oslo.'

'Naturally,' said Porta, dryly. 'I suppose they promised you glorious victory and little flags to wave and tin trumpets to blow? And the enemy was just a bunch of toy soldiers waiting to be knocked down like a load of skittles? Jesus Christ Almighty, the things some people believe!'

'We died like flies,' said the Professor. 'They sent us into battle totally unprepared. Before we'd even had a chance to discover the danger we were in most of us were already dead.'

'Heard it all before,' muttered Barcelona.

'Yeah. They made you think the war was some sort of Sunday school outing,' said Porta. 'What sort of training did they bother to give you?'

'Six weeks,' said the Professor.

We all turned to look at him.

'Six weeks?'

'That's all.'

'My God, we had three years of it,' said Alte slowly. 'For us the war began easily enough with Poland. Just like manoeuvres, only real bullets instead of blanks ... six weeks! God in heaven! How many of you survived the first onslaught?'

'There were two hundred and thirty-five of us at the beginning. All volunteers. All in the Viking Division in the Ukraine. The first day, one hundred and twenty-one of us were killed. More were lost when the road was strafed by Russian fighters and some of the ambulances went up in flames ... The C.O. went mad and put a bullet through his brain. Two days later, eight of us were shot for "desertion in the face of the enemy". Nine more of us were sent to disciplinary regiments for having said that our officers were more to blame than we were. They were professional soldiers and they knew what to expect. We were volunteers and we'd been misled ... I was beaten for six hours non-stop in the prison at Lemberg. At first I thought I was lucky to be left alive. I'm not so sure now.'

'So long as there are whores in the world, it's worth being alive,' said Little John, bracingly.

The Professor smiled, and we all, automatically, perked up at the sound of the word 'whore'. Sex was a subject of which we never tired. We all knew each other's preferences by heart, we lived intimately with each other's day dreams, yet somehow they never ceased to be an enthralling topic of conversation.

It was not long before we heard a volley of shots away to our right, and instantly we were on the alert.

'Probably a search party out looking for us,' whispered Alte. 'Take cover and stay hidden.'

Silently we crept on our stomachs back into the shelter of the undergrowth. It was dusk now, and our nerves were on edge at the prospect of being hunted. The search party were obviously also nervous. They fired a few shots into the bushes, retreated, came on again, fired at random at nothing at all. Doubtless they would willingly have given us up for lost had not their officers urged them on with the usual mixture of threats and curses.

We caught a quick glimpse of them as they came through the trees. They were gauche young recruits, it was probably their first action. We heard one, more confident than the others, boastfully declare his intention to shoot on sight. The officer in charge turned on him wrathfully.

'You wait until then, you'll be dead! In cases like this you shoot by instinct not by sight. Now shut up talking and keep your ears pinned back.'

The Legionnaire silently rose up from the bushes and sent a volley of shots in the direction of the voices. We heard a cry, then someone cursing. The undergrowth crackled, then there was silence. We could sense the presence of someone not far away. The Legionnaire frowned intently through the darkness. Heide began to slide stealthily forward along a narrow path, followed closely by Porta and Little John, Barcelona covering them with his machine gun. A twig snapped in two and we saw a dark figure step out from the bushes. Barcelona at once opened fire. The man screamed and clasped his hands to his eyes. It was a Russian officer, a lieutenant. He came blundering up the path towards us, blood streaming down his face. Barcelona fired again and put the man out of his misery, and at the same moment the rest of us opened fire on several figures that loomed up in the darkness. They were an easy prey. Those that did not fall turned and ran, and from some distance away we heard a Russian voice raised in anger. Doubtless the C.O. attempting to restore order. Alte jerked his head.

'All right. Let's go.'

For the rest of the night and the following day we remained hidden and undisturbed in the wood. Towards evening, we prepared ourselves for our journey to the German front line. We had evolved a plan that was simple enough in theory, though whether it would work in practice seemed, to me at least, highly problematical.

We approached the line of Russian trenches. Naturally we were stopped and questioned. To each question Alte gave the same reply: we had been sent out in capacity of a mine-clearing unit. No one batted an eyelid. We were provided with equipment and even wished good luck.

'Rather you than me,' said the sergeant who guided us on the last stage of our journey through the front line of Russian trenches. 'I just hope the saints are looking out for you!'

'Spassibo pan,' replied Porta, unctuously.

Then we were in no-man's land, crawling rapidly across it towards the German lines. A hail of machine gun bullets ploughed up the ground all about us and we fell in a huddle into a shell hole. We leapfrogged from shell hole to shell hole, until at length Alte insisted on leaving us behind and going it alone. We hardly dared to watch his progress. We just lay chewing our finger nails and waiting for the fun to start. And then, after what seemed an eternity, an unknown voice yelled at us in German.

'O.K., you can start moving across, but don't try any funny business. I'll have one man at a time, a minute between each man.'

They were evidently fearful of a trap, for as each one of us jumped down into the trench we were met by the sharp end of a bayonet pricking our chests. A young infantry lieutenant questioned us and remained highly sceptical – as who could blame him? German soldiers dressed in Russian uniforms? German soldiers appearing in no-man's land from behind the Russian lines? Now that we were back, we could hardly believe it ourselves.

'You'd be amazed at the things that go on in the German Army,' said Barcelona, cheerfully.

The Lieutenant turned on him.

'Hold your tongue, Feldwebel! You may have been racketing round the country enjoying yourselves for the past few weeks, but you're back in the army now and you'll do well to remember it.'

'We're back all right,' muttered Steiner. 'Who else would give us such a nice warm welcome? Red carpets and all! I tell you, Lieutenant, it's a real treat to get back home again.'

Captain Lander was, if anything, even less welcoming. We had the odd feeling that he was not really pleased to see us. However, three days later his body was found riddled with bullets in a thicket, and it hardly seemed respectful to the dead to go on doubting him.

As usual, it was the partisans who were held responsible for the murder, although some people did, indeed, raise their eyebrows in the direction of Porta and Little John. In the end they had to take the extreme measure of attending the Captain's funeral in order to prove their innocence.

He came to us from the military prison at Glatz. The court martial had sentenced him to serve ten years in a disciplinary regiment for having dared to say that war was the means by which a second-class housepainter had come to be called a genius.

From lieutenant-general, he was demoted to major. In Africa he lost his left eye, in Finland he left behind a part of his stomach. He was an excellent tank commander, capable of leading a whole division, but he had never learnt to guard his tongue against what he believed to be the truth.

Major Mercedes was the best officer we had ever had. Standing upright before us on an old packing case, bareheaded and in his shirt sleeves, he introduced himself.

'O.K. I'm your new officer. Karl Ulrich Mercedes. Like you, I'm in the shit right up to my neck. I'm thirty-five years old and I weigh 15½ stone. Any questions? No. I've nothing else to say to you, except this: you pull your weight and I'll pull mine and we'll all get along fine.'

At Lugansk he was wounded in the belly and had half his jaw shot away. He was one of the very few officers we ever respected.

CHAPTER FIVE

LUGANSK was a sea of flames when we drove through in the tanks. Bodies spilled across the streets and lay in the gutters like so much rubbish tipped out of the dustbins. Columns of soldiers, torn and bleeding, dived for the illusory safety of burning houses and crumbling piles of masonry.

A shot. And then another, and then more. Shells, hand grenades, anti-tank guns, incendiary bombs. A whole barrage aimed at destruction and death.

The interior of our tank, a 52-ton Tiger, resounded with the harsh noise of metal on metal: mess tins, water containers, tin mugs, spanners, wrenches, empty boxes that had once held hand grenades. Porta stepped on the gas, the Tiger ground forward and the whole range of ironmongery rattled and clanked at our feet.

Mechanics, covered in mud and blood and oil, sought desperately through the devastated streets for their units. An infantry captain, shouting orders in the middle of the road, was caught by one of the Tigers and thrown to the ground. The following tank was unable to avoid him. All that remained visible were his legs and his leather boots with their shining spurs.

No one said anything. No one cared. What was the death of one more man when set against the wholesale slaughter at Lugansk on the night of 14th March? We were past the stage of emotion, our feelings were dead.

Somewhere a roof collapsed with a thunderous roar and a shower of sparks rained down upon us. We pressed on, in line, until a sharp cry from Little John brought us to a halt. In one bound he was out of the tank and running back hell for leather up the burning street.

'What's got into him?' demanded Heide. 'What's he think this is, a joy ride?'

The radio crackled angrily into life. It was Lt. Ohlsen, asking roughly the same question as Heide and adding the curt command that we should get started again and stop holding up the column. Porta shrugged his shoulders and put his foot down. The tank moved forward, at the same moment as Little John reappeared. He threw something down the hatch and himself after it. We sat gaping at a grubby urchin, not more than four or five years old, who gaped back at us uncertainly.

'What's the meaning of this?' snapped Alte.

Little John pulled the child on to his lap.

'He was sitting in the gutter all by himself. I couldn't just leave the kid out there to get killed. A second later and he'd've been buried under half a ton of burning timber.' He glared round at us. 'He's mine, see? And from now on you can all contribute part of your rations ... You and me,' he told the boy, 'we're together now. O.K.?'

'Yes, I can just imagine the Major's expression of delight when he hears about it,' said Alte, sarcastically. 'He'll be overjoyed.'

'I don't give a monkey's cuss,' said Little John, 'for him or for anyone else. This kid is mine and we're sticking together ... Imagine that, I'm a father! Poor little sod, he's scared to death. Turn your ugly mug the other way, Julius, it's enough to put the shits up anyone.' He turned the boy to face him and pointed a finger at himself. 'Hey, tovaritch! Toi pljemjanjik! Me, Little John Otschoenasch!'

Porta gave a derisory laugh.

'You cretinous great oaf ... That means you're God the Father.'

'All right, you explain to him,' said Little John, heatedly. 'Tell him I'm his father. Go on!'

Porta obligingly let loose a stream of fluent Russian. The boy bit his finger, evidently soothed by the sound of his own language but generally uncertain what to make of the situation. He was in rags, filthy dirty, with burns on his bare feet and a nasty gash running down his cheek. The Legionnaire cleaned him up a bit and dressed his various wounds, and Heide gave

68

him an apple, which he ate ravenously, core and all. We had nothing else to offer him, but in any case there were more pressing matters requiring our attention.

Shells and incendiary bombs were exploding all about us, houses were toppling down like packs of cards, burning roof beams lay in our path and débris littered the nose of the tank. We pushed on our way out of town, moving slowly and cautiously. A bunch of soldiers rushed at us from some ruins, and it was not until we had mown down the last of them that we realized our mistake: we had shot at our own soldiers. They had obviously taken refuge in the burnt-out houses and must have thought themselves saved on seeing their own tanks approaching. Unfortunately, in the heat of the moment it was difficult to distinguish between the camouflaged tunics worn by the Germans and the khaki uniforms of the Russians.

The tanks hurled themselves out through the suburbs at full speed. We took a left turn through what had once been a beautifully laid-out garden. An ornamental pond was cracked in two beneath the weight of the tank. The surrounding fields were a mass of khaki. Everyone, on foot, by tank, by lorry, by motorcycle, had but one idea: to put as much distance as possible between himself and the burning hell of Lugansk.

'Advance!' screamed the Major's voice over the radio.

We advanced, mercilessly; a line of fifty tanks ploughing through the sea of khaki. All round us was the staccato rattle of machine guns, the bursting of shells. Flame throwers set the very air alight, soaked as it was in the escaping petrol of various wrecked and abandoned vehicles. Russian infantry troops surged about us in a state of panic, milling first this way, then that, hurling themselves to the ground and clawing with their fingernails in a despairing attempt to dig themselves into the earth. But our artillery was always one step ahead, ploughing the ground into deep furrows and the men with it. The tanks churned onwards, crushing whatever and whoever stood in their path.

And then, suddenly, silence. The shooting stopped. There was no more need for it. The Russians were fleeing before us and we rounded them up like so many sheep, pushing them on towards the German lines. A sense of madness, of sheer exhilaration, almost a blood lust, overcame even the least aggressive amongst us. It was inevitable, and, indeed, necessary to survival in this kind of warfare.

And then, with a harsh metallic cry, our exultation was shattered. The tank was hit by a shell from an anti-tank gun, with such force that for a moment the vehicle was out of control. By some curious miracle, the grenade did not penetrate the outer rim of steel.

'Get the hell out of here!' shouted Alte, his eye still glued to the observation panel.

The anti-tank gun was obviously in the immediate vicinity and we lived the next few seconds in agonized expectation of another grenade. None came. Perhaps some kind soul had put the gun out of action for us. At any rate, we forged ahead with the tank still intact and made for our own lines.

We were sent off to a new position on the outskirts of Novoajdar, but had barely arrived there when Lt. Ohlsen's voice crackled across the radio ordering us to turn about and take a different direction.

'Jesus Christ,' muttered Porta. 'This war gets bloody boring at times.'

We moved off again, Little John doing his best to comfort his newly-adopted son, who was crying fit to break your heart. Our Tigers joined up with a group of armoured cars that had been sent on ahead in support of an infantry regiment. We were to remain stationary, in wait for the enemy troops. The cold was intense. Little John had given his jacket to the boy and was now running in circles outside trying to keep warm.

Suddenly, from nowhere it seemed, a hail of grenades rained down on the assembled tanks. The cries of the wounded mingled with the sound of explosions. Little John gave a blood-curdling shriek and hurled himself back into the tank. His right ear had completely disappeared. His face was awash with blood.

'My ear!' he was bellowing. 'The buggers have nicked my sodding ear off!'

'Does it hurt?' I unwisely inquired.

Little John turned on me in a fury.

'What do you think, you stupid flaming bastard?'

It was a foolish question, of course. I realize that.

Once again, we were in the thick of the action. The tanks moved forward through a barrage of shells and grenades. Houses burnt, men screamed, the noise of cannons and machine guns filled what for a short while had been a beautiful silence.

'Something big brewing this time,' mused Alte. 'I don't like the look of it.'

When Alte said he didn't like the look of anything, then you knew it must be pretty bad. Veteran of the front line that he was, he could sense the danger in a situation long before the rest of us had even realized that a situation existed.

Lt. Ohlsen came through again.

'What do you make of it, Beier? What do you think?'

Alte shook his head.

'Not too good, if you ask me. Ivan's preparing for some piece of tomfoolery ... it's just a question of what and how. The damned smoke's so thick it's like a fog out there. You can't see more than a few yards ahead.'

'Well, keep your eyes skinned.'

'Will do.'

The company of tanks advanced cautiously. One by one we crossed a small wooden bridge that creaked and groaned under our weight. Radios crackled incessantly and men spoke nervously of attack. There was an uncertainty abroad that night, and it set all our nerves on edge.

An attack in the dark is a terrifying ordeal for a tank regiment. Here we were at a most particular disadvantage in that the road we were on was narrow and winding, and on either side of it lay treacherous marshland. It was obvious that the Russians had us in their sights for their bombardments followed us with nasty precision.

One of the tanks left the track and became stuck in the boggy ground at the side of the road. We tried hoisting her out with cables, but she was too deep in the mud and the cables snapped under the pressure. Major Mercedes came running up to us, using language unbefitting to an officer; demanding, in effect, what the hell we were playing at. He set to work himself, fixing a new cable. He was wearing thick gauntlets, like a docker.

Before we had a chance to try out the new cable, the Russians brought their heavy artillery into action. The Major was up and inside our tank with a turn of speed I should frankly not have thought possible for a man of his bulk. We closed up the side panels and the tank reverberated unpleasantly under the bombardment. The Russians were hurling all they had against us. Not surprisingly, Little John's adopted son began to scream with fear, and it was all we could do not to join him in a demented chorus. Barcelona's voice came over the radio:

'Old Man! Can you see anything?'

'Damn fool question,' grunted Porta.

'Not a flaming thing,' replied Alte, cheerfully.

'Where the hell are they attacking from? The whole of the Fourth Company have already been wiped out.'

There was a sudden and unnerving silence. In our panic we began firing blindly into the darkness. Our own infantry remained quiet, doubtless waiting to see what would happen next. The initiative was with the Russians now.

It started up again, with renewed fury. It was as if a volcano had erupted, belching out not rocks and fire but shells and bullets and grenades. The air was full of the sound of death. It came at us from all sides, and we sat silent and horrified in the midst of it, trapped in a steel box that could explode and send us sky high at any moment. No one attempted to speak. Probably no one was capable of it. We just held on tight as the tank shuddered and heaved beneath the onslaught. Our eyes were wide open, our throats were dry and painful. We felt ourselves to be alone in the inferno, cut off from the rest of the world. It seemed only a question of time, of minutes or even seconds, before a missile found its mark and 1,500 litres of petrol went up in a solid sheet of flame. We knew how it would be. We had seen it happen to our friends and comrades, and we had no illusions as to the manner of our death. It was usual for tank crews to end up as charred skeletons: only ten per cent of us survived the war.

All about us, shells were thudding down and great gouts of earth were catapulting into the air. Death seemed to cling at the nape of our necks, to plant clammy cold feet up the length of our spines. We could have retreated, but the thought did not occur to us. We were not heroes, we had no desire for heroism. An iron discipline had been drilled into us, it had become an integral part of us over the years, and it was that alone which kept us at our posts in the middle of hell. That, and fear for our own skins. We fought not for Hitler, not for the Fatherland, but simply to stay alive. It was a case of probable death at the hands of the Russians as against certain death before the firing squad if we dared to withdraw. Again, we were familiar with the story. We had known other crews in other tanks who had broken under the pressure of extreme fear. We had not blamed them, but they had met their death fast enough at dawn the next day. 'Desertion in the face of the enemy'. We were always given the full details. It was the best method of discouraging others from following their example.

A fresh blast hit the tank. The boy suddenly screamed. He hurled himself to the ground, kicking, gnashing his teeth, foam specking his lips. Before we could restrain him he had dashed his head against the breech of the machine gun. Little John snatched the child into his arms while the rest of us stared, aghast, at this new horror in our midst. Heide groped nervously for his revolver. The child arched his body, threw back his head, jerked himself out of Little John's arms and went crashing to the floor.

'Do something!' ordered Little John, frantically. 'Don't just bloody stand there! Do something!'

Alte bent over the child, then slowly shook his head.

'There's nothing we can do. He's dead.'

Bruised and torn and bleeding, the little body lay still on the oily floor of the tank. It looked like nothing so much as a bundle of empty rags. Little John stared, as one unable to believe the evidence of his eyes. He suddenly hit himself hard on the forehead with a clenched fist and let out a roar of desperation. Before any of us could move he had gathered the child's body to him and was up and out of the tank, brandishing his revolver and shooting wildly in all directions.

'Come and get it, you lousy stinking load of swine!'

We stared out at him, mesmerized. He never was a pretty figure to look upon, but now, with a bloodstained bandage flapping over his forehead and a dead child clutched to his chest, he was quite horrifying.

'He's gone barmy,' muttered Porta. 'He won't last two seconds out there.'

'I'll get him.'

The Legionnaire, swift, silent and surefooted, followed Little John out of the tank. With one well-placed blow he had knocked him senseless, and Heide and Porta between them managed to drag his body back to safety. The child fell from his grip and remained lying in the road. The Legionnaire left it there without a backward glance.

Once more we entered upon a period of watching, listening, waiting ... From somewhere ahead of us, a mass of tattered and bleeding humanity emerged from the trenches. It was our infantry.

Slowly a grey dawn began to break. A damp and stifling mist hung in the air, but at least we could see what was going on. Flares were being sent up from behind the Russian lines; green and white. We knew what that indicated: it was the signal for attack. Little John had regained his senses and was vaingloriously threatening to kill all and sundry. It looked as if his hour had not come.

The attack began. Wave upon wave of Russian infantry swarmed across to our trenches. We heard their exultant cries of 'Uhrae!' as they rushed in for the kill. They stretched as far as the eye could see, and our own infantry were no more than tiny islands in the enemy ocean. Abandoning their positions, jettisoning cannons and machine guns, they fled for their lives. There was nothing else they could do against such an onslaught.

It was a day of mist and grey, overhung skies. A day like many others. And yet, for thousand upon thousand of men in that section of the front it was to be their last day on earth. No one ever dared calculate the exact number of losses that were incurred. Both sides suffered, and both sides destroyed the casualty lists rather than face the truth. The battle of Lugansk had been too dear. The official communiqué stated, simply: 'Local attack in the Lugansk sector repelled by our artillery. Position held.'

The voice of Mercedes came over the radio:

'All Tigers to go into the attack with everything available. Make for the railway embankment 400 metres ahead ... Good luck!'

The railway line and the embankment were a chaos of overturned trucks and locomotives. Long sections of the track were buckled or had been viciously ripped up, so that now they pointed heavenwards like accusing iron fingers. Signals flapped aimlessly, burning oil drums added to the chaos. The body of a German soldier, propelled no doubt by the force of an explosion, was impaled on an upturned rail and now swung back and forth like a human weathercock.

From the top of the embankment we had a balcony view of the entire scene. The Russian infantry stretched out to the horizon, the massed khaki interspersed here and there by anti-aircraft batteries and anti-tank guns drawn by horses.

'God in heaven,' murmured Alte. 'It doesn't seem possible there could be so many of them.'

The Tigers moved in to attack. From afar they must have resembled some strange and hideous pack of prehistoric monsters. There was no time, now, to reflect and be scared. Mechanically we set about our task of destruction. The earth trembled beneath us, the heavy guns roared and blasted. Stream upon stream of bullets tore their way into the mass of enemy soldiers. For a moment, the great sea hesitated. A ripple ran through it and then a tidal wave as those nearest the tanks turned to flee. Many were crushed in the general panic. Many more were shattered by the heavy shells that landed in their midst, throwing up great geysers of earth and humanity.

Inside the tanks we were half suffocated. The air was hot and acrid, burning our eyes and our throats. Heide worked like a maniac, loading and reloading the gun. His heavy gauntlets were singed, and a cloud of smoke rose up from them. Several times our clothes caught alight and we had to beat out the flames with our bare hands. Our faces were black, we were bathed in sweat. In normal circumstances we should have found the conditions unbearable, but now we scarcely noticed.

The tank rocked and vibrated, and the fury of the chase was

upon us. We knew it of old, but always it burst upon us as a new experience. Danger was forgotten, death was forgotten, the very war itself was forgotten. We knew only that we had to kill. The figures in khaki were no longer men, no longer soldiers like ourselves, but wild beasts to be hunted and crushed. We were the hunters, hunting and killing for the sheer, primitive joy of it. We laughed aloud as we crushed our prey beneath us. We shouted in triumph as we saw them cowering in their holes, and we turned towards them and we blasted them out of existence.

We worked bareheaded and barechested, caps and tunics abandoned. Teeth shone white in oily, grimed faces. Eyes gleamed dementedly. Little John was howling like a wolf. We killed and killed again, with every weapon at our disposal, with cannon, machine gun and flame thrower. And the Russians turned on us, wounded animals at bay, and fought back with desperate fervour. Mortally wounded, they still hurled everything they had into the battle. But their revolvers and their rifles had no more effect than pea shooters. Even the anti-tank guns were useless at any range less than a hundred metres. Some of them, indeed, hurled themselves upon us in suicidal attacks with Molotov cocktails and magnetic bombs, but it's difficult to make a magnetic bomb stick to a tank, and the Molotovs generally did more harm to their own side than to ours.

'Tigers, pull your bloody fingers out!' roared the Major over the radio. 'We haven't got all day to waste mopping this lot up!'

Incensed, we pressed on with an even greater fury. Now the Russians were fleeing before us, our shells exploding in their midst, broken bodies hanging puppetlike in the air and thudding down upon the tanks. The hum of the ventilator showed that the fan was still functioning, but nevertheless the stench of blood and sweat and burning humanity was enough to turn your stomach. At one point Alte turned his head aside and vomited. Some of it caught me in the face. I wiped it off with the back of my hand and never realized until much later.

'Last shell going in,' announced Heide, suddenly.

'And only thirty litres of petrol left,' added Porta.

Following in the rear, in the wake of the carnage, were the refuelling tanks. We turned back and in record time were stocked up once more with ammunition. New orders came over the radio: Russian tanks to our right. Distance 1,200 metres. Deal with them.

It was a whole formation of T.34s. We could see them massed on the far side of the railway line, and as we brought our guns to bear I felt fear returning to me. At moments like that it is sheer hell to be trapped in a tank.

'Fire!' commanded Alte.

The heavy guns roared. Almost at once, the leading T.34s were in flames – but on our side, also, vast torches had been set alight. Within minutes we were surrounded by burning masses of steel. Few men managed to escape from the inferno before the ammunition exploded and blew both tank and occupants into a million unrecognizable pieces. It was the light tanks that suffered: the Tigers withstood the onslaught, while the others were wiped out almost completely.

After an hour's hard fighting, the Russians were defeated. The cost to both sides had been devastating.

The enemy had discovered that a breakthrough at that section of the front was not possible: we had discovered that we could hold out against a concerted attack. We opened up the hatches and gulped in the cold air; lords, for the moment, of all we surveyed, which was nothing but a tangled mass of burnt-out tanks, charred bodies, and the maimed and bloody wrecks of humanity that were still left alive.

We had but a moment to savour our victory. It was Alte who first noticed the T.34s once again massing on the far side of the railway line. There must have been more than a hundred of them. Their aim was immediately obvious: to cut off our means of retreat. The Russians were past-masters at such tactics, as we knew from previous bitter experience.

There was no time to reflect upon our situation. Alte passed the message straight on to Major Mercedes, and he at once gave the order to withdraw. It was a race to beat death. We turned and fled, each tank heading on its own course for the safety of the German lines.

There was a T.34 ahead of us. We had it in our sights . . .

Fire! The tank shuddered. Flame roared out of the mouth of the cannon. A second later, an answering flame shot heavenwards from the T.34 and a black cloud of smoke mushroomed after it. Then the explosion, which destroyed both tank and men.

Two more we disposed of in similar fashion, but the luck could not hold out indefinitely. We pushed on at full speed, passing the blackened remains of several of our own tanks. At one point we came upon a band of German soldiers, blood-smeared and limping, the lame and the blind supporting each other. We slowed down to take them on board and within seconds the turret and the bonnet were swarming with men. Inevitably some lost their grip and fell back into the road, but we had no alternative but to abandon them. This was no time for sentiment. If we stopped to pick up everyone, we should all end our days as a heap of charred bones. Nevertheless, it required a strong man to move on and leave his companions to the mercy of the enemy. Hands clawed piteously at the sides of the tank, voices were raised in despairing cries. Porta instinctively put his foot on the brake and Alte turned furiously on him.

'Keep going, you bloody fool.'

For a moment, Porta looked mutinous.

'I said, keep going!' repeated Alte. 'And that, my friend, is an order.'

Porta opened his mouth to speak but his words were drowned by the impact of some heavy metallic object on the outside of the tank. The whole thing shuddered and shook. Inside, we fell about in a mass of unco-ordinated arms and legs. Outside, the wounded soldiers shrieked in agony.

'Dive bombers,' hissed Alte. 'Now perhaps you'll bloody get a move on.'

Porta hunched a shoulder indifferently, but none the less the tank started up again. I think we all let out sighs of relief. Porta was the best driver in the whole regiment, and if anyone could get us safely back, he could. A blood-chilling scream ripped the air as we moved on our way. There was a moment's stillness. Then the Legionnaire hunched a shoulder.

'Someone caught underneath,' he said, laconically.

We rolled on across the steppes, now crunching our way through a sea of ruins, fallen masonry, broken glass, now ploughing across abandoned trenches, through shellholes and craters. Far ahead of us were the other Tigers. Only Barcelona was at our side, his own tank submerged beneath a horde of wounded infantrymen.

Alte kept muttering beneath his breath. We caught the word 'bridge', and we knew what was running through his mind. There was a certain bridge we had to cross, to reach the other side of the river. Much depended on whether we or the Russians reached it first.

A fresh obstacle came our way: Barcelona's tank ran into a patch of marshy ground and was soon completely bogged down. We passed him a cable, but as we were only able to pull crossways, and not straight ahead, it was of very little use. Even as we watched, the heavy tank sank lower in the mud, and Mercedes, when called up on the radio and informed of the situation, gave orders that it should be abandoned and destroyed. Barcelona and his crew were installed with us and we set off again, once more with a mass of bodies clinging to every foothold on the exterior of the tank.

We ran into a Russian battery and were upon it before they had time to scatter themselves. We caught only a glimpse of horrified faces, contorted with fear, as we plunged our way through the centre of them.

Shortly afterwards, it was our turn to start trembling: the tank began losing speed. Porta and Little John worked feverishly, to no avail. The distance between us and the rest of the Tigers widened still further.

'What the hell's happening?' we demanded, made irritable and unreasoning through sheer terror at our likely predicament. 'Get it moving, for Chrissake!'

'I'm not a bleeding magician!' snarled Porta.

Alte called up Lt. Ohlsen on the radio: no reply. We saw the last of our fellow tanks disappear over the brow of a hill, far ahead of us. It seemed unlikely, now, that we should ever reach the bridge . . . And then, suddenly, the motor started up again. It coughed and spluttered, cut out altogether, came back to life. The tank jerked forward. For the umpteenth time, Porta had worked a miracle. We showered him with extravagant praise, and he merely spat contemptuously and changed gear.

'We are heroes,' announced Little John. 'It is our duty to die a hero's death . . . Heil Adolf! What luck for you that we were born at this hour . What luck for us that we're still alive to fight another bleeding day.'

'What the flaming hell are we fighting for, anyway?' grumbled Barcelona, who was crouching in a corner to be out of our way.

'Don't ask damn fool questions,' advised Alte.

In a cloud of dust, we reached the bridge. It was still intact, guarded by a section of Russian infantry. We didn't wait to exchange pleasantries, we literally drove through and over them. Two daring spirits hurled themselves on to the front of the tank: one had an arm torn off, and our passengers dealt with the other.

Across the bridge, we had to pass through a village that was heavily defended. Somehow we managed to survive constant barrage from the enemy anti-tank guns, but judging from the shrieks and yells, many of those on the outside must have suffered appallingly. There was nothing we could do for them.

Outside the village we came face to face with a T.34. The first we knew was when a shell exploded on the armour-plating on the forefront of the tank. Fortunately it was not of sufficient strength to harm us, but the remainder of our passengers were swept off like straws in a high wind. I fixed the Russian tank in our sights. Before I could fire, Porta had pressed his foot down and was moving head-on towards them. The two tanks met with a hideous crash and rebounded off each other. Inside the Tiger we fell about all over the place. I nearly knocked myself senseless hitting my head on the sharp corner of an ammunition box. The lighter Russian tank was in worse case than our 52-tonner. She had slewed right round, and two members of her crew, who had been half in and half out of the hatch at the time of the collision, were sliced in two as the impact closed the heavy cover of the hatch on their legs.

After a bit we overtook a section of German infantry which had obviously seen some heavy fighting at some time during the day. All were half dead with fatigue, their eyes sunk deep into their sockets, their faces grey and haggard; most of them wore filthy bloodstained bandages, some had lost an arm, a leg, an eye. They knew the whereabouts of neither the Russian nor the German lines. They called out to us as we passed, appealing to us to take them up. We waved and shouted words of helpless encouragement, and as they saw we had no intention of stopping, their appeals turned to threats and vituperation. A captain of artillery drew his revolver and fired several shots at us, and an Oberwachtmeister planted himself four-square in the middle of the road with a machine gun and bawled at us to stop. We moved on inexorably. The Oberwachtmeister refused to give ground, and the result was inevitable. A howl of fury rose up behind us from his companions.

Some time later we met up with the rest of the Tigers in a wood a few kilometres to the south of Lichnovskoj. Under cover of darkness the mechanics set to work on the battered tanks. Ours was given a new engine and fresh plating, and one of the tracks was changed. Barcelona took over a Tiger that had been abandoned by the S.S. The gun had been put out of action but was swiftly replaced by a more modern weapon taken from a tank that had been too damaged to be worth repairing.

Lt. Ohlsen joined our group and handed round cigarettes.

'How about giving us a tune?' he demanded of Porta.

'Such as what?' asked Porta, pulling out his flute.

'Something gay. Whatever you like.'

'Horst Wessel,' suggested the Professor.

General hoots and jeers.

'The Lieutenant said something gay,' Porta reminded him.

A bottle of vodka was passed round in the wake of the cigarettes. Slowly, we began to relax after the rigours of the day.

'Let's sing, "I was born and brought up in a brothel",' proposed Porta.

We roared it out at the tops of our voices, savouring the mounting crudity as verse succeeded verse. The vodka bottle circulated. A sense of peace and well-being gradually stole over us.

'If only they'd provide us with a tankload of whores,' sighed Little John.

For a while, we discussed the possibility with all the enthusiasm we generally brought to affairs sexual. As usual, the discussion deteriorated and finally broke up in a riot of fighting and disorder. Lt. Ohlsen grew bored with us. He told us to shut up and then wandered away to a more peaceable group while we continued with our skirmishes. Someone hit Porta over the head with the handle of a grenade. Little John quietly finished off the vodka while the rest of us were otherwise engaged. Someone else then bashed Heide with a spade, and the Professor, as usual, ended up with a bloody nose. In the middle of it all, the order came through: prepare for departure. We heard the first tanks set off through the trees and saw the long tongues of flame licking out of their exhausts.

Once again we moved into action. We left the shelter of the wood and took our place on the road, part of a long column of vehicles – tanks, lorries, armoured cars, amphibious VWs, jeeps – all heading east for an unspecified destination.

We pulled up again some miles further on. Porta leaned out of the tank and yelled at an infantry division that had joined us.

'Hey, be a pal and tell us if we're on the right road for the war! We'd like to have a bash, if we're not too late.'

'You'll bleeding find out where it is soon enough,' came the disgruntled reply.

In the distance were the familiar rumblings of heavy artillery. The sky was criss-crossed with searchlights, and away beyond the treetops coloured flares lit up the night.

The Tigers mustered together and stood patiently awaiting orders, a long line of tanks stretching far back down the road. Porta and Little John left the comparative comfort of the interior and ventured outside, where they installed themselves in a ditch and played dice for vast sums of money that neither possessed. They were joined after a while by Heide and the Legionnaire, and the game swiftly became the opportunity for a fresh bout of brawling.

Somewhere too close for comfort a cannon gave a short, dry bark.

'T.34,' said Alte, calmly.

The order came through to move forward. The four gamblers forgot their differences and leapt back into the tank, Barcelona gave us the thumbs-up sign. Ahead of us, a stream of white and green tracer bullets rose into the blackness. It was the signal for attack.

Slowly we edged forward into the thick undergrowth, crushing bushes and young trees beneath us. Our guns fired in short bursts. Somewhere a T.34 exploded and rained down a red-hot shower of steel upon us. All around us the anti-tank guns were hard at work. Each time we heard one we instinctively sunk our heads into our shoulders.

Suddenly the booming and roaring of the heavy artillery stopped, and there came instead the cracking of automatics and the rattle of machine guns. From the raucous shouts of encouragement we heard, we gathered that the infantry had gone into the attack.

'Tigers, forward!'

We increased speed. Thick gouts of mud were thrown up, trees were knocked down like so many skittles. We halted momentarily to let a column of infantry pass through, then advanced in formation on the Russians ahead of us. The fever of the chase was on us again, but with this difference: no one was sure whether we were the hunters or the hunted. Everything was in a state of confusion.

We came to a small village, a railway crossroads, where there was fierce fighting. The steady chattering of machine gunfire; hand grenades, rockets, flame throwers; harsh cries in Russian and German; screams and yells and thick columns of smoke. An ammunition dump went up in a sheet of flame. Gigantic torches that were burning houses lit our path. We were given a warm welcome by a couple of anti-tank guns, both of which had to be wiped out before we could continue. The usual carnage littered the streets. Dead soldiers, dead horses, dead civilians. Pieces of equipment that had been abandoned. A Russian captain trapped beneath an overturned vehicle, screaming with his mouth wide open and his eyes staring, unseeing. Many of the wounded, unable to crawl away fast enough, were crushed beneath our tracks. A constant fine shower of burning cinders fell over everything, even penetrating to the interior of the tank. We drove through hell with our arms held protectively across our faces, but for those outside it was far worse. We saw many soldiers yelling with pain and staggering across the street with both hands clapped to their eyes.

Half-way through the village there was hand to hand fighting; we had to turn aside and plough across a row of houses. The walls slowly crumbled beneath the impact of fifty-two tons. In one house, a bed, with two dead bodies; between them, still alive, a small girl. Porta was unable to brake in time to avoid her. No one said a word. We lied to each other by our very silence. No one spoke for the simple reason that no one had the courage to admit what he had seen. This was not war, it was murder. It was one of those things you would never talk about.

The villagers had lost everything; including, in many cases, their lives. An old woman sat amongst the ruins of her home, amongst a few broken sticks of wood that had once been her furniture. Her long grey hair was charred, her arms and legs covered in burns. She followed the passage of the tanks with eyes that opened wide in terror, but she made no attempt to hide from us. There was nowhere left to hide, in any case. Three civilians lay dead in the middle of the road. Further on, the bodies of a dead child and a dead soldier lay together, their blood mingling, still warm and red.

Without knowing why, we were ordered to a halt in the centre of a street. Nearby was a square, a cobbled courtyard with a well in the middle. At this well a German soldier was relieving himself. He must have been holding it in for a long time, because the operation continued indefinitely. We sat watching him in silence, as if he were performing some curious ceremony. Why did he have to pollute the supply of drinking water? There was no malice in his action. He urinated into the well because the well was there, because the well was convenient, because he didn't think; and for no other reason. When he had finished he tied up his flies and stepped back with a deep sigh of satisfaction, as if the world were now a better place.

On the other side of the well a small boy was playing in the sand, seemingly unmoved by the war that was taking place all round him. The soldier walked over to him, said a few words, patted him on the head. He turned and saw the tanks, waved cheerfully towards us; lit a cigarette, leaned back against the well, smoking. Then he glanced over his shoulder again at the child, pulled something from his pocket and tossed it into the sand. The child clawed it up and instantly crammed it into his mouth. The soldier grinned and nodded. Next moment, with an expression of sheer amazement on his face, he slowly folded in upon himself and sank to the ground. His legs twitched, a spout of blood came from his open mouth. The child stood up and took a few uncertain steps forward, then he, also, collapsed. None of us had heard the shell that killed them both until it actually reached the spot and exploded. It threw up a surprisingly small quantity of sand, and the dust soon settled again.

The scene was almost as before. A couple of chickens wandered out into the open and began pecking hopefully for food near the two bodies.

Under cover of the tanks, our infantry pressed forward in another attack. From innumerable holes, men in brown uniforms suddenly made their appearance. Porta leaned out of the side of the tank and waved them on.

'See you in Moscow, lads!'

A hail of bullets rained about his head and he withdrew it quickly amidst jeers from the troops.

The attack advanced, retreated, advanced again and then hesitated in the face of fierce Russian opposition. The Russian artillery now began to join in the fun. Our troops threw themselves to the ground, flat on their bellies, but still the shock of the explosions hurled them up into the air and tossed them back again like broken puppets. With my forehead pressed against the rubber surround of the observation panel. I watched the whole macabre scene as if it were a cinema show.

'Enemy anti-tank to our right,' announced Alte, suddenly.

There was a battery of them concealed behind the walls of a farm. In company with the other Tigers we advanced upon them, subjecting them to a concerted bombardment. They held out for a while, inflicting serious damage on us, but soon we were on top of them, crushing the guns beneath our heavy tracks. The crews had fled, and we picked them off with machine gun fire. Lt. Ohlsen's tank received four direct hits simultaneously and the explosion reverberated through our own Tiger. We saw one of the crew flung up into the air in a mass of flames. Whether anyone survived, we were not then certain. Four other tanks were left as burning wrecks. Of the entire First Company, only six tanks now remained. The whole of the Fourth Company had been wiped out some time back.

Once again, we had become the hunted. We moved away from the area of immediate danger and reformed, in positions of attack, several kilometres further on. The divisional commander, General Keller, turned up in an open car and quickly restored order from a state of chaos. Reinforcements arrived from other armoured sections and we were sent off once more.

The atmosphere inside the tank was suffocating. The ventilating system had ceased to function and we were all choking and red-eyed from the constant discharge each time the guns were fired. Heide was overcome by the fumes after a while and collapsed on the floor at our feet. We kicked him out of the way and left him there. We had neither the time nor the opportunity to do more for him.

Coming up on the left, along a strip of road bordered by poplars, I sighted a long column of familiar black shapes, and in spite of the heat I felt the goose pimples break out like a rash on my arms.

'T.34s!'

'Thats all we wanted,' said Alte, bitterly.

'Some party,' commented Porta. 'Anyone feel it's time to go home yet?'

'Twelve hundred metres,' murmured Alte. 'Have you got them, Sven? If you shit this one up, we've had it.'

I was too well aware of the fact for comfort. I had the leading T.34 in my sights. The image was clear. I fired, without even realizing that I had done so.

The sound of an explosion. The welcome sight of smoke and flames. I fell backwards with the recoil of the gun, hardly able to believe my luck.

'You did it!' yelled Porta, fetching me a thump on the back. 'You bloody did it!'

The long column of T.34s had come to a confused halt. They turned their guns to the right, obviously not sure what had hit them nor where the enemy was situated. They probably took us for a battery of anti-tank guns concealed behind the poplars.

Once again I had them in my sights; once again I fired; and once again the missile found its mark. The other Tigers were joining in, we had the enemy at a disadvantage, and the air was soon thick with clouds of dense black smoke, shot through with red and yellow flames.

'That's it!' yelled Little John, suddenly. 'Firework display over!'

Alte looked at him in astonishment.

'What the hell are you talking about?'

'No more ammo,' said Little John, cheerfully. He sank on to the floor beside the unconscious Heide and gave him a contemptuous kick. 'You can wake up now, you've missed all the fun.'

We withdrew from the battle and Alte called up the refuelling wagons. By the time they had arrived and we were provided with a further stock of ammunition the T.34s had been effectively wiped out and the rest of our section were moving forward to a new destination.

We emerged from a thicket of trees and found ourselves on the edge of a plain that was black with a dense mass of assembled tanks. It was a breathtaking vision, a display of sheer force. There must have been at least two hundred Tigers gathered there, obviously called up from a number of regiments.

An S.S. man, an Obersturmführer, watched us go by and spat disdainfully on the death's head painted on our tower. The death's head was the emblem of the disciplinary regiments. The Obersturmführer belonged to the Second Division of S.S. tanks, 'Das Reich', probably one of the most arrogant in the entire Germany army. By way of showing him that we were every bit as coarse as we looked, we gave him the two fingers as we passed.

The orders were to proceed towards the south-west, in the

direction of Sinegorsky, where an entire division was encircled by the enemy. We were able to pick up their desperate appeals for help over the radio.

We reached them within the hour. In the absence of enemy tanks we were soon able to deal with the opposition and were given a heroes' welcome by our own troops. The only trouble was, they turned out to be members of the S.S. And as Porta said, had we known that we should never have bothered to rescue them. It was a fine point which we detested more: the S.S. or the Russians.

The order came through to reassemble and retreat from the area while the going was good. Within minutes we were on our way, but we were not long left in peace. A squadron of JL2s appeared and began dive bombing us. We promptly dispersed into the wooded areas bordering the road, but when the bombers finally departed, disappearing towards the east, they left behind them a scene of appalling carnage. To add to the misery, several divisions of Russians troops had been sighted in the distance.

Major Mercedes consulted the map, then conferred with Lt. Gaun, his ordnance officer.

'I think we'd better get the hell out of here while there's still a chance. If we hang about too long, they'll cut us off.'

'What about the wounded?'

The Major picked up his field glasses, surveyed the advancing Russians, glanced back at the map, then shook his head and climbed back into his tank.

'All those not capable of marching under their own steam will have to be abandoned.'

Lt. Gaun took a protesting step forward.

'Sir, we can't leave them here like that. You know the Russians won't take prisoners. It's certain death. We might just as well have left them in the first place.'

The Major gave him a brief look.

'It'll be certain death for a lot more of us if we don't pull out of here.'

He disappeared into the tank and it moved slowly forward. For a moment the Lieutenant stood watching it, then he turned and let his gaze travel over the various groups of wounded men sitting or lying on the ground. Admittedly they were the S.S., admittedly we loathed them, but still it was a pitiful sight. Many were in a bad way and would obviously not last long without expert attention. There had not been time to apply proper dressings to the wounds. Several men nursed shattered limbs that were nothing but raw pulpy masses of flesh covered with makeshift bandages, already soaked with blood. Here and there the sharp edge of a bone protruded, gleaming white and jagged. But on the whole, the troops were cheerful. It obviously never occurred to them that they would be left to the mercies of the oncoming Russians. They spoke longingly of the peace and quiet of a hospital room; they were already seeing visions of beautiful nurses, cool hands upon their brow, clean sheets, soft blankets; no more stinking trenches, no more fighting, no more horror. On the whole, those who had lost arms or legs were inclined to rejoice. For them, it meant permanent retirement from the nightmare of the front line trenches, a return to Germany, to their wives and their children. Those of us who had overheard the Major looked sympathetically upon Lt. Gaun and did not envy him his task.

The orders for departure were given. Ponderously the big tanks moved off, each covered in as many soldiers as could find a foothold. It took a moment for those left behind to accept the truth. When they did so, the reaction was worse than any battle I had yet known. Screams of rage and terror mingled with desperate cries of appeal. Supplicating hands clawed unbelievingly at those who had been lucky enough to find a position on the outside of a tank. Men with blood pouring from open wounds came tottering towards us, shrieking with pain and with sheer incredulity at this thing we were doing to them. Some crawled, some used each other as crutches. Others just lay and stared, with eyes that were vacant and glassy. Three officers hurled themselves into the path of an oncoming tank and were instantly crushed. It was our final farewell to thousands of our own wounded. That was all the thanks you could expect in wartime. Heil Hitler and try to die like a hero.

For us, it was a race against time. On both sides the Russian tanks were closing in on us in an attempt to cut off our means of retreat. Their shells rained down upon us. The sky was full of flak and tracer, and over and above everything else we slowly became aware of the droning of enemy aircraft.

They came screaming at us from out of the clouds. We barely had time to take note of them before the entire tank was lifted off the ground, as if by some unseen excavator, thoroughly pounded and then flung back again with a jolt that jarred every bone in our bodies.

One of the enemy bombers had found its mark: a bomb had exploded just under our tower. It was a miracle that the tank itself did not explode. We were thrown up to the ceiling, back to the floor, one on top of another. Wires and pipes were ripped away, the gun was torn bodily from its mountings, pieces of glass embedded themselves in our flesh. The world became a whirling mass of bombs, earth, rocks, steel, all performing some crazy flying dance through the air.

The Jabos came screaming back from another direction. For the men outside, it must have been wholesale slaughter. It was hellish enough inside. Trapped in a pitch black hole, unable to see, unable to breathe, our eyes and throats burning with the acrid vapours that swirled round us. There was an almost overwhelming urge to burst out into the sea of bombs and meet death head on rather than sit waiting for it in the dark, expecting at any moment to be blown into a million pieces.

But when, at last, it was all over, we none of us moved or spoke. The sudden silence was strange and unnerving. It seemed impossible that we should be still living. For a long time we were scared to move, scared to see what horrors lay in wait outside.

We emerged slowly, almost reluctantly, into the fresh air. Of those who had clung to the outside of the tanks, scarcely a man remained alive. Many of the tanks themselves were mere smouldering heaps of wreckage. From those that remained, grimy, unrecognizable figures were painfully pulling themselves into the open. We saw a man come crawling out of a tangled pile of steel with blood pouring from a wound in his throat. We saw another with half his face burnt away, the charred flesh hanging in ribbons. Little John's right hand had been split open, Porta had a hole the size of a fist in his forehead. The Russian bombers had done their work well. It was a wholesale massacre.

Barcelona staggered towards us, followed by the rest of his crew. He looked at our tank, then looked at us, as if unable to believe that we had come out of it alive. We turned and followed his gaze, seeing the Tiger for the first time and sharing his incredulity. The gun had been torn completely away; the tracks were buckled like switchbacks; the bonnet was staved in; most of the wheels were missing, the petrol tanks were flattened, and the vehicle as a whole simply no longer existed.

We stood staring for several minutes, until at last Porta shook his head and wiped the blood from his eyes.

'God, that was a tank and a half,' he said, sadly.

Torgau. Called a prison; in fact a hell. A cold grey hell, staffed by sadistic maniacs with whips and jackboots, with the unfortunate inmates reduced to the level of a herd of cattle and treated a great deal worse.

There were but two exits from Torgau: one led to the firing squad and one to a disciplinary battalion and the Russian front. Ninety per cent of the prisoners took the former way out. Perhaps, in the long run, they were the lucky ones.

CHAPTER SIX

THOSE of the regiment who survived were sent back to Germany. It was felt, perhaps, that we had earned a rest.

Our company were put on guard duties at the military prison at Torgau. It was a forbidding place, where everything was grey: the stark stone walls were grey, the main gates were grey, the uniforms were grey, the bars across the windows were grey. The very sky itself, when you were lucky enough to get a glimpse of it, was grey.

The great double doors were swung open to admit another prisoner, marched in in handcuffs between two guards. He jumped nervously as the doors clanged shut behind him. For a moment his mouth twisted, his face contorted, we thought he was going to shout aloud. But he just muttered to himself, and we caught the words 'a living death'.

'Hold your tongue!' screamed the feldwebel. 'In this place, you speak when you're spoken to and not before ... And as a general rule the only time they bother to speak to you is to ask whether you want a bandage tied round your eyes.'

Feldwebel Schmidt sniggered with self-satisfied laughter. He was always laughing. His fellow warders called him 'the Joker'. He might have been taken for a jolly, jesting fellow, except that his sense of humour unfortunately operated only at other people's expense. He was not, in that respect, altogether normal. His desire to be constantly laughing at other people's expense amounted to a definite obsession. But there again, he was not so very unusual: none of the warders employed in Hitler's prisons could ever, by any stretch of the imagination, have been described as 'normal'.

Feldwebel Schmidt pressed the bell that rang far away in the depths of the prison, in the room marked 'Reception', which was the domain of Hauptfeldwebel Dorn. The prisoner was marched off.

The Hauptfeldwebel lived his life in a carefully contrived muddle of papers and documents. Filing cabinets stood in all four corners of his office. Wire trays filled with papers stood before him on the desk. Files marked 'For Signature', 'Urgent', 'Pending', 'Top Priority' and so on lay scattered about for all to see, proclaiming to the world that Hauptfeldwebel Dorn was a man much occupied by prison affairs. There was an impressive array of pens, pencils, rubber stamps, bottles of ink, rulers, and other office paraphernalia. And behind it all sat Hauptfeldwebel Dorn, conscientiously doing as little work as possible. In the third drawer of his desk, hidden beneath the pile of the 'Völkischer Beobachter', which no one would ever think of reading, was a dark green bottle marked 'Glue'. In fact it was cognac, which always proved a good restorative if ever Dorn found himself with his back to the wall and having to pick up a pen and sign a few letters.

The office door opened to admit Schmidt and his fellow warder and the handcuffed prisoner.

'Heil Hitler!' barked Schmidt.

As a matter of principle, Dorn ignored him. He sat hunched behind his desk, apparently fully absorbed in the contents of a file that he was studying. Inside the file, typed on several sheets of official paper stamped 'Gekados' (Secret) was a pornographic story.

Feldwebel Schmidt scraped his throat, deferentially, to call attention to his presence.

'Silence!' snapped Dorn. 'You can see that I'm busy.'

For the next few moments there came only the sound of heavy breathing and the important rustling of the secret papers. At length Dorn closed the file, placed it in the drawer with the bottle of Glue beneath the 'Völkischer Beobachter', and turned majestically to survey the prisoner. Without a word he held out a hand to Schmidt. Schmidt silently passed over the prisoner's papers. Dorn glanced at them and said 'Hm!' in tones of contempt and importance. He tossed them nonchalantly into one of his wire baskets, stood up, paused a moment for effect, then

94

strolled slowly round the desk and placed himself before the prisoner.

'Well?' he demanded.

The prisoner stiffened.

'Lt. Heinz Berner, 76th Artillery,' he said.

'Well?' asked Dorn, once again. 'May one inquire what it is that brings you to Torgau? Or is it, perhaps, sehr gekados?'

Lt. Berner looked down at the floor.

'Sentenced to death for murder . . . sir.'

'An officer turned murderer?' Dorn raised his thin eyebrows. 'An officer of the German Army? It scarcely seems credible . . . Who, if it's not too much trouble, was the unfortunate victim?'

'My fiancée.'

'Your fiancée?' Dorn threw back his head and whinnied like a horse confronted with a bag of oats. 'That's good! I like it! It's the best thing I've heard in a long time! Well, never mind, Lt. Heinz Berner: you'll soon be reunited with her. We have no place for men like you in the German Army.'

Lt. Berner was taken to the third floor and shut up in a cell measuring 3 by $1\frac{1}{2}$ metres. He felt as if he were in a sardine tin. Any minute now someone would turn the key and peel back the lid, and that moment would mean death to Lt. Berner.

He sank heavily on to a wooden stool, put his head in his hands and sat without moving for almost half an hour. It seemed to him that his life was over, almost before it had even begun. Most of his friends had turned against him; for them, he was already dead. At any minute he could expect to hear the man with the key and he would know that they had come for him, that the firing squad was waiting somewhere in the yard outside.

It seemed impossible that it was such a short time ago that he had left the military school in Potsdam covered in glory, promoted to lieutenant, sent home on leave, met at the station by his proud parents and devoted Else. Even now, looking back, it was difficult to see exactly how it had all happened, where it had really started to go wrong. He thought, perhaps, the first inkling of trouble had appeared that day he had taken Else out to dinner. He had kissed her in the vestibule of the restaurant.

A lingering kiss with the tip of his tongue exploring inside her mouth. Such a kiss as he had read about in that book by – who was it? Some American name. Müller? Miller? Yes, that was it. Henry Miller. The book had been confiscated and ostentatiously burnt after half the camp had read it. Else had reacted to the kiss like an outraged virgin. Upon reflection, she probably was a virgin, and she had most certainly been outraged. For two days she had refused to speak to him, and had then only resumed the relationship on the strict understanding he should not lay so much as a finger on her, never mind a tongue. Else was a member of the B.D.M.(*) And according to their doctrine, no officer should ever demand 'that sort of thing' from one of their girls. Chastity until marriage. Desire should not exist. And if by some misfortune, by some freak of nature, it did rear its horrible head, then it should be firmly extinguished until a couple were safely wed. Did the Führer, they asked, go about subjecting young girls to gross behaviour? Obviously not. It was unthinkable.

Heinz had done his best to extinguish his freakish desire to possess Else. After all, he owed it to the Führer. Unfortunately his desires refused to be extinguished.

'An officer of the German Army should simply not behave that way,' Else told him.

'What way?'

'You know quite well, Heinz.'

'Then how should he behave?'

'He should wait until he's married.'

Heinz accepted it, since he had no choice, although as far as he could recall they had never laid down any specific rules on the subject at the military school at Potsdam.

'Let's get married, then,' he suggested. 'From the moment we belong to each other physically, you can count yourself as my wife. Surely that would be all right?'

Else flung herself upon him and for several moments they kissed each other with all the forbidden fervour described in the Henry Miller book. And then, suddenly, she had thrust him away from her and was staring with revulsion in her eyes, as if he were some hideous monster.

(*) Bunn Deutscher Mädel – League of German Girls

'So? Is that the only reason you want to marry me? Because you want to go to bed with me? How disgusting! I find that sort of thing utterly contemptible. I've just reported one of my best friends for having sexual relations with a man.'

It took him the next few hours to convince her that she was misjudging him. By the time he had succeeded, it was almost true: desire had, at least for the moment, been repressed.

And then, the next day – how had it happened? How had it possibly happened? They had been so happy together. The brutes of the Kripo, they refused to believe that he really couldn't remember. They'd beaten him up and threatened him with 'a little outing', which, they assured him, would quickly restore his memory. He hadn't understood what they meant, but he had gathered it was something unpleasant. The Chief Inspector had punched him several times in the face and accused him of murdering other people besides Else.

'Tell us about it,' he said. 'Take us into your confidence and we'll do all we can for you. We'll have your case heard here at Hamburg instead of Berlin. You'll do better in Hamburg. We treat people fairly here.'

They had thrown him about the room and kicked him in the guts, until at last he had vomited up blood. He thought they must be mad. They made him lick up his own vomit, and several other things he preferred to forget. Finally, he was put in preventive detention and a new set of warders occupied themselves with him. They broke two of his fingers, one on each hand, choosing the middle finger because that was the one that gave most pain, and because it could successfully be broken in three places. The doctor who examined him afterwards thought it quite amusing.

'Slipped on the floor, eh? Amazing the number of people who've done that just recently. I keep telling them they shouldn't put such a high polish on it. They'll have a really serious accident one of these days.'

And so, now here he was, in Torgau ... Torgau! My God, was it really true? Was he really in Torgau, of all places? Torgau, a name that was synonymous with hell, with torture, with death ...

Once again, the Lieutenant buried his face in his hands; and this time he sobbed like a child. He didn't want to die, not even the death of an officer, and please God they would at least grant him that – but he wasn't ready for death, he was too young. Only twenty, and full of patriotic fervour. Why did they have to kill him? He wanted to fight, for the Fatherland, for the Führer, for the sheer honour and glory of it. It would be idiocy to waste so valiant an officer. What could he do? Write to Generaloberst Halder? Yes. Halder would help him. Sure to. It was his duty to write to him. He owed it not only to himself but to Germany.

The Lieutenant jumped up and ran to the door of his cell. He clutched at the bars and shouted at the top of his voice.

'I want to write a letter! I want to write a letter!'

Outside in the passage, someone beat on his door.

'Stop that flaming row in there!'

The Lieutenant fell back. He sank in a kind of daze on to his wooden stool. For a long time there was silence. Now and again he heard footsteps in the corridor, the jingle of keys. It was a sound that drove him to the very edge of panic. Each time, he imagined they were coming for him.

The brutes of the Kripo had treated him as some kind of sex maniac. The court martial had expressed the regret that he could die only one death and not be killed ten times over. And yet even now he could not remember clearly how it had all happened. He had loved Else. He had had no wish to harm her.

He had been drunk, he knew that. Too drunk to have full control of himself; not so drunk he did not know what he was doing. And he had torn off his clothes, he knew that, also. Else had screamed and fought, but no one had heard her. Or if they had, they had taken no notice. It was the fault of the war. You became accustomed to violence and accepted it as a normal part of life. In the end it made no impact on you and you failed even to notice it.

Else had kicked him hard on the shins. It had hurt, but he had only laughed and tightened his grip on her wrists.

'Let me go! Let me go!'

And he hadn't. No, he definitely hadn't. He could remember holding on to her. She had fought like a creature demented. She had called him a swine, a brute and a Jew, which were the three worst insults she knew. She had punched him in the face, and a Sèvres vase had fallen from the mantelshelf and shattered, he remembered all that. He seemed also to recall the untimely end of a piece of Dresden china, an ornate looking-glass and several other valuable knick-knacks.

He remembered all that, but what he did not remember were the things that followed. He did not, for instance. remember pulling out Else's hair by the roots, or tearing at her flesh until she bled; or hurling her to the ground, or firing twice at point-blank range upon a portrait of the Kaiser. He did not remember sinking his teeth into Else's throat, nor licking up the blood, hers mingled with his; nor the warm salty taste of the blood, nor the strange rattling in Else's torn throat, nor the sudden softness of her previously unyielding body. All this he did not remember.

When he had come to his senses he had snatched the girl into his arms and sat rocking to and fro, crying over her, as her head lolled back and forth like that of a puppet. There seemed to be broken glass and congealing blood all about him, and he was frightened and wondered what had happened. He had called to Else to help him, but she had not replied. Slowly it had come upon him that she was dead.

'You're playing games with me!' he shouted, and he shook her broken body to and fro. 'You're pretending! You can't be dead! You're not dead!'

But she was. And he had run from the room, half naked and covered in blood, and rushed blindly about the streets until they picked him up.

Heavy boots along the corridor. The Lieutenant sat rigid and strained, the sweat pouring off his forehead. Was this it? Were they coming for him?

Someone swearing. More footsteps. Silence.

The Lieutenant ran across to the door and tried to see out. He put his finger on the bell. Would they object if he rang it? Just to see what was going on? Surely a man condemned to death had a right to know what was going on? But did he really want to know? He hesitated, his finger trembling. If he rang, who would come? One of the guards. A corporal, or some other lowly person. Was not he a lieutenant in an artillery regiment, and therefore above associating with such people?

He heard the sound of something heavy being dragged past his door. A body? Perhaps they had come to fetch some other poor devil for his last journey and he had fainted through sheer terror? Would he himself faint when they came to fetch him? He imagined them with their rifles and their steel helmets and he knew for a certainty that he would not be able to face them with any show of courage. They would have to drag him, as they were dragging this one . . .

More footsteps. Lt. Heinz Berner huddled shivering against the wall and called for his mother. His heart almost stopped beating as the footsteps stopped. A key turned in the door. This was it, at last. This was how it felt. They had come for him . . .

An immense Obergefreiter stood in the doorway. He was wearing the black uniform of the tank regiments, with the death's head insignia. He surveyed the Lieutenant pityingly for a moment or two, then shrugged his shoulders and closed the door behind him.

'Things not going so well, eh? Not so hot being an officer at a time like this? Personally I'd sooner be an ordinary soldier and have my freedom than a lieutenant and locked up in a prison cell.'

The young Heinz Berner watched in amazement as the Obergefreiter sat casually on the wooden bench that served as a bed and gestured to the prisoner to do likewise. A conversation between an officer and an ordinary soldier? Unimaginable. Where was the respect due to his uniform? The respect he had been taught about in the military school at Potsdam? He stared down at himself, as if to check that he was, indeed, wearing the uniform of a lieutenant of artillery. And this great oaf of an Obergefreiter lolling nonchalantly before him . . . For the first time in his life, Heinz Berner began to doubt the truth of all he had been taught.

'Listen to me, laddie,' said the Obergefreiter, turning his head and spitting on the cell floor.

Laddie! And him a lieutenant! He was about to remonstrate with the man, but just in time he recalled his unhappy situation and kept his mouth closed. He collapsed on to the bench, all strength gone. The Obergefreiter was still talking. Berner had no idea what he was on about. He stared numbly ahead, and slowly, very slowly, the realization came to him that barely a foot away and within easy reach was the Obergefreiter's revolver. Just hanging there, in its holster. Hanging there unnoticed. Waiting to be snatched up and used. Not to mention the bunch of keys attached to his belt ... Visions of freedom rose up before Heinz Berner and almost blinded him in their intensity. The Obergefreiter was a large man. A giant of a man. Such people, it was commonly acknowledged, were always slow in their reactions. Slow physically, probably slow mentally as well. One well-placed blow on the head from the butt of the revolver and that would be the end of the Obergefreiter. And no great loss to anyone. Heinz Berner's breath came and went in quick gasps of excitement. The Obergefreiter went on talking.

'The thing is, laddie, you just got to find courage somewhere. You get in a panic, you make it worse for yourself. I mean, once they got you out there, it's all over before you know where you are. Nothing messy, no hanging about, no pain, nothing like that ... Mind you, you get on good terms with the medico, he might be persuaded to give you a little jab of something beforehand. Put you out, like. That's what he did yesterday for the major who was going. You can nearly always get these little extra perks if you set about it the right way. Like if you need anything particular, you just ask me and I'll see what I can do for you – only not a word to anyone, mind.'

He turned and spat on the floor once again. In that moment, Heinz Berner had seized the revolver and sprang to his feet, covering the guard.

'Hands up!'

Little John very slowly pulled his immense body off the bench. He stared at the Lieutenant, his mouth gaping open. With one hand, he groped for his revolver and found the case empty. The Lieutenant snapped his fingers nervously.

'Keys,' he demanded.

Little John shook his head, rather sadly. He unhooked the bunch of keys and held them out. At the same time, with a swift and agile movement that directly contradicted all the Lieutenant's surmises, he brought down his right hand in a vicious chopping motion. Little John never needed to hit people twice. The inexperienced artillery officer fell heavily to the floor and Little John stepped over the inanimate body and picked up his revolver.

'Stupid bugger,' he said, without rancour.

He slammed the door of the cell behind him and crashed his way back along the corridor. Meeting up with Porta, he stood for some time watching a group of prisoners in ragged grey uniforms rinsing out their mess tins under a cold water tap.

'839 just had a go at me,' remarked Little John, idly. 'Didn't get him anywhere.'

'Ah-huh.' Porta grunted, then jerked his thumb over his shoulder. 'Fancy a game of pontoon?'

They made their way to the lavatories, the only place where they could reasonably be assured of privacy, thanks to a mirror set at an angle opposite the door, which allowed them to see in good time who might be approaching. Porta pulled out a pack of dogeared cards and a couple of cigarettes cut down to a size that could conveniently be held inside the mouth should a superior officer come upon them. Oberstleutnant Vogel, the Prison Governor, had long ago decided that smoking should be one of a long list of 'strictly forbidden' activities. Any soldier caught indulging was subject to severe punishment. Vogel not only enjoyed meting out severe punishment, he had a positive psychological need to do so, and this was one method by which he could assure himself of a constant supply of offenders.

The pontoon session continued uninterrupted for perhaps twenty minutes and was brought to a hasty finish only by the arrival of the prison Chaplain, von Gerdesheim.

'Peace be with you.'

He nodded amiably at Porta and Little John. There was no trace, now, of either cards or cigarettes. Little John bent his head, unctuously. In fact he hated priests.

'And with you, Father. I hope the world's treating you well.'

The Chaplain frowned, evidently suspicious of Little

John's sudden and new-found piety. Little John smiled and folded his hands in a priestly way. The Chaplain cleared his throat.

'Tell me, my son. Do you – ah – believe in God?'

Little John opened wide his eyes and did his best to register shocked indignation that such a question should be thought necessary.

'I should just hope I do, Father!'

'I confess I find it a pleasant surprise to come across a believer in the ranks – particularly in a regiment such as yours. It is, to say the least, unusual.'

Little John stared heavenwards with a saintly smile on his lips.

'I – ah – I don't seem to recall seeing you at communion, however?'

The Chaplain's tone was hesitant, almost apologetic; as if Little John had surely been there and it was simply that he had missed him. Little John withdrew his gaze from heaven and directed a bland stare at the priest.

'I assure you, Father, I attend church regularly every 15th August.'

'Indeed? May I ask what special significance is attached to 15th August?'

'It's the Holy Virgin,' exclaimed Little John, earnestly. 'Every 15th August, regular as clockwork, I go to church in her honour, don't I?'

The Chaplain shook his head.

'My dear fellow, I'm sorry, but I simply don't see the connection!'

'Well, put it this way,' said Little John, in reasonable tones. 'Do you or do you not believe in the Holy Virgin? Because frankly that's what it all boils down to.'

The Chaplain grew slowly crimson.

'I beg your pardon?' he said.

'Herod was a shit,' affirmed Little John, with stout irrelevance. 'And St. Bernard used to get pissed as a newt drinking holy schnaps in the snow.'

It was, perhaps, the sum total of Little John's religious knowledge, and he displayed it proudly.

'Have you gone mad?' demanded the Chaplain.

He controlled himself with a very obvious effort, and his voice once again took on its smooth, benevolent, coaxing tone.

'Why do you say such things, my son? What pleasure does it give you?'

Little John was all smiles.

'Look, Father, it's like this, isn't it? Let me tell you. When I was a little kid about so high I had this crazy urge to go into the Ursuline Convent at Eger. You know why? Because I'd once heard someone say they'd got several litres of the Holy Virgin's milk stashed away there. Well, the way I reckoned it, what with Jesus having kicked the bucket a few centuries back, this milk should be in a pretty high old state by now. Know what I mean? Well—'

'That's quite enough.' The Chaplain stepped away from Little John as if he might be contaminated. 'What is your name, Obergefreiter?'

Little John came to attention.

'Wolfgang Creutzfeld, 27th Tank Regiment. Ist Battalion, Fifth Company. At present doing guard duties at the Military Prison at Torgau, Section C ... And if you find it any easier, Padre, all my pals call me Little John.'

Little John leaned forward, interested to see what it was the Chaplain was writing in his notebook.

'You shall hear more of this.'

The Chaplain closed the notebook with an irritable bang. It turned out to be a book of psalms, which he had used for writing down Little John's particulars. Little John looked suitably impressed.

As a result of the Chaplain's confusion following upon this incident a certain Stabswachtmeister Kraus, of the Schutzpolizei, was executed without receiving the blessing of the church – not that he had asked for it, nor would have accepted had it been offered. His last words were a defiant, 'Death to Hitler!'

As a further result, Little John was sentenced to eight days' solitary confinement. Three days after his release, he and Porta became ingloriously and incapably drunk and beat up the

Chaplain. Shortly afterwards, suffering from almost total amnesia, the Chaplain was transferred to the Military Prison at Glatz. It was there that the Russians arrested him, in May 1945, and there that he subsequently hanged himself.

Gustav Dürer had been in the army for thirty-one years and Head Warder at the military prison of Torgau for twenty-eight years. According to Hauptfeldwebel Dorn, who thought highly of him, he and men like him were the very backbone of the invincible German Army.

But, alas for the German Army, there came a day when Gustav Dürer was assassinated. And as if this in itself were not disgrace enough, the assassin was one of the very prisoners he was guarding. The name of Gustav Dürer became, overnight, anathema to Hauptfeldwebel Dorn. He had his name removed from the Roll of Honour of the Prison, he had a bonfire made of all the deceased's belongings, and he did his best to forget that the cretin had ever existed. The backbone of the German Army would do better without such men as Gustav Dürer.

The only mementoes he kept of his ex-Head Warder were two bottles of vodka and four of cognac. He confiscated these as being property of the state and he locked them away in his drawer beneath the copies of the "Völkischer Beobachter" which no one ever read. They were, so to speak, a proof of Gustav Dürer's unworthiness: it was quite obvious the man could never have come by them honestly.

CHAPTER SEVEN

IT was a cold, grey morning. The air was heavy with mist and the stones of the courtyard were damp and icy. Alte stood huddled in a doorway, the prisoners shuffled about in groups, their lips blue with cold. Those who still had the energy, or the will power, ran up and down in an effort to keep fit and warm. One or two had cigarettes carefully hidden in the palms of their hands. Alte always allowed the men to smoke during their short periods of exercise, 'strictly forbidden' though it was.

Standing apart from the others, his shoulders hunched up, his eyes fixed in a blank stare, was Feldwebel Lindenberg. A wavering trail of smoke from his right hand betrayed the presence of a cigarette, given to him by Porta. It was a present which would earn the donor sixty days' solitary if anyone discovered.

The rest of the prisoners respectfully left Lindenberg alone with his thoughts. Word had already spread that his execution had been fixed for the following morning. It was known throughout the prison that the Chaplain had visited him the previous day, and the roster of guard duties included a command that the first section, second group, should present themselves at the armoury at 4.15 on Friday morning. They knew what that meant: they would be issued with two bullets each; two bullets of the old, round-headed type. No one ever knew why it was that round-headed bullets should be used for executions. That was just the way it was.

Lieutenant Heinz Berner looked across at Lindenberg and wondered how it felt to know that your hour was fixed. He shivered, with cold and with fear. He had been at Torgau for four weeks now, and still he lived in the daily expectation that today would be THE day, the day when he received his visit from the angel of death and knew that within thirty-six hours he would be no more. Time did not dull the sharp edge of fear. Each day brought him nearer to his ultimate fate, and each day was predictably worse than the one before.

The young lieutenant had learnt much in four weeks. He knew what it meant when the Chaplain came to see you in your cell. He knew all about the pink files, with their signed and countersigned execution orders, that arrived from headquarters and found their way to the desk in Hauptfeldwebel Dorn's office. He knew where the executions took place, and he knew that they were carried out by the tank regiment who were on guard duty at the prison. He knew more about executions in general, and executions at Torgau in particular, than ever they had taught him at the military school.

Lieutenant Berner was sitting on the damp flagstones, his back against the stone wall of the latrines. Next to him was a young peasant farmer, Kurt Schwartz. They sat together, but neither of them spoke. It was generally believed that Schwartz was simple, not to say downright retarded. He had been at Torgau for more than six months. Two appeals against sentence of death had already been rejected: a third one was in the process of being rejected. It was doubtful if Schwartz was even aware of them. The first eighteen years of his life had been passed more in the company of cattle than of human beings, and on being drafted into the Services he had totally failed to grasp the fact that he was now army property and no longer free to come and go as he pleased. He stayed as long as it suited him, but with the arrival of spring he knew that his first duty was to the farm, and one Friday evening he quite simply packed up his bags, shouldered his rifle and walked out. Once back at the farm he hid the rifle and the rest of his army equipment beneath a stack of potatoes in the barn and went about his daily business much as he had done before the war interrupted him. The military police had no trouble in tracing him: he had done nothing to cover his tracks. He greeted them happily, as if they were old friends come on a visit.

'Grüss Gott!'

'Heil Hitler,' replied the Feldwebel who was leading the party. 'We're looking for a Kurt Schwartz. Would that be you, by any chance?'

'Yes, that's me,' said Kurt, readily. 'What can I do for you? Whatever it is, I'm afraid I can't hang about too long, it's coming on to rain and there's a lot to be done out here.'

'Rain be damned!' retorted the Feldwebel. 'You're coming with us, and you're coming right now. There's a court martial waiting for you.'

'For me?' Kurt looked at him, puzzled. 'Why should they be waiting for me? No one's told me anything about it.'

It was not until the Feldwebel lost all patience and began hitting him about and demanding to know where he had hidden his rifle that Kurt, in his turn, began vaguely to suspect that all was not well. These four men in their steel helmets filled him with a sense of unease. He wondered what he could have done to displease them. Perhaps he should not have left the barracks without first saying goodbye?

The Feldwebel became quite threatening on the subject of the lost rifle. With primitive cunning and mulish obstinacy, Kurt at once closed his mouth and kept its hiding place a secret. The Feldwebel hectored and cajoled, but Kurt remained dumb. There was talk of desertion and its dire consequences, but Kurt merely stared with blank eyes, being unable to grasp the fine degree of difference between 'absence without leave' and 'desertion', or the fact that one merely involved prison and transfer to a disciplinary regiment while the other meant death.

Now he was at Torgau waiting to be executed. Each day when Little John opened the door of his cell for the exercise period, the same conversation took place:

'Is this it?' Kurt would say.

And Little John would shake his head and reply:

'Not this time.'

And Kurt would hunch his shoulders philosophically and say:

'Ah, well. Tomorrow, perhaps?'

And Little John would agree:

'Tomorrow, perhaps.'

But they remained at cross purposes. Little John was thinking of the execution order: Kurt was thinking of his return to the farm.

Round and round the courtyard ran a blond and much decorated Oberleutnant. He had been at Torgau for two months. He had lost his family, his wife and three children, during a raid on Berlin. They had been burnt alive in a cellar. Compassionate leave had been refused, so the Oberleutnant had taken matters into his own hands, forged the necessary documents and returned to Berlin. He had been picked up almost at once and it had taken a court martial barely ten minutes to reach a verdict: desertion, falsification of papers, sentenced to death.

Sitting at the top of a flight of stone steps was an elderly lieutenant-colonel, his faded blue eyes staring into the far distance. In direct defiance of orders from above, he had evacuated his regiment from an impossible situation hemmed in by Russian troops. The court martial had had no doubts on the matter: sabotage, cowardice in the face of the enemy, sentenced to death.

Rape, mutiny, murder, theft, so-called cowardice, so-called desertion – all these crimes, and many more, had been committed by the miserable inmates of Torgau.

'Do you not find it an unpleasant task,' a cavalry officer once politely asked Julius Heide, 'having to shoot people that you have come to know personally?'

'What kind of a question's that supposed to be?' grumbled Heide.

'It interests me to know. It seems to me that there's a considerable difference between fighting for your life when you're at the front – killing men you've never met, because if you don't kill them they'll almost certainly kill you – and shooting down in cold blood people you've lived with day by day over a period of months. I know you're carrying out orders, you can't do anything else but obey them, but how do you feel when the moment actually comes?'

'What a bloody fool thing to ask!' Heide was visibly disconcerted. 'What's it to you, how I feel? I don't go around asking you how you feel, do I?'

'No, but you could if you wished. I shouldn't object,' said the officer, gently. 'In fact, I don't in the least mind telling you: I'm scared stiff. Sometimes when I'm alone in my cell, just lying there wondering if it's going to be today that they come for me, I get so shit scared I can hardly stop myself from screaming . . . Funny thing is, I never felt that sort of fear at the front. You know you stand a good chance of dying, but—'

'Will you shut up?' demanded Heide, fiercely. 'I've got plenty enough worries of my own without hearing all yours as well. Stop beefing, and just get this into your head: I don't know you, I never did know you, I don't want to know you. You're nothing to me except another bloody number!'

The officer shook his head and smiled.

'You know me all right. And all the other poor devils they've got locked up here. You know us all, and you'll never forget us.'

Outside, in the courtyard, Alte blew his whistle. The precious hour was over and it was back to their cells for another day of waiting. The prisoners mutely formed up in twos, long since accustomed to the routine, but today something occurred to break the monotony: Gustav Dürer, Feldwebel of the section, appeared in the doorway and brought the long column of men to a standstill. Slowly his eyes roved over them, and each prisoner shivered and did his best to hide behind his neighbour. It was generally accepted that Gustav Dürer was not human. Guards and prisoners alike went in terror of him. It was said that he had a direct link with the Gestapo, and certainly it seemed as if even the Prison Governor was sometimes uneasy in his company.

'You!' Dürer shot out an arm and pointed to Lindenberg. 'You over there! Come with me.'

Lindenberg's face was abruptly drained of all colour. He swayed and would have fallen but for the willing hands of his comrades. Every man there, including Alte, believed that Lindenberg was being led away to his death in the middle of the afternoon. It was the sort of trick that would delight Gustav Dürer: accustom the prisoners to a routine – a visit from the Chaplain equals thirty-six hours to live – then suddenly shatter it all and create panic and uncertainty.

As Lindenberg was led off, it seemed certain to all who watched that it was the last they would see of him. It seemed no less certain to Lindenberg himself. He was unable, at first, to grasp the fact that the Stabsfeldwebel had brought him not to the firing squad but to one of the administration offices of the prison. It took him several minutes to adjust. A woman was standing in the room. A typical Party woman, tall and masculine, with an ivory complexion and hair the colour of sunbleached corn. She wore a brown uniform and carried a document case, and Lindenberg was too numb with panic to understand that she was speaking to him. With an impatient gesture, she repeated her question.

'Are you or are you not Feldwebel Hermann Lindenberg?'

'I am.' He bowed his head before her. 'Yes.'

'I have some papers for you to sign. Here, take them.' She thrust them into his unwilling hands. 'There's no necessity for me to explain them to you, you'll sign them in any case, but just for the record it's a document authorizing the State to take full control of your son and of his education.'

'What?'

Lindenberg jerked up his head and stared at the woman. She curled back her upper lip and uncovered a row of large white teeth.

'I think you heard me ... Your wife has been found incapable of bringing up the child. No German woman who shelters a deserter and saboteur such as yourself is worthy of the honour ... I shall be glad if you'll sign at once, it will save us both a great deal of trouble.'

Lindenberg wiped the back of his hand across his forehead, mainly for something to do, something that would prevent him from striking the creature.

'If I don't sign?' he hazarded.

'You will sign. It's an order. As far as society is concerned, you and your wife have ceased to exist. The boy belongs to the State. The State will clothe him and feed him and see that he grows up to be a worthy citizen.'

Lindenberg took a step nearer the woman. Coldly, contemptuously, he spat in her face. 'That's all you'll get out of me,' he said.

Predictably, Gustav Dürer's rubber truncheon came crashing down upon him, raining blows on head and shoulders. The woman wiped her face and stood smiling at the sound of Lindenberg's gasps of pain.

'Are you ready to sign now?'

'I shan't sign anything,' panted Lindenberg.

More blows. More pain.

'I shan't sign anything!'

'This is ridiculous,' said the woman, abruptly. 'I should have thought you had more control over your prisoners. In any event, I can't waste any more of my time. Get him to sign these before tomorrow.'

Dürer smiled significantly.

'He'll sign.'

'Well, make sure of it.'

'I'll make sure. No need to worry ... We have our own methods here. Sehr gekados ...'

'I'll leave it to you, then.'

'Please do. It will be a pleasure.'

The woman went out and Dürer closed the door; softly, menacingly, behind her. He turned to Lindenberg.

'Now ... shall you and I get down to business together?'

'Do what you like,' said Lindenberg, through clenched teeth. 'I shall be dead anyway within a few hours. You have no more power over me.'

'You think not?'

'I know not.'

'We shall see, my friend ... At least, we can do our best to make your few remaining hours as uncomfortable as possible ... and that, I think you'll find, will be very uncomfortable indeed.'

He looked at Lindenberg and laughed, exultantly, as if savouring the delights to come.

'We shall begin, I think, by breaking every bone in your body ... by every bone, I mean every bone ... There are over two hundred bones in the human body – and that, mark you, will be only the beginning. By the time I've finished with you, you'll be crying out for death.'

Quite suddenly, Lindenberg went mad. With a wild cry he hurled himself upon Dürer and seized him by the throat. Dürer, bowled over by surprise rather than by the ferocity of the attack, lost his footing and fell backwards, with Lindenberg still clinging to him. Both men were snarling with rage, more like wild animals than human beings. Lindenberg's fingers hooked themselves into the flesh of Dürer's neck, tearing and kneading. The guard's eyes were red with broken blood vessels, his breath coming in a series of rattles and gasps.

Little John, up on the third floor in a room directly above, heard the thuds and bangs, the stifled shouts and the clicking of Dürer's bunch of keys, and went running down the stairs to investigate. He opened the door, took one look, silently closed it behind him and rushed off again to the latrines, where Heide and Porta were playing an illicit game of dice. He came upon them in such a hurry that he caught them guiltily in the act, and they cursed him roundly for his idiocy.

'Never mind that!' Little John rushed into one of the cabinets, flushed the water, backed out and ran into the next. 'Start making a row – any sort of row – Lindenberg's in the middle of murdering Dürer!'

'You're joking!'

'Go and look for yourself if you don't believe me.'

'I don't,' said Heide, but in any case the appeal of making a loud noise was too strong to be denied. 'I'll throttle you if you're having us on.'

He picked up a scrubbing brush and hurled it through a window, kicked a bucket round the floor, banged the door two or three times. Porta turned on the taps in all the washbasins and began running the water at full burst, splashing and singing as he did so. Little John crashed up and down in his army boots and flushed the water in all the cabinets.

'Surely to God,' said Porta, 'he must have done it by now?'

'If he's doing it at all,' said Heide, with a look at Little John. 'Personally I doubt it.'

Little John held up a hand for silence and they all stood listening.

'Surely he must have done it by now?' repeated Porta.

'Let's hope so. We've given him enough time.' Little John opened the door and beckoned to the others. 'Come on. Let's take a look.'

There was fortunately no one else about. They crept up the

passage, paused for a moment outside the room, and then, hearing no sound, opened the door and looked in.

Lindenberg was sitting on Dürer's chest, his fingers still locked round his victim's throat. The guard was plainly dead. His face was mottle blue, his bloodshot eyes burst alarmingly from their sockets, his tongue protruded between his teeth.

The three men stood in silence. Slowly Lindenberg pulled himself to his feet. He detached the dead man's bunch of keys, turned, smiled almost apologetically and held them out to Porta.

'I strangled him.'

'So we see,' murmured Porta. 'There's not much to say except thanks very much, is there?'

'What are you going to do about it?'

They looked at each other. Heide cleared his throat.

'We'll have to report it. You realize that. We'll have to tell Dorn.'

'Of course.'

'You'll go down into history for this,' said Little John, earnestly. 'It's the only decent thing anyone's ever done in this place.'

Lindenburg smiled, rather wearily.

'You'd better take me back to my cell, hadn't you? And if I were you, I'd report the incident at once. It looks better that way. I don't want you to get yourselves into any sort of trouble.'

'You're probably right.' Porta turned to Heide. 'Will you go and make the report while we take him back?'

'Like hell I will! I'm on duty, I can't leave my post.'

'Little John—'

'Nothing to do with me,' said Little John, firmly. 'He's not in my wing. This is your pigeon, you deal with it.'

'He may not be in your wing, but you were the one who was supposed to be on guard duty in this corridor. And you were the one who saw him do it and made no attempt to stop him.'

'And you were one of the ones that helped drown the sound of the crime!' retorted Little John.

Heide suddenly snapped his heels together and puffed out his chest.

'I'm the senior man round here, and I'm ordering you to go and report the incident to Hauptfeldwebel Dorn.' He looked at Little John. 'Immediately, Creutzfeld!'

'Oh, get stuffed!' came the indifferent retort.

In the circumstances, there was little that Heide could do in the face of such flagrant disobedience. He could not physically force Little John into making a report to Dorn, and he knew from past experience that threats left him cold.

'Oh, for Christ's sake!' he exclaimed, irritably. 'What's your suggestion. Leave the corpse lying here to rot and say nothing to anyone?'

Little John shrugged his shoulders.

'Why not? What's it to us?'

'What about him?' Heide jerked his head towards Lindenberg, who was slumped in a chair and seemed quite uninterested in the whole affair. 'What do we do about him?'

'What do YOU do about him,' corrected Porta. 'You're the senior man round here, remember? It's up to you.' He slowly took out a cigarette and lit it, at the same time studying with interest a large printed card that said 'NO SMOKING' in bright red letters. 'Sorry, mate, but it looks like you're in the shit right up to your neck.'

'Put out that cigarette!' yelled Heide, pointing to the notice.

Porta ignored him. He turned earnestly to Little John.

'Glad I'm not a sergeant,' he said. 'Only gets you into hot water all the time. Take you and me, for instance. No responsibility. Treated like idiots. Never understand anything without it's repeated three times . . . Oh, it's a grand life, I tell you! But him—' He gestured towards Heide – 'him with his stripes and all! He's the one who carries the can, poor idiot.'

'Tell you what,' suggested Little John. 'Let's take Lindenberg back to his cell and then knock off for a game of pontoon. How about it?'

It seemed the best idea anyone had yet had. And yet somehow the corpse of Gustav Dürer prayed on their minds.

'We're storing up trouble,' said Heide. 'I'm warning you.'

'You're the senior man . . . Give us another card.'

'We'll all be in this together when they find out.'

'Twist,' said Little John, imperturbably.

'They go mad when things like this happen—'

'And another.'

'It's all very well for you—'

'Now I'll stick.'

'I've got a good idea,' said Porta. 'Why don't we tell the Old Man what's happened and leave him to deal with it? Little John, you go and tell him right now.'

'Why me?' said Little John, suspiciously.

'Why not you? I'm not asking you to go and see Dorn, am I?'

'Just as well, because I shouldn't go . . . Well, O.K., I'll tell him, but that's my lot. After that, you do your own dirty work.'

Little John disappeared. He was back a few moments later with both Alte and Barcelona Blum.

'This is bad,' said Alte. 'What the hell do you expect me to do? Where's Lindenberg now?'

'Back in his cell.'

'Back in his cell. O.K. None of you lot saw anything. None of you heard anything. O.K. Didn't know a thing about it until the prisoner came to find you. O.K. But what about the man who was supposed to be on guard duty in this section? How do we explain him away? Why wasn't he doing his job properly?'

Heide and Porta both turned to look at Little John. Little John spat briefly on the floor.

'No good asking me. I got the runs. Spent half the morning in the bog. That's where I was when Gustav got clobbered. Shitting in the bog.'

'I see.' Alte breathed deeply. 'That's very helpful. You've been to the M.O. about it, of course?'

'No. Completely slipped my mind.'

'That's a pity,' said Alte, drily. 'I rather thought that at – say – eight o'clock this morning, during the exercise period, you'd gone to see Obergefreiter Holzermann and that he'd given you some tablets to take for a stomach upset?'

'Eh?'

For a moment Little John looked puzzled; then, slowly, his face cleared.

'Yeah. You're right. He gave me some tablets and I swallowed the lot. I been in and out of the bog ever since.'

'They'll believe it,' said Alte. 'They'd believe anything of you ... As for Porta, you I take it were up in Lindenberg's cell making a search during his absence ... Is that right? I like to get all the facts straight.'

'Absolutely,' agreed Porta. 'Quite right. Making a search. That's exactly what I was doing.'

'And what about me?' asked Heide, anxiously.

'You ... Yes. You were taking an inventory of the cutlery. Get hold of the old one and start copying it out again. Little John, get up to Lindenberg's cell and make it look as though a hurricane hit it. Tell him what's happening.'

'O.K.'

Little John hurried off, but turned back at the door.

'Here, just a minute – who's going to tell Dorn?'

'I am,' said Barcelona. 'No, no, don't thank me, I couldn't bear it! I already know I'm a saint.'

'You're a bloody fool,' said Little John, disappearing.

Hauptfeldwebel Dorn was sitting at his desk with his feet up and one of Major Divalordy's cigars clamped between his teeth. The Hauptfeldwebel liked cigars. Especially Major Divalordy's cigars. He liked the expensive aroma of the smoke and he liked the sense of social superiority that accompanied them. His desk was as usual piled high with letters and files. A book of pornographic studies lay open on his lap.

He ignored Barcelona's first tap at the door. It was obvious from the manner of the knock that it was not an officer out there, so according to his custom Dorn let him wait. Not until Barcelona's third attempt did he drawl a languid, 'Come in.'

Barcelona had barely entered the room when there came a further three rapid knocks on the door. Before Dorn had time enough to raise an inquiring brow, Porta was also in the room. He clicked his heels together and gave an abrupt salute.

'Stabsgefreiter Porta, sir, Fifth Tank Company, reporting on the Governor's orders.'

'What the hell for?' demanded Dorn.

'Orders to check all typewriters and other office equipment, sir.'

Dorn's mouth sagged slightly.

'Whose orders, if you please?'

'Colonel Vogel,' said Porta, with untruthful aplomb.

It seemed doubtful if the lie would ever be brought home to him. A variety of curious and unlikely orders were frequently issued by Colonel Vogel. No one was likely to check up on this particular one.

'Oh, very well, get on with it!' snapped Dorn. 'And don't take all day about it.'

Humming busily to himself, Porta dumped his bag of tools on the ground and began taking the typewriter to pieces. He unscrewed everything that was unscrewable, removed rollers and platens, pulled out yards of ribbon, poked here and pulled there and generally oiled everything in sight. Dorn watched him with a sense of growing horror.

'I hope to God you can put that thing back together again.'

'So do I, sir,' agreed Porta, fervently.

Dorn clicked his tongue against his teeth and turned to Barcelona.

'Well, Feldwebel? What do you want?'

'Sir,' began Barcelona, earnestly. 'Feldwebel Blom, sir. Following the orders given to me by my Section Chief – that is to say, Feldwebel Beier, sir – Feldwebel Beier being my Section Chief, sir—'

'For God's sake!' snapped Dorn.

Barcelona looked puzzled.

'Sir?'

'Speak normally, man! Get to the point, can't you?'

'Sir! Strabsfeldwebel Gustav Dürer has been killed. He's in one of the rooms leading off the main corridor of Block 6 ... sir.'

Dorn's cigar quivered between his lips. He snatched it out and glared up at Barcelona.

'What's that you said?'

'Strabsfeldwebel Dürer, sir. Strangled.'

'You're mad! Where did you get this absurd story from?

Dürer would never allow a thing like that to happen ... Who did it? Explain it to me!'

With a certain amount of barely concealed relish, Barcelona did so. Porta, meanwhile, examined each separate part of the dismantled typewriter in turn and kept one ear cocked for a suitable point of entry into the conversation. He waited until Dorn's questions became a little too probing for safety.

'Sir!'

Dorn swung round on him.

'Well? What do you want?'

'I've done the typewriter, sir. May I have a look at your desk, now?'

'What the devil for?'

'Colonel's orders, sir. He said to examine every—'

'Oh, very well, very well, if you must! Get on with it and stop interrupting me!' Dorn turned back irritably to Barcelona. 'Who was on guard at the time of Dürer's – ah – murder?'

Barcelona shook his head.

'I don't know, sir.'

'Christ Almighty, if we go on like this the war's as good as lost!' Dorn thumped a fist on his desk and Porta gave an exaggerated start. 'Nothing but a bunch of saboteurs and traitors! In league with the prisoners, every single one of you! Going behind my back, neglecting your duties ... God knows I've been reasonable enough up until now, but this is the turning point. Mark me well, Feldwebel, this is the turning point!'

His cigar had gone out. He tossed it away and looked for another one in Major Divalordy's desk. An almost imperceptible chalk mark allowed him to check whether anyone else had had the temerity to open the drawer.

'Who promoted you to the rank of Feldwebel?' he suddenly demanded of Barcelona.

'When I was with the 36th at Bamberg, sir. The C.O. there, he—'

'Hm,' said Dorn, plainly not very interested. 'It's curious, Feldwebel, but you bear a strong resemblance to a badly cooked steak. Such things are fit only for swine and curs.'

'Yes, sir,' agreed Barcelona, placidly.

'Sir!' Porta re-entered the conversation, his face a-beam

with happiness and goodwill. 'I've dusted all the drawers in your desk with talcum powder, sir. You can pull them in and out as easy as anything . . . Shall I do the Major's desk as well, sir?'

'Be quiet!' hissed Dorn. 'I'm sick of your everlasting prattle. Do the job you came for and then get out. I have more important matters to deal with.'

Dorn abruptly left the room and went off to find Alte and view the corpse.

'This is going to cost someone his life!' he declared dramatically. 'I shall not rest until I have uncovered the culprit. Not a moment's peace will there be in this establishment—'

'Actually,' said Alte, 'we already have the criminal. He's upstairs locked in his cell.'

Dorn glared at him and left the room.

In a way, he found that he was almost glad that Dürer had been murdered: it was Dorn's chance to prove himself, to show his mettle, as it were. He took long, involved statements from everyone who had been directly, indirectly, and even just very remotely connected with the affair. He checked and he double-checked. He adopted an attitude of lofty and judicial calm . . . until, that is, he came to interview Little John, and Little John defeated him. He totally lost his way in the rambling maze of Little John's discourse – what he had done, why he had done it; where he had done it, how he had done it; where he had been, where he had come from; who had said what and what he had said back and what he WOULD have said back if—

'Obergefreiter Creutzfeld!' screamed Dorn. 'I am strongly beginning to doubt your sanity! Your proper place is in a lunatic asylum, not in the German Army!' He turned to Alte. 'Feldwebel Beier, get rid of this man. Give him some simple task to do and see that he sticks to it. But kindly ensure that I do not have to set eyes on him again!'

Ultimately, he interviewed Lindenberg in his cell. He threatened him with death and told him in no uncertain terms what happened to people who dared to lay hands on members of the Gestapo. Lindenberg sat silent throughout the tirade, then calmly told Dorn he might go to hell, adding by way of an afterthought that he had thoroughly enjoyed strangling Gustav

Dürer and wished only that he might do it all over again.

Very much shaken, Dorn left the cell. Quite obviously the man Lindenberg was a raving maniac. The authorities had had no right to confine him in a military prison. The personnel of Torgau could hardly be held responsible for the actions of a madman.

There now only remained the signing of certain documents, the filling in of certain forms in triplicate and quadruplicate, and Gustav Dürer could be finally eliminated from the records. Dorn returned to his office in a thoroughly bad temper and slammed the door behind him.

'I say, anything wrong?' inquired a mildly reproachful voice.

Dorn bit back the oaths that automatically rose to his lips. He clicked his heels together.

'Heil Hitler! Did you pass a good night, sir?'

'Fair to middling, thank you, Dorn.'

Major Divalordy was an ex-insurance man from Innsbruck. He tended to confuse the army with his insurance company, and he treated Dorn with the same bone-headed amiability that he showed towards his colleagues there. It never crossed his mind that the Prussian professional soldier felt for him a profound scorn.

The Major smiled affably and stroked at the corners of his silky blond moustache.

'Well, how goes it? What's on the menu for today? Anything juicy to report?'

'More than you know,' thought Dorn, furiously.

He straightened up and began to bark out the events of the day in the best military manner.

'Strabsfeldwebel Gustav Dürer has been strangled by one of the prisoners. Feldwebel Lindenberg. Obviously a lunatic. Death occurred only a short while ago, I have already completed an examination of the facts. The body has been left undisturbed in a room on Block 6 – I thought you might care to take a look at it. The typewriter in this office has been cleaned and overhauled on the orders of the Colonel. The drawers of the desks have been dusted with powder and may now be opened and closed without difficulty. In your in-tray, sir, you'll find two files that require your attention – rejected appeals. There is also an execution order that needs your signature, and a cutlery inventory you might care to look at ... I think that's the lot, sir.'

Dorn stood stiffly to attention, watching the Major's reaction. He noted the sudden beads of sweat on his brow, and he was satisfied.

'I find this news most distressing. Really most distressing ... Gustav Dürer murdered! It seems scarcely credible ... That such a thing could happen in a civilized establishment ... Really, a most shocking business! Are you quite sure of your facts, my dear fellow?'

'Absolutely positive. The prisoner Lindenberg has confessed to the murder.'

'But why should he do such a thing in the first place? What could he possibly hope to gain by it?'

'I really don't know,' said Dorn, who in fact had not thought of inquiring into Lindenberg's motives. 'I think it very likely, sir, that he just couldn't stand the sight of the Strabsfeldwebel.'

'Really?' The Major twisted the ends of his moustache in rapid agitation. 'What an extraordinary state of affairs! I cannot myself say that I cared overmuch for Gustav Dürer, but it hardly seems an adequate reason for murdering a person.'

'As I said sir, the prisoner is obviously a lunatic.'

'Obviously. Obviously. But even so—'

Dorn enjoyed seeing the Major so obviously suffering. He leaned across his desk and began efficiently laying out various letters and documents awaiting signature. The Major picked up his pen and wrote his name where Dorn indicated. He had, for the most part, no idea what he was signing. Without his adjutant to show him the way round, he would have been totally lost in this jungle. It was the greatest fear of his life that he should one day be alone in the office when the telephone rang. He would then be forced to answer it, and sooner or later it was bound to be one of Colonel Vogel's staff officers at the other end of the line. They never used the telephone except to complain, but worse than that, Major Divalordy could never understand a word that any of them were saying. They spoke in weird military jargon, of which the Major had as yet mastered only the most common of everyday phrases.

Dorn smiled and held out a pink file. He opened it with a servile flourish. The Major nodded his thanks, leant forward, scrawled his signature at the foot of a page. It was a death warrant that he signed so blithely, as he had signed many others before. He closed the file and handed it back, without ever seeing the thick Gothic print on the outside of the pale pink folder:

Feldwebel Hermann Lindenberg
  43rd Infantry Regiment
Date of Decease . . . .
Delivered to Crematorium . . . . .

Dorn collected up the signed papers and shuffled them together.

'There'll be forms to be filled in, sir, for Dürer's death. Do you want to see to them or shall I?'

'No, no, I leave it all to you. You'll know what to do about it.'

The Major opened his drawer and took out a couple of cigars, one of which he handed to Dorn. They each had a glass of cognac from the bottle that was kept in the corner cupboard. The contents of this bottle had visibly diminished since the previous night. Both men noticed the fact; neither mentioned it.

'Poor chap,' thought the Major. 'He'll have needed something to buck him up after all that's happened.'

'They're all the bloody same,' thought Dorn. 'Tell you in public they don't touch either alcohol or women, while in private they do bugger all except whore and drink. Bloody typical.'

Dorn settled himself comfortably behind his desk. The day's post was brought in and he flipped through it and extracted one particular letter, tossing the rest into one of his many in-trays. The contents of the letter kept him happily occupied for some little while. Ultimately, and with obvious reluctance, he hid the envelope in his cache beneath the 'Völkisdher Beobachter' and turned his attention to the forms that had to be filled in. At the top of the page he wrote, 'Inquiry carried out by Haupt-feldwebel Dorn into the Death of Strabsfeldwebel Gustav Dürer'. Under that, against the heading 'Cause of Death', he wrote the one word, 'Murder'. He sat and stared at it for several minutes, pleased with the effect, then gloatingly continued with the rest of the report. Who knew but it might not end up before S.S. Reichsführer Heinrich Himmler himself? Dorn already saw himself transferred to the Gestapo.

He was interrupted by the shrill ring of the telephone at his elbow. Somewhat abruptly, Major Divalordy left the room. Dorn sneered at his passing back, snatched up the telephone and snarled down it.

'Yes? Who is it? What do you want?'

'I want to know what the hell is going on in your section.'

It was the voice of Colonel Vogel. Dorn dropped the receiver in a panic and it clattered to the floor.

'Hallo? Is that you, Dorn? What the devil's going on? Are you still there?'

'Yes, sir.'

Nervously Dorn gave his version of Dürer's death and his own handling of the affair.

'The whole thing sounds like a bloody botch up to me,' said the Colonel.

Dorn hastened to add that Major Divalordy was now in full possession of the facts and was dealing with the matter himself. The Colonel merely grunted and put the receiver down.

For a few moments Dorn sat stunned and immobile in his chair, but it was not long before he rallied and began doing a little telephoning on his own account. Having vented his wrath on subordinates all over the building he began to regain some of his lost confidence, and he walked out abroad to vent a little more wrath on anyone of a lower rank who might conceivably cross his path. To give himself the air of being on official business, he snatched up the contents of one of his trays and stuffed them haphazard into a brief case. Thus armed, he roamed the building in search of someone to terrorise.

At the end of the first corridor he was lucky enough to come upon a group of prisoners lethargically scrubbing the floor. He gave them a good five minutes of his time, rounded off his lecture by picking up their bucket of water and throwing it over them, and went on his way feeling a great deal happier with life.

As he rounded the corner he bumped into Major Divalordy, whose face, even in the dim prison light, was of a ghostly pallor. Dorn saluted stiffly. The Major shook his head.

'These are terrible times to be living. Terrible times, my dear fellow ... I've been called to the Colonel's office. Eleven o-seven I have to be there ... I fear this matter of Dürer can scarcely have pleased him.'

Dorn made a vague noise indicative of sympathy and continued along the corridor to the arms depot, which was in the charge of Overfeldwebel Thomas. Thomas was assisted by the Legionnaire, who in his turn, three days a week, was assisted by Little John. It was a good place to work in, the arms depot. Orders were to keep the doors locked and bolted from the inside. Almost any activity, therefore, could safely be indulged in on the right side of the doors. When Dorn arrived there was a game of cards in process. By the time Thomas had opened the door to him the cards had disappeared and both Little John and the Legionnaire were industriously cleaning equipment.

'You call this place an arms depot?'

Dorn let his gaze wander magnificently round it. He had no authority here, but it was always worth a try.

'It looks more like a rubbish dump than an arms depot.'

He kicked an empty cartridge box across the room and turned on Thomas.

'How would you like it if I were to make a report of all this – this mess, this – this chaos? Eh? I could, you know. If I felt so inclined I could make things very awkward for you with Colonel Vogel. I shouldn't like to, of course, but really, Thomas, I would advise you to pull your finger out and get things smartened up in here.'

'Suits me the way it is,' said Thomas, laconically.

There was a silence. Dorn nodded, warningly, and turned to go. As he did so, the Legionnaire's voice arrested him.

'Bit awkward, this bother about Gustav isn't it?'

'Don't talk to me about that!' snapped Dorn, his composure suddenly cracking. 'What a thing to happen! Bloody swine!'

'Who? Feldwebel Lindenberg, you mean?'

'Not at all. I was referring to Gustav Dürer. What a damn fool thing for an experienced warder to do! Over twenty years in the service and then he gets himself strangled by some madman . . .'

'Very careless,' commented the Legionnaire. 'Of course, it could only happen in a place like this.'

Dorn's eyes glinted dangerously.

'Just what are you trying to infer? Are you attempting to insult me?'

The Legionnaire looked shocked.

'Good grief, no! I shouldn't dream of such a thing.'

'After all,' put in Little John, helpfully, 'it wasn't your fault it happened, was it? No one could blame you. It's just unfortunate it happened to happen in your section, if you see what I mean? Still,' he added, with comfortable philosophy, 'there always has to be a first time, doesn't there? That's what I say. There always has to be a first time. It could happen to the best of us. I shouldn't worry about it too much if I were you.'

Dorn suddenly realized that Little John was the same prattling nincompoop who had confused him earlier on.

'I thought I told you to keep out of my way?'

'That's right,' agreed Little John, with a ready smile. 'You said I was to be given simple tasks, being as I'm not up to tackling anything complicated . . . I'm cleaning the guns, sir.'

'Then get on and clean them!' roared Dorn.

He marched out and slammed the door behind him. His sense of well-being, his personal satisfaction, had been shattered by that great cretinous oaf. Now he would have to start all over again.

He stormed off down the corridor, and it seemed to his suspicious mind that he heard loud bursts of uncouth laughter coming from behind the locked doors of the arms depot.

Katz and Schröder arrived at Torgau early in the morning direct from Berlin. They walked side by side with purposeful steps, heads down, hands in pockets.

They left again some hours later. They were on their way back to Berlin, but something in their step was different. The stride was shorter, less buoyant, less assured; their feet seemed to drag, as if unwilling to move. Their heads were hanging dejectedly, their shoulders humped up round their ears.

'What a shit,' muttered Katz. 'A lousy stinking shit of a Colonel.'

'Artillery, at that.'

'And Army, not even S.S.'

There was a silence.

'You don't suppose.'

'What?'

'You don't suppose there's anything in it?'

'The Russian front?'

'Mm.'

Another silence.

'How could a lousy stinking shit of a Colonel have any influence? I ask you? It's not even as if he's S.S.'

Katz pinched his lips together.

'Lousy stinking shits of Colonels sometimes have more influence than you might think.'

'You reckon?'

'Could well be.'

They slouched on in silence towards the station.

'What a shit!' said Schröder, bitterly.

CHAPTER EIGHT

EARLY next morning, Feldwebel Lindenberg was led out to be shot. Little John and Porta accompanied him, one at each elbow.

Lindenberg was dressed in his own green uniform, but his head was bare, as laid down in the regulations. Little John and Porta wore steel helmets, which glistened malevolently in the cold grey dawn. Their rifles were slung over their shoulders and their heavy boots crashed uncompromisingly on the cobblestones.

The first platoon, under the command of Lt. Ohlsen, was already in place. Standing near the wall were a captain of the garrison with the Prison Chaplain and Medical Officer. On the far side of the courtyard, near a small doorway, two medical auxiliaries were waiting, seated on a stretcher.

Lindenberg glanced nervously about him. Until now, he had preserved his dignity. Was his courage going to fail him at the last moment? Out of the side of his mouth, Little John sent messages of encouragement.

'Keep your pecker up, mate. Don't give the buggers anything to gloat about. We're all on your side.'

Lindenberg managed a smile. He held his head high and stepped out defiantly on his way to the firing squad. When they arrived at the appointed place he calmly positioned himself, raising his arms for Little John to attach the strap that would hold him upright until the moment of firing. The captain approached him with a scarf to bind round his eyes, and Lindenberg shook his head.

'Take it away, I don't need that. I prefer to see what's going on.'

'As you wish.'

The captain hunched an indifferent shoulder and returned to

his position by the wall. Lindenberg spat contemptuously at his retreating back. A moment of silence, then Lt. Ohlsen held up a hand. Lindenberg found himself staring into the barrels of what suddenly seemed to be thousands of rifles, all pointing directly at the small piece of white rag that had been pinned on his chest and marked his heart. It was a heart that beat so furiously, so erratically, that for a moment Lindenberg thought he might die of a seizure before their bullets could reach him. A burst of blind panic came upon him. He began to lose consciousness, felt his head swimming, felt the blood pounding in his ears, thought for a moment that the ground was coming up to meet him, only he was strapped upright and he knew it was impossible.

He must master this weakness. There must be no going under at the last moment. He owed it to Little John, to Porta, to all the others out there – all those men who were so firmly on his side, who identified themselves with him and yet whose job it was to fire upon him. The sailors in blue, the boys of the tank regiment in black, and the condemned man in green. A pretty picture.

Lindenberg raised his head and his eyes met those of Little John, standing at the end of the platoon, towering above the rest of his companions. Lindenberg signalled him a last, forgiving smile. Almost imperceptibly, Little John raised his rifle until it was no longer pointing at the small piece of white rag, but at a point over and above Lindenberg's left shoulder. There was nothing that Little John could personally do to stop the execution, but at least he would not fire on a friend. Seconds later, Porta's rifle took the same direction as Little John's. A profound sense of gratitude filled Lindenberg. He was moved by their simple act of friendship, and the tears that trickled so warmly down his cheeks were not the tears of weakness and he felt no shame.

One of the soldiers suddenly fainted. A young boy, scarcely more than eighteen years old. He crumpled and fell forward on to his face. His spectacles tinkled on the flagstones, his rifle clattered from his hand. No one paid the least attention.

'Poor little devil, he's far too young for this sort of thing.'

130

It was Lindenberg's last conscious thought. The next moment, the rifles cracked. There was one anguished cry, then silence.

Lt. Ohlsen stepped forward, revolver in hand, but the coup de grâce was not necessary: Lindenberg was dead. Ohlsen stood for a moment looking down at the body, his face set and expressionless, then quietly stepped back into line. At a sign from the Medical Officer the two orderlies picked up their stretcher, heaved the body upon it and disappeared through the small door that led to the crematorium. The first platoon was marched off towards the barracks. The Professor was hauled to his feet. Nearby, very quietly and with no fuss or bother, someone was vomiting.

Little John and Porta walked back side by side.

'You just wait,' muttered Little John. 'You just wait until it's our turn to have a go at them. The bastards.'

There was no need to explain who 'they' were: Porta knew automatically.

'That'll be the day,' he said. 'And we'll bloody well make sure we know what we're aiming at, too. I should hate to miss!'

Five o'clock was striking. Exactly twenty minutes had passed since Lindenberg had been marched from his cell. By eleven o'clock that morning Hauptfeldwebel Dorn had tied up the whole affair and was able to dismiss it from his mind. The relevant papers had been filled in, all the necessary forms completed. The total cost of the operation he had calculated at 1,290.05 marks. Major Divalordy's rubber stamp had been used wherever a signature was required, and the whole lot had been sealed in an official envelope and put out for posting. That was that. The matter was over and done with, and a good morning's work. The Hauptfeldwebel was able to relax.

Dorn lolled back in his chair, his feet on the table, one of the Major's cigars between his fingers. He opened one of his desk drawers and fumbled furtively beneath the 'Völkischer Beobachter' for pornography, then settled down with a contented sigh to study the more lewd of the pictures through a magnifying glass.

The middle of the day was Dorn's best time. Everyone else was fully occupied, going about his work, and no one came to disturb him. Those who dared intrude too often upon his privacy were soon made aware of Dorn's displeasure, and none but the most stupid or the most zealous ever came to him with prison business during the middle hours of the day. The telephone was an exception: it did, occasionally, trouble him by ringing, and annoying though it was it could hardly be ignored. It rang now, barely ten minutes after Dorn had lit his cigar and settled down to enjoy his well-earned rest. He answered irritably.

'Dorn here. Who's speaking?'

It was a feldwebel, wanting to know what he should do with Lindenberg's belongings.

'What sort of belongings? Anything interesting?'

'Not really, sir. Only a load of sloppy letters and other bits of tat.'

'Send it all to the court martial,' said Dorn, studying one of his pornographic photographs through the magnifying glass and feeling a pleasant sensation run through his body. 'They might find it useful for wiping their arses on ... Oh, and feldwebel—' His voice took on a more stringent note – 'while I've got you on the phone, perhaps you'd like to be reminded of the fact that I am an extremely busy man and do not care to be disturbed on account of trivialities. Use your initiative, feldwebel. I shan't tell you again.'

'Very well, sir.'

Dorn replaced the receiver and returned to his cigar and his photographs. Five minutes later, there was a second interruption. A sharp rap at the door and two men entered, without waiting for an invitation. They were dressed like twins. Each wore a soft felt hat, with the brim turned well down, brown shoes that squeaked as they walked, and long leather coats buttoned to the neck. Their faces were different, but their eyes were the same: light grey in colour, cold and menacing in expression. Dorn looked across at them, insolently, without removing his feet from the table. At the same time he felt regiments of cold wet feet marching up and down his spine, and involuntarily he shivered.

'To what do I owe this interruption?' he demanded.

'Difficult to say, really.' The taller of the two men turned to his companion. 'To what do you suppose he owes this interruption?'

'It could be we want to have a few words with him, perhaps?'

'What is this?' said Dorn. 'Who are you?'

'Katz and Schröder.' It sounded like a music hall comedy team. 'Katz and Schröder, come to pay you a visit. That's who we are.'

The taller man, who appeared to be Katz, smiled smoothly at Dorn.

'Aren't you going to offer us a drink, Hauptfeldwebel?'

Dorn regarded the two men with astonishment. There was something about them that made him feel definitely uneasy, but he was determined not to capitulate. His conscience, after all, was clear. Whoever they were, whoever had sent them, he had nothing to fear. Nevertheless, they did make him feel uneasy. He slowly removed his feet from the desk and slid the pornography back into its hiding place.

'I'm sorry, gentlemen. I have only water to offer you. You can always get beer from the canteen, of course.'

'Of course,' agreed Schröder, with a smile. 'That is as it should be. You're doing quite well so far ... But while I think of it, Hauptfeldwebel: no more feet on the table, eh? It is, after all, the property of the Führer.'

'What do you want here?' asked Dorn, cautiously. 'This is a military establishment. Nothing to do with civilians.'

The two civilians exchanged delighted smiles and said nothing. Dorn stood up and leaned towards them, hands on the desk.

'If you don't intend explaining yourselves I shall be forced to call the guard and have you removed. This is my office and I am a busy man. I strongly resent your manner, and your behaviour. You have absolutely no right to come bursting in here without permission. Either state your case or get out.'

Dorn had delivered his threat. There was nothing else he could do. He stood back to await results.

'Bravo,' murmured Schröder, vaguely.

He sniffed the air and turned to Katz.

'He may not be able to offer us a drink,' he said, 'but by the smell of things the man smokes a good cigar. And by the laws of hospitality,' he told Dorn, 'I think you should at least hand round the box.'

It was almost as if Dorn had never spoken. It was a direct insult and he was left with no alternative. Tight-lipped, he reached out a hand and pressed the bell for the guard. Katz laughed in his face.

'One guard won't be nearly enough ... we'll need at least three! Three strong and stupid men. The stronger and stupider they are, the better ... And we shall also require a table, a typewriter, three chairs and two lamps with 500 watt bulbs. Do you have all that? Because it's your job, Hauptfeldwebel, to supply it.'

Dorn gaped at the man.

'What on earth are you talking about? What have you come here for?'

'Really,' said Schröder, smothering a yawn, 'if he only had the strength to match his stupidity—'

He was interrupted by the arrival of the guard, marched up to the office by a sergeant.

'Here's your guard,' said Schröder, without turning round. 'What do you want him for?'

Dorn swallowed a few times, then shot out a finger.

'Get out, you idiots! Can't you see I have company?'

The guard opened his eyes wide and the sergeant was heard to mutter the word 'alarm'. The sight of the two cretinous, staring faces was too much for Dorn.

'Get out!' he screamed. 'How many times do I have to repeat an order before you decide to obey it?'

The guard and the sergeant hastily saluted and left the room. Dorn mopped his brow with the back of his hand and wondered whether he would have more authority standing up or sitting down. He decided, for the moment, to remain standing, but his arms presented a problem. They dangled at his side and were a nuisance. He put them behind his back and felt like a school-boy; then he clasped them in front and felt like a priest; then he let them fall limply of their own accord and they hung down to his knees, with his hands like ton weights at the end of each wrist, and embarrassed him. He was aware, all the time, of Katz and Schröder watching him and smiling at his discomfiture.

'Are you ready?' asked Schröder, softly.

'Ready for what?' Dorn turned on his questioner with a last attempt at keeping control of the situation. 'I don't know where you two gentlemen have come from, but I suggest you go back there immediately. You can have no possible business with me. In fact, you annoy me.'

'Did you hear that?' said Schröder. 'Can he really be so stupid as not to know where we come from?'

'It is possible,' said Katz. 'A lot of these people are extremely slow-witted.'

'I am at the end of my patience!' snapped Dorn. 'Either you leave my office immediately or I shall call Colonel Vogel – and that, I can promise you, will have most unpleasant consequences.'

'For Colonel Vogel.' Schröder nodded. 'Not for us. However, if he knew we were here I'm sure he would have enough sense to keep out of our way.'

Katz walked round the desk and sat himself down in Dorn's chair. He put his feet up on Dorn's desk. He opened a drawer and rummaged idly inside it. Then he undid the top button of his coat and leaned back, very much at ease. Dorn felt powerless to protest. Watching Katz, he had noticed a menacing bulge beneath his left arm, which could mean only one thing: the man was carrying a revolver. He glanced at Schröder and saw the same tell-tale signs. The sweat poured in great torrents down his back as he realized the truth.

'Are you from the Gestapo?'

The two men promptly fell about with laughter, as if Dorn had made the biggest joke of all time.

'He's quick,' spluttered Schröder. 'By Dachau, he's quick! You live on those sharp wits of yours, friend, and they should keep you going a good long time.'

'That is,' amended Katz, 'if he dies a natural death.'

'Of course.'

'And now—' Katz looked across at Dorn, trembling on the

other side of the desk – 'let's get down to business. Katz and I are from the R.S.H.A. 4-2A and we should like to have a few words with you about the things that are going on inside this prison.'

'Things? What – things?'

'The assassination.'

Schröder spat vehemently on the floor and ground it in with his foot.

'He is not a gentleman,' thought Dorn, helplessly. 'He is not a gentleman or he wouldn't spit on my floor.'

'Where is he?' demanded Katz, suddenly.

Dorn forced himself to look away from the appalling spectacle of Schröder grinding his spittle into the carpet.

'Where is who?'

Katz snapped his fingers.

'The Madman of Torgau ... the lunatic ... the assassin. Where is he?'

Dorn stared dumbly from one man to another.

'All right,' said Katz, patiently. 'If the question's too complicated for you, don't bother to answer. Just get the man sent up here.'

'You want to speak to him?'

'That was the general idea.' Katz gave Dorn a kind smile that had no humour, no understanding behind it. 'Not that we don't find your company intensely stimulating, but unfortunately we can't spend all day in pursuit of pleasure. I know that you, as an avowedly very busy man, will appreciate our point of view. So just get the prisoner sent up here and let us be done with it.'

Dorn swallowed, hard. His instestines suddenly underwent a violent spasm and he felt sick.

'It's not – not possible—'

'What is not possible?' asked Katz, pleasantly.

'The criminal – he was sent before the firing squad this morning.' Dorn lifted a helpless hand. 'Dead and buried. The whole affair's closed.'

Schröder walked softly across the floor towards Dorn.

'Is this your idea of a joke?'

'Certainly not,' said Dorn. 'The man has been executed.'

Schröder exchanged glances with Katz and breathed heavily through his nose.

'In that case, my very busy friend, I have to tell you that you have personally sabotaged an inquiry into a crime committed against the State and at the same time infringed paragraph 1019 of the Criminal Code. I take it you know what that means?'

Dorn's sweat glands redoubled their efforts. He felt cold and wet and sick.

'I can't possibly be held responsible. I don't give the orders round here, I simply prepared the papers.'

'Precisely. *You* prepared the papers.' Schröder whipped out a hand and seized Dorn by the collar of his tunic. 'I'm warning you, unless you can produce the murderer you're liable to find yourself facing a firing squad before very long. You prepared the papers, you took down the statements, you sifted the evidence, you did all the work – so you produce the murderer. Any murderer will do, but we've got to have one. Is that clear?'

Dorn's lips opened and closed silently, like the fronds of a sea anemone. His brain was in a state of terror and confusion. Visions of the firing squad, of the Russian front, danced like spots before the eyes. And it was all the fault of that wretched Gustav Dürer. Nothing but trouble when he was alive, nothing but trouble now that he was dead. What irony to reflect that he himself had requested that the man be posted to his section!

Dorn suddenly drew himself up straight. If this was the end, then very well, it was the end. But they should see how a good Hauptfeldwebel conducted himself. Enough of this lenience towards his inferiors. And towards his superiors, come to that. For too long he had shouldered more than his fair share of the burden. From now on he would be hard, hard as the steel from the Krupp works.

Schröder released his hold on Dorn's tunic and waved a none too clean finger in his face.

'I'm telling you for the last time: either produce a murderer, or you can count yourself as a dead man.'

Silence. Dorn stood stiffly, his arms rigid at his side, hard as the steel from the Krupp works. Katz suddenly came to life.

'Sit down.' He nodded curtly towards a stool in the centre of the room. 'Consider yourself under arrest.'

Even steel from the Krupp works might have wavered beneath the blow. Dorn's heart missed a beat then went wildly on its way, sending the blood pounding in his ears. No more peaceful days idled away with the Major's cigars and a book of titillating photographs. Instead he saw himself scrubbing floors, slopping about in the filth of prison latrines, shut up in a cell at Glatz like a common criminal. Or even – and this was the worst horror of all – even committed to Torgau itself, where all the prisoners knew him as a Hauptfeldwebel and where the humiliation would be unbearable.

Katz seated himself at the typewriter and inserted a sheet of paper.

'Name? Age? Religion?'

He made out a lengthy report under four main headings: sabotage, illegal conduct, neglect of duties, falsification of documents. When it was finished to his satisfaction he handed Dorn a pen and told him to sign it. Through force of habit, Dorn added the word 'Hauptfeldwebel' after his signature. Katz at once snatched the pen from him and scored through it.

'You can forget that. You're no longer a Hauptfeldwebel. You're under arrest, you're a person of no importance whatsoever.'

At this humiliating moment the door opened and an officer entered. In stature he was insignificant; in presence he was the largest man in the room. A colonel, wearing the pale grey uniform of the assault corps, decorated with two silver death's heads. Round his waist was a broad leather belt and a holster containing a black P.38 revolver. On such a small man, the revolver seemed to take on the proportions of a machine-gun. The colonel's left sleeve was empty; round his neck hung the Croix de Chevalier. He advanced magnificently into the room, sure of himself and of his authority. Dorn jumped at once to attention.

'Hauptfeldwebel Joa—' He stopped, abruptly, and corrected himself. 'Joachim Dorn, under arrest, sir.'

Not a flicker passed across the Colonel's face. He stood rigid, his eyes coldly regarding the two Gestapo men. Katz and Schröder had instinctively come to their feet. Already they seemed less certain of their superiority. Dorn was hardly able to keep his kneecaps from leaping up and down. He braced his legs and found himself shivering. He was always ill at ease in the Colonel's presence. The silence continued, prolonged itself unbearably. It was the Colonel himself who broke it.

'These men—' He glanced distastefully at Katz and Schröder – 'they belong to the Secret Police, I presume?'

'Yes, sir,' confirmed Katz, with an uneasy frown. He disliked the expression 'Secret police'. 'S.S. Stabscharführer Katz, accompanied by S.S. Oberscharführer Schröder as assistant. We have been sent here to make a report on the incident that took place yesterday in the 2nd section of this prison, when a certain Gustav Dürer was murdered by one of your prisoners.'

'I take it you have now gathered sufficient information to allow you to make your report?'

The Colonel's question was in fact more in the nature of a statement. His tone was polite, but menacing.

'With regard to Haupfeldwebel Dorn – may I ask if you consider him to be in any way implicated in the murder?'

'No, sir. Not in the murder itself.'

'Oh?' The Colonel arched an eyebrow. His nostrils quivered slightly, like those of a dog who suddenly finds itself on the right scent. 'May I therefore further inquire what business you two gentlemen have to conduct in this particular office?'

He pulled a gold watch from his pocket, checked the time with that shown by the clock on the wall.

'If my information is correct – which I have no reason to doubt – you passed the guardhouse at 9.37. It is now 17.14. You have been inside the prison for 7 hours and 37 minutes, yet not until this moment do I have the pleasure of meeting you – and even now it is I who have had to come to you, which hardly seems to me to be a very satisfactory state of affairs.'

Katz opened his mouth to speak, and then changed his mind. The Colonel gently arched a second eyebrow.

'Possibly you were not informed that it was I, and not the 2nd Section, who caused you to be sent here?'

'Oh, yes, sir,' said Schröder, with unwise enthusiasm. 'We

were told that you wanted an outside inquiry to be conducted into the affair.'

'Indeed?' The Colonel permitted himself a frostbitten smile. 'In that case, I really am at a loss to understand how it is that you failed to present yourselves to me on your arrival here?'

Katz was spared the embarrassing task of finding a suitable reply to this question. The door opened and Major Divalordy thrust his beaming person upon the scene.

'Good morning, good morning!' he began, in his usual cheersome fashion. 'And how are we this fine—'

His speech stopped short. His smile faded. He looked at Dorn, at the Colonel, at the two Gestapo agents. A series of nervous tics twitched his eyebrows and mouth convulsively. He had suddenly become the focal point of attention. From the silence that fell, it was obvious that he had burst in in the middle of something important, and feeling the need to express himself the Major began babbling a stream of inanities. Everyone stood gravely listening, until at length his voice faded awkwardly away in the middle of a sentence. Again, there was that nasty silence.

'Nothing special to report, sir,' concluded the Major, timidly.

'Really?' The Colonel's eyebrows went up again, both together this time. 'In the midst of all this excitement, you have nothing special to report? I see.'

The Major shuffled his feet uncomfortably. He murmured something about the 'unfortunate incident that had occurred yesterday'.

'More than unfortunate,' interrupted the Colonel. 'I should say catastrophic, rather. The consequences of that "unfortunate incident", Major Divalordy, are likely to be extremely disagreeable.'

'Indeed yes, sir.' The Major nodded, heartily. 'Just what I was thinking myself, sir. Extremely disagreeable.'

'Not so much for me—' said the Colonel.

'No, sir?'

'No, Major. Not so much for me, as for you.'

Major Divalordy gulped down a mouthful of air. He felt bubbles of hot sweat bursting out all over him. The Colonel calmly screwed a monocle into his eye and held out his hand for the papers that Katz was still clutching. Katz silently passed them to him and joined the rest of the room in standing stiffly to attention.

The Colonel ran his eye swiftly down the first page, then tossed the bundle of papers contemptuously on to the desk. He removed his monocle and studied first Katz, then Schröder.

'You have deliberately disobeyed my orders. You were told to report to the Kommandantur – to me, personally. Instead of so doing, you seem to have taken it upon yourselves to play at private detectives in the 2nd Section and to sit in judgment upon one of my hauptfeldwebels.'

Katz and Schröder said nothing. They stared fixedly ahead at a photograph of Adolf Hitler, as if seeking courage and inspiration.

'Very well,' said the Colonel. 'I take your silence to mean that you accept the charge. In a few moments you will be called in to see my adjutant. He has himself conducted an inquiry into the matter and has certain documents for which he requires your signature. You are expected back at Berlin this evening. From there, you will be transferred to another section – somewhere on the eastern front. I wish you well of it, gentlemen.'

The heroes of the Gestapo were dismissed. The Colonel turned his back on them and they left the room without a word. It was for Dorn, now, to take his turn on the rack.

'You've been a hauptfeldwebel for some considerable time now,' began the Colonel, deceptively gentle. 'I've been keeping my eye on you, Dorn, and it has seemed to me that of recent months you've been finding your duties rather – taxing, shall we say? Rather irksome? You're a good soldier, I know that. I sense in you an eagerness to be done with office work, to come personally to grips with the enemies of the Führer ... Am I right?'

Dorn nodded his agreement. What else, after all, could he do?

'Your talents are wasted in paper work,' continued the Colonel, lyrically. 'A man with your gifts, a man with your zeal, your burning loyalty and devotion to the Fatherland, should sooner be engaged on active duties. Out with the men, fighting at the front ... You've been very patient all these years, Dorn. It has not gone unnoticed. Now it is to be rewarded: you chance has come ...' The Colonel's voice took on a brisker tone. 'Your papers have already been transferred. Be ready to leave within the hour. Bon voyage, and good luck.'

Stunned and horrified, Dorn saluted and crept from the room. Nothing had ever been further from his thoughts or his desires than a personal confrontation with the enemies of the Führer – unless they should be safely behind bars, as at Torgau. His blood boiled in helpless anger against the Colonel. All those years of devoted service, and this was his reward! Sent to the front line, to die like a common soldier! If the Führer only knew how his most loyal of servants were treated ...

The door closed behind Dorn, and Major Divalordy was left, still sweating, alone with the Colonel. He gave an ingratiating smile, but the Colonel did not return it.

'Well, Major, this is a most unsatisfactory turn of events ... Who, I wonder, had the absurd notion of placing you in charge of this section? You are evidently quite unfitted to the task. You have allowed yourself to be led by the nose by a mere feldwebel, and I will not tolerate such a state of affairs. One is either an officer or a plain soldier. Which do you consider yourself to be?'

Major Divalordy swallowed convulsively.

'An officer, sir.'

He had attempted a gallant cry: it left his lips as a faint bleat.

'An officer? I wonder?'

The Colonel considered the matter a moment.

'I'm interested in you, Major. I should like to give you a chance to prove yourself, and for this reason I have personally gone to no small amount of trouble on your behalf. You will be glad to hear that I have found a post for you in an engineering regiment. You should see plenty of action and have plenty of scope to show the stuff you're made of. I myself have grave doubts that you are officer material: I shall be only too happy if you prove me wrong.'

To the Major's horror, Colonel Vogel pulled out a Request for Transfer form and threw it on to the desk.

'I knew you would be anxious not to waste time, so I've already made all the necessary arrangements. You have only to sign this form and give it to my adjutant and I think you'll find there should be no delay in effecting the transfer ... To you also, Major Divalordy, I say bon voyage and good luck.'

The Colonel left the room, and Major Divalordy remained standing in position for many minutes, wildly contemplating suicide.

He died of dysentery in 1948, in a prisoner of war camp at Tobolsk.

All the sentences passed by courts martial were sent for verification to the Judicial Department of the Army. Each case had to receive the official signature of the Head of the Department, General von Grabach, before sentence could be carried out.

Von Grabach was known for his expensive tastes rather than for his legal wisdom. He was known for his whoring and for his addiction to the cognac bottle. He affected a gracious way of life, was more concerned with the set of his jacket, the gloss on his creaking leather boots, the glitter of his silver spurs, than with the more mundane aspects of army life.

It was many years, now, since he had troubled to read any of the documents to which he so lightly appended his name. Death sentences or deliveries of sausages, they were all one to him.

CHAPTER NINE

GENERAL VON GRABACH paced eagerly up and down the thick pile carpet of his office, staring out upon, but not seeing, the magnificent view over the Landwehr Kanal. Instead of the water, instead of the trees, he was gazing upon a vision of Frau von Zirlitz wearing her pink silk panties. General von Grabach had a passion for pink: he even went so far as to wear pink underclothes himself. He also had a passion for Ebba von Zirlitz: she was his mistress of the moment.

As he paced, he glanced impatiently at his watch and subtracted another five minutes from the long hours he must wait before the delights of the evening which lay ahead. The watch was gold, with a heavy gold strap. It was a present from the town council of Bucharest, where he had been stationed for four glorious months. Bucharest! There was a cushy number, if you like. Endless days of dances, parties, free drink, free tobacco. Endless nights of frolic and debauchery. It seemed to von Grabach, looking back upon those halcyon days, that every other woman you met in Bucharest was a beautiful nymphomaniac.

It was different here in Berlin. You had to fight for your women here, and a damned hard fight it was, too. But the worst thing of all was the way you simply couldn't move for the S.S. men that swarmed all over the city. Ghastly types. An uncouth rabble that in his opinion had no place in the German Army.

Von Grabach pulled a sour face at the thought of them. He turned to the window and gazed out, watching an asthmatic tug boat slowly pulling a string of barges through the sluggish waters of the canal. His thoughts returned pleasurably to Frau von Zirlitz. He really must remember to send a note to his friend, the General commanding the division to which Captain von Zirlitz belonged. There must be no chance of the gallant

Captain arriving home unexpectedly. Scenes could lead only to unpleasantness, and it would be disastrous if the echoes reached as far as Prinz Albrecht Strasse. Certainly no sane man would consider it a crime to be found sleeping with the wife of an officer who was fighting at the front – indeed it was perfectly natural and only to be expected – but unfortunately some of the men who held the reins of the Third Reich could not, in the General's opinion, be considered as sane.

He turned back from the window and began pacing again, up and down on the thick pile carpet. The General's office, as befitted his rank and station, more resembled an elegant drawing-room than an office. It was here, at his delicately carved writing desk, that he signed the death warrants of the prisoners in Torgau. But for the moment his mind was not on death warrants it was on Ebba von Zirlitz in her pink silk panties.

His dream was terminated by the arrival of his staff officer, who pointedly placed two rose-coloured folders on the writing desk.

'Sorry to bother you, sir. These have just come in. A couple of appeals from Torgau. One we've seen before – an infantry feldwebel, charged with desertion. The other's new – an artillery lieutenant, found guilty of murder.'

'Thank you, Walther, just leave them there. I'll take a look at them later, if I have the time. I wish they wouldn't keep pestering us with these constant appeals, they know full well we never let them go through.' Complacently the General pulled out his gold cigarette case. 'Others might, but we're made of sterner stuff, Walther. Sterner stuff. These miserable creatures don't deserve pity. They've committed their crimes, they must pay for them. An iron discipline, Walther: I practise what I preach ... Here, have a cigarette. I think you'll find them to your liking, they came from America via the Red Cross.' He laughed, merrily. 'What wouldn't I give to see their faces in Washington if they knew where their precious cigarettes had ended up!'

'Thank you,' said Walther, with a faint smile.

The two men stood side by side at the windows and watched a company of new cavalry recruits swinging past, singing lustily as they went.

'Good lads,' murmured the General. 'Damned good lads. The youth of Germany, Walther. The youth of Germany ... God bless 'em!'

'Yes, indeed,' said Walther, echoing the general's fervour. 'I was watching them training only yesterday. It does your heart good to see such enthusiasm – every single one of them ready to die for the Führer.'

'The Hitler Jugend.' Von Grabach inhaled deeply and with an air of personal satisfaction. 'Tell me, Walther ... to change the subject: have you been along to the gypsy quarter recently?'

'I was there only yesterday evening, sir.'

The General made a strange whinnying noise of anticipation.

'Anything – interesting? Anyone you could – ah – particularly recommend?'

'I would say not, sir.'

Walther shook his head, regretfully, and the General let out his breath on a long sigh. 'There's no shortage of women, of course, so long as you're not too choosy. But no one I should care to recommend to you personally, sir. Not quite up to your class, if you know what I mean?'

'A pity. I trust your judgment in these matters, Walther ... By the way, have you ever met an Ebba von Zirlitz in your travels?'

There was that in the General's tone which indicated to the alert Walther that the question was not altogether as casual as it sounded. He hesitated.

'Ebba von Zirlitz?' Carefully, he considered her. 'I can't say I recall the name. Am I likely to have come across her anywhere?'

'Possibly not. In any case, no matter.' The General waved his cigarette through the air. 'It's not important. I merely inquired on behalf of a friend of mine. He has a penchant for the lady.'

Walther joined in the General's laugh, while metaphorically thumbing his nose. What an old fool! Almost everyone knew Ebba von Zirlitz. He himself had been to a party with her only a couple of months before, and he knew for a fact that at least a dozen men had already been through her.

'All right, Walther. That'll be all for now. I'll send for you if I need you.'

The General dismissed him and turned back to the window, to his silent contemplation of the inner vision of Ebba in her panties. Slowly and luxuriously, his mind began to strip her naked, but the General fortunately managed to put a stop to it before things had gone too far. Breathing lustily through his heavy nostrils, he turned back to his writing desk, picked up one of the rose-coloured files, flung it down without even looking at it and reached out for the telephone.

'Ebba? Is that you, my little love? It's Claude here ... just counting the hours, my sweet, until tonight.'

He sent a loud slopping kiss down the line to her. Ebba laughed gaily.

'Don't forget that fur you so rashly promised me!'

'You shall have it, my pet. Never fear.'

For the next three days the rose-coloured folders lay untouched and forgotten on General von Grabach's writing desk. They were joined by others, from other prisons, until at last there was a little pile of them. Each file represented a condemned man and his friends or family, all anxiously waiting for news. Each file represented days, weeks, perhaps months of endeavour and sacrifice – constant visits to those in authority, endless train journeys from far distant places, letters, telephone calls, tears and humiliation. A man's sister had sold her body; a man's father had sold his soul. Wives and mothers and sweethearts had left their homes and taken up work in Berlin factories, to be near at hand and able to pursue their endeavours with more vigour. Families had parted with precious possessions in the hope that bribery might work where personal supplication had failed. It was a long, heartbreaking battle before the right to appeal could be won, but when at last the appeal was approved and had gone through for consideration by those at the top – what then? Only waiting. Day after day, waiting for news that never came, knowing that you had done all that was possible and that the matter was now out of your hands.

Out of your hands and into those of General von Grabach.

But the General was a busy man, he had no time to spare for minor matters. A large notice had been pinned to his door: 'ENGAGED. ON NO ACCOUNT TO BE DISTURBED.' Even Walther saw him for no more than a few minutes each day. Sometimes he had time only to say 'good morning' or 'good evening' as the General hurried in and out of his office. The fact was, as Walther well knew, that the affair von Zirlitz was prospering. It had been helped along by the arrival of the promised fur – a sable, supplied by the Head of the Commissariat from a stock that had been confiscated during the course of an S.S. inquiry. The confiscated furs were designated for the troops fighting on the eastern front, but none ever reached them. In Berlin the higher-ranking officers had the pick of the bunch for their wives, their girl-friends and their mistresses. The rest went on as far as Poland, where the occupying army shared them out amongst themselves. The troops in the trenches went cold, but who should worry?

The Head of the Commissariat took one fur for himself and one for his friend the General. He had no special love for the General, but he did believe in keeping up a good relationship with those who might one day prove useful to know.

'You must find your work very absorbing?' he hazarded.

'Oh, it's well enough in its way,' agreed the General, more interested in picking his teeth with a silver toothpick than in discussing the intricacies of his work. 'Something new always turning up. Keeps you on your toes all right.'

He leaned back in his comfortable chair and sipped his cognac contentedly. The Head of the Commissariat had one of the most elegant offices in all Berlin; more elegant, even, than the General's own.

'Fine cognac,' he commented.

'Not too bad, is it?' agreed the Commissar, complacently. 'It was requisitioned in France for hospital use ... I sent one of my feldwebels off to Spandau yesterday. Caught the fellow stealing.' He gazed across at the General. 'I hope the court martial takes as serious a view of the matter as I do. Such men must be made an example of. In my opinion, a death sentence would not be out of place.'

'Rest assured. It shall be seen to. I personally shall keep an eye on the man's case.'

'I wish you would. I find there is an unwholesome disregard to discipline creeping into the Service these days.'

'Not from my quarter, I can promise you that. Iron discipline is my creed. I practise what I preach ... Only the other day a member of my own staff came back from leave three days late. He attempted some garbled excuse, but I'm not a man for half measures. All or nothing, it's the only way. The country has no use for layabouts and parasites.'

'So what did you do about it?'

'Why, I called in the Military Police and told them to arrest him. Suspected desertion. I've asked for the death penalty. Paragraph 1133, clause 9.'

The General rubbed his hands together and hopefully edged his empty glass towards the bottle of cognac.

'Where would the country be if we let people come and go as they pleased? Before you knew where you were whole regiments would be bowling off home whenever they felt like it.'

'Quite so. To my way of thinking, the Military Code is far too indulgent. How many times does one hear of the death penalty being commuted and some useless wastrel sent off to idle away the rest of the war in a so-called "disciplinary" battalion?'

'Speaking for myself,' said von Grabach, 'I can tell you that I very rarely uphold appeals for clemency. I might almost say never.' He picked up his second glass of cognac. 'At this very moment, for instance, we have a case of persistent refusal to obey orders on our hands. A young captain from an infantry regiment. The chap's got some pretty powerful relatives, and frankly it's causing us no end of a headache, one way or another. The matter's due for hearing in three weeks' time. However, I shall not allow myself to be swayed by any outside pressures. I firmly believe in imposing the death penalty whenever and wherever the law makes provision for it. I mean to say, it makes a mockery of the whole idea of discipline if you let these people get away with things all the time ... Matter of fact, in this particular case I've already prepared the necessary documents.'

'Before the hearing?' The Commissar looked, for a moment, almost shocked. 'You mean, the verdict's known in advance?'

General von Grabach laughed, airily.

'I wouldn't put it quite like that,' he said, with a certain amount of condescension in his voice. 'But the court martial almost always passes the sentences we ask for. Those who sin against the state must pay the penalty no matter who their relatives are. I am swayed by no one. I do my duty as I see it, and none shall deflect me from my course – except, perhaps, the Führer himself and Heinrich Himmler,' he added. 'But I can assure you that they are iron disciplinarians both. We are cast in the same mould. I am proud to be as I am ... You see this cross?' He fingered the decoration round his neck. 'You know why they gave me this, General Schroll? Because I run my service efficiently. Because in 99 cases out of a hundred I demand the death penalty. The Feldmarschall himself said to me, "War needs men who are hard, and such men must be rewarded". I think you'll agree with me that any moron is capable of fighting on the front line. But when it comes to doing my job—' He shook his head, wearily, as if at times the responsibility weighed heavy on his shoulders – 'ah, then it's a different matter. Not just a question of signing papers, you know. You need a definite cultural background. A good grip of psychology. Understanding of human nature. A lifetime's experience of dealing with people—'

'How right you are, my dear General. There is none of the sinecure about your job – or, indeed, about mine. To be honest with you, I myself have been sadly out of sorts just lately. Overwork, you know. And the strain ... The doctor advises at least six weeks in Baden-Baden if I'm to avoid a complete breakdown ... I suppose you know of no addresses down there?'

Von Grabach screwed up his eyes and followed the smoke of his cigar as it coiled up to the ceiling.

'Baden-Baden?' He took a sip of cognac and rolled it thoughtfully round his mouth. 'I must say you have an excellent taste in cigars! If you ever lay your hands on any more of them—'

'You like them? I'll send you round five boxes first thing tomorrow.'

'Really? How perfectly delightful! How very generous of you.' The empty cognac glass was once again pushed hopefully towards the bottle. 'Baden-Baden. Now let me see . . . I do have one or two addresses I could let you have. I'll send someone round with a list for you tomorrow.'

'I should be most grateful. By the way—' General Schroll picked up the bottle of cognac and leaned forward confidentially – 'have you heard the rumours that are going round Berlin? That our troops in the Caucasus have been routed? If it's true, then it certainly makes one wonder if the final victory is to be achieved quite as—'

He was interrupted by General von Grabach sitting bolt upright in his chair and banging down his glass.

'I beg your pardon, sir? One hesitates to believe the evidence of one's own ears! May I inquire if you are in any doubt as to the final outcome of the war?'

'Not at all!' cried the Commissar, his neck already growing red above the collar of his uniform. 'My dear General, I wonder at you for even suggesting such a thing . . . It is simply,' he continued, with desperate improvisation, 'that here, in the Commissariat, we have an oberfeldwebel who is rather too much given to pessimism. I myself have overheard him speaking defeatist claptrap on more than one occasion. I abhor that kind of thing, as you well know. This rumour about the Caucasus was the last straw: I decided then and there that he must be got rid of.'

'But surely,' murmured von Grabach, intently studying the glowing butt of his cigar, 'he is in good hands here? I feel certain that you, of all people, would know how to put a hasty end to such treachery.'

Schroll's neck became red all over, up to his double chin and the lobes of his ears. He muttered a few incoherent words, then seized desperately on the first exit that presented itself: the telephone.

'Excuse me, my dear General! A most important matter that had completely slipped my memory.'

He spoke feverishly for some moments to Oberstintendant Schmidt, head of the Special Supplies Depot.

'Incidentally,' he ended up, 'be so good as to send eight cases of cigars and six bottles of champagne over to my office as soon as possible. The same cigars as I had the other day. Will you give it your urgent attention? Thank you . . . And by the way, Schmidt – that leave request you put in. I don't think you need have any worries about it. I'll see that it's passed.'

He replaced the receiver and smiled confidently at von Grabach.

'The cigars are on their way. Be with you tomorrow. And I take it you won't find a case of champagne amiss? I suddenly remembered a consignment we've just had from France.'

They shook hands amiably. At the door, von Grabach turned.

'Let me have a full report on your traitor.'

'My traitor?'

'Have you forgotten so soon? Your oberfeldwebel who talks of defeat . . . As soon as I receive your report I'll deal with the matter personally. We've had instructions to come down very heavily on that sort of thing.'

The one general left the room; the other stayed behind, hot under his high collar. Von Grabach was well aware that in fact there was no traitor. The Commissar was equally well aware that he had fooled no one with his improvisation. Simply, he had made a tactical error. He had opened his mouth too wide, and von Grabach had found a new game to play. Cigars and champagne were not enough, he wanted to turn the screw and see what happened. Someone would plainly have to be sacrificed. Schroll called for his adjutant and settled back into his chair to think of a suitable lamb.

Stabsintendant Brandt, the General's adjutant, had been a bank clerk before the war. He was the soul of obedience and discretion, without an original thought in his head.

'Ah, Brandt,' said the General. 'We have a certain ober-feldwebel attached to the Commissariat – he talks constantly of strategic withdrawals and the like. You know the one I mean?'

Brandt folded his smooth forehead into concertina creases.

'I believe so, sir.'

'Good. In that case, I want him put under immediate arrest.'

Brandt's eyes bulged in amazement from their sockets.

'Arrest him, sir? What for?'

'Defeatist talk. Undermining the morale of the troops. Such men are a threat to the entire German Army.'

'But sir, I don't believe he's ever spoken to any of the troops. About defeat, I mean. I've never heard him speak about defeat to anyone.'

'Strategic withdrawals?'

'It's hardly the same thing,' protested Brandt.

'It may not seem so to you, Brandt. To me they are synonymous. For all practical purposes, that is. It's all of a piece with the propaganda they put out from London and Moscow.'

Brandt frowned. He was not bent on arguing with the General on any matter of principle; he simply had a neat and well documented mind, a place for everything and everything in its place, and here were a few facts that were definitely not in their place.

'Excuse me, sir,' he said, in the firm but respectful tones of a clerk who had discovered an error in his superior's arithmetical calculations, 'but if you remember, there was an occasion when you yourself were in favour of the strategic withdrawal. That was at the time of—'

'That was quite different.' Schroll frowned. 'The situation was different, the time was different. It was at a different phase of the war altogether.'

'I see, sir.'

Brandt fell silent. He was very far from seeing, but then it was not up to him to see. It was up to him to point out errors and inconsistencies, not to interpret them.

'About this oberfeldwebel,' continued Schroll. 'A certain person has taken a rather unhealthy interest in him. Unhealthy for him, unhealthy for us. Upon reflection, I think it might be best if he were to disappear rather suddenly. And his papers as well, of course.'

Brandt stiffened.

'Sir! Excuse me, sir, but that is quite impossible. It's against all the regulations. You can't just get rid of papers like that. Papers are necessary to the running of the entire Army. Where should we be without them? In a fine muddle! Maybe you don't realize it, sir, but—'

'God damn it!' burst out Schroll, losing patience. 'Who do you think you are, Brandt, lecturing me like that? Do what I tell you, and you'd better make it snappy if you don't want to find yourself out in the trenches!'

General and adjutant stood facing each other mutinously. Brandt's smooth, shiny face was full of reproach.

'Get and do it!' cried Schroll, turning away. 'I want that damned oberfeldwebel out of Berlin and on his way somewhere else within the hour!'

'Very good, sir. I think I could arrange a quick transfer to an infantry section in Greece.'

'Greece?' screamed Schroll, contemptuously. 'That's no good, you bloody idiot! There's only one place to send him, and that's the Russian front. When I say get rid of him, I mean get rid of him ... Finland would do, I suppose. Anywhere, so long as it gets him out of our hair. As for the papers – do what you like with 'em. Burn 'em, stuff 'em up the chimney, stuff 'em anywhere you wish. I leave it entirely to you, but those papers have got to go.'

'Yes, sir, said Brandt, weakly.

His safe, regulated world of filing cabinets and carbon copies had been toppled by a sudden earthquake. Make out false documents! Burn papers! He had never done such a thing in his life before. Papers were records, and records were the lifeblood of civilization. Brandt felt as if he was going mad.

He tottered from the room, and in his place the General sent for his ordnance officer, a young infantry lieutenant who had greatly distinguished himself on the battlefield and lost a leg in doing so. Schroll waved him into a chair.

'Sit down, Brücker. Make yourself comfortable. Cigar?'

Brücker settled himself into the depths of an armchair and watched as Schroll paced back and forth, back and forth, tapping the palm of his left hand with a ruler.

'It's very difficult to steer a straight course through the troubled waters of this world ... Don't you find it so, Lieutenant?'

Brücker laughed, easily.

'I don't altogether care for your choice of metaphor, sir, but
– yes, on the whole I would agree with you.'

The General paced a bit more. Brücker narrowed his eyes.
What was the old devil planning now, in that mean little brain
of his? Whatever it was, he could do nothing to harm Brücker.
The Lieutenant had a brother in the S.S., and the brother had
influence. If anything, it was rather Brücker who could harm
the General.

'My adjutant,' said Schroll, abruptly. 'I find him to be quite
astoundingly idle.'

'The man's a moron,' said Brücker.

'A moron! Yes, you've hit on the exact word.' Schroll turned
eagerly on Brücker. 'I wonder – could you manage to get rid of
him for me? Without any fuss or bother, you know. Without
implicating me in any way. I should have to give every appearance of wishing to keep him here ... You understand
me?'

Brücker looked at him coldly. Schroll gave a nervous neigh
and began washing his hands in the air.

'The man gets on my nerves. I can't work properly with him
around. I—'

'Say no more, General. I know what to do. There's an S.S.
unit out in the Ukraine—'

'Excellent! The very thing! If you can bring this off, my
dear boy, you'll be doing us both a favour. You'll find yourself
promoted before the end of the month, I can promise you
that.'

'Thank you, sir.'

Brücker trod thoughtfully from the room. Promotion
interested him not at all: he had his own means of obtaining it
virtually whenever he wished. The fate of the adjutant left him
unmoved: the man was a fool and deserved whatever was
coming to him. But it would be interesting to find out what it
was that he knew about the General. It was obviously something dangerous. Obviously something worth knowing.

Four hours later, a message came over the teleprinter to the
effect that Stabsintendant Brandt had been transferred to a
special unit in the Ukraine. General Schroll, with a fine show
of indignation, spent twenty minutes raising heaven and earth

to keep his adjutant with him in Berlin. When the reply came through that the order was 'from above', and when he discovered just how far above – right up towards the cloud-covered summit, higher than he had ever dreamed of climbing – he ceased his efforts and sat back instead to mop his brow and ponder uncomfortably upon the influence wielded by the young Lieutenant Brücker.

Some time afterwards, von Grabach made inquiries about the oberfeldwebel who (so it now seemed to General Schroll) had started all the trouble.

'Transferred?' he murmured, on hearing the news. 'Your adjutant also, I believe? How very sudden!'

'They mess you about,' said the Commissar, vaguely. 'Of course, I daresay we could always get hold of him again if you think the matter really worth pursuing?'

General von Grabach only smiled and mentally raised his hat to his colleague. The man was quick off the mark, you had to give him that.

Later that same day von Grabach received two cases of cognac sent round from the Commissariat. General Schroll left for a well-earned rest in Baden-Baden.

The cognac had arrived shortly before lunch. At four o'clock in the afternoon von Grabach, in a state of complete euphoria, received a visit from a certain Councillor Berner. Had it not been for the cognac-coloured clouds surrounding him, he would never have consented to see the man in the first place. He gathered, through the haze, that Councillor Berner's son was at present lodged in Torgau Military Prison awaiting death by the firing squad. Councillor Berner, not unnaturally, was anxious that his son's life should be spared. He had come in person to bring the names of several influential relatives in support of his son's appeal for mercy.

The General listened to Councillor Berner's supplication and was unmoved. Then he listened to the names of the influential relatives and grudgingly agreed that something might perhaps be done. He nodded his head gravely from the Olympian heights of his power.

'I shall do my best for you, but understand that the matter is not entirely in my hands. Like anyone else, I receive my orders from above . . . If it were left to me, of course, I should have no hesitation whatsoever in upholding the appeal. Personally I am against all forms of violence and brutality. If I had my way I should abolish the death penalty altogether. However—' He shrugged a shoulder – 'discipline is discipline, as I think you will agree. One can but obey one's orders.'

The Councillor distractedly played the piano in the air as he talked.

'My son's crime was not committed against the State, you know, General. It was a crime of passion. The girl led him on. He was not altogether sane when he did it . . . He's a good soldier. We can't afford to throw away men like that. Only save his life and give him a chance to prove his loyalty. Even if it means sending him to the Russian front, at least let him have a chance—'

'Yes, yes. I shall do my best, I do assure you.'

'May I rely on you, General?'

'I give you my word,' said von Grabach, his vision blurred by cognac. 'Your son's life shall be spared.'

There were celebrations in the Berner household that night. Champagne flowed, the telephone rang unceasingly. The Councillor told everyone who would listen that Germany should be proud of her generals: they were wise and humane and none could say otherwise. He wrote that same night to his son, telling him the news, and his heart overflowed with gratitude.

The particular wise and humane General in question lit up a cigar, poured himself a generous glass of cognac and sat back comfortably in the remote depths of an arm chair. All was well in von Grabach's limited but expensive world. He had passed a night of fantasy and excitement with Ebba von Zirlitz, and only the same morning he had heard that he had been granted a long rest period at Berchtesgaden. Life was treating him well. Perhaps he ought to make a small token effort and look at the rose-coloured folders that still lay on his desk. Between two puffs on his cigar he reached out a hand and clawed up the first of them.

'Lieutenant Heinz Berner, demoted to private. Prisoner, 2nd

Section Cell 476, Torgau, Saxony. Condemned to death.'

The General thumbed listlessly through the pages. His eye skimmed over the words, but his brain did not absorb them. One rose-coloured folder was much like another, and he had seen a great many in his time. He flung down Heinz Berner and picked up Paul-Nicolas Grün. Identical. Von Grabach neither knew nor cared what crimes had taken them to Torgau. They were prisoners, they were condemned to death, and as far as he was concerned that was an end to the matter.

He threw the last of his cognac down his throat. He glanced at his watch. Time to go and supervise his packing if he were to leave for Berchtesgaden that same day. He picked up his pen and carelessly scrawled his signature across the two folders. Heinz Berner and Paul-Nicolas Grün had been finally condemned and nothing short of an act of God could save them. The Russians themselves could be knocking at the gates of Torgau, but Berner and Grün would still have to face the firing squad. Iron discipline. An order was an order.

General von Grabach laid one file neatly on top of the other, with the air of one who has completed a good day's work. For a moment he was filled with a vague feeling of disturbance, which he traced, much later at Berchtesgaden, to Councillor Berner and a couple of reckless hours spent over a cognac bottle. Once traced to its source, the feeling of disturbance instantly disappeared and was replaced by one of annoyance. What right had the man Berner to come meddling in military affairs? He had extorted a false promise from General von Grabach, taking advantage of the General's temporary inebriation. Everyone knew the General's principles. Everyone knew that he was an iron disciplinarian, who never went against the findings of a court martial. The very idea of upholding an appeal was abhorrent to him. In any case, no matter what he may have said to the Councillor under the influence of cognac, it was too late now to stop the natural sequence of events that followed from his signing of the death warrant. War was war and others beside the Councillor had had to suffer the inconvenience of it.

Von Grabach decided to make one magnanimous concession: he would arrange for the parents to pay a last visit to their son before he faced the firing squad. It was more than they deserved, but he was not inhumane, he was not unjust. He would grant them this one last favour, though God knows he would probably get little enough thanks for it. He thus dispatched a message to Berlin and put the matter from his mind, never to think of it again. His sleep was disturbed only by dreams, never by nightmares, and his conscience was at peace.

It was Frau Berner who opened the official communication from Berlin:

'If you wish to pay a final visit to the prisoner Heinz Berner, whose execution is fixed for 5 a.m. May 24, you should present yourself to the Kommandantur of Torgau Prison at 18.00 hours on May 23. This authorization is valid for four persons. The length of the visit is limited to ten minutes.'

Frau Berner, with no one to support her in this moment of crisis, gave a heartrending cry and crumpled to the floor. Frau Grün, on the other hand, mother of the other condemned prisoner, was in the middle of her twelve-hour day as a chambermaid at the Graf Moltke Hotel and could not therefore, afford the luxury of losing consciousness. She bore the news bravely, but the beds were ill-made that day and the floors ill-swept. They threatened to report her to the Inspector of Works Department, which would have meant immediate transfer to a munitions factory. Frau Grün shrugged her shoulders and seemed not to care where she was sent. Three months later, she killed herself, beneath an underground train at St. Paul's Station.

At Torgau we had all read the letter or heard the news and were convinced that Heinz Berner, by some miracle, had been granted a reprieve.

'Well, strike me rigid!' said Heide. 'I never thought I'd live to see the day. You're a lucky bugger, Heinz.'

Heinz Berner was beside himself with joy. He capered about the cell like a young carthorse, while the rest of us sat on his bed and discussed the wonders of the situation.

'Well, at least you're one of us now,' said Little John,

smugly. 'And better for it, if you ask me. Who wants to be a bleeding officer, anyhow?'

Alte alone remained sceptical.

'It's too good to be true,' he said, when we had left the cell and were safely out of earshot. 'I don't see how his father could know about it when we haven't heard anything here. We should have had it over the teleprinter by now.'

'Anything's possible,' said the Legionnaire. 'Allah works in strange ways. I've seen this sort of thing happen before. When I was in the Legion, it was. One of the lads was saved right at the last moment. The reprieve came through literally seconds before he was due to be shot.'

Alte shook his head.

'I don't like it. I just don't like it. I only hope to God no one's being sadistic enough to pull the boy's leg.'

'It'll be O.K.,' said Porta. 'Take a bet?'

'I wouldn't care to bet on a man's life,' said Alte, gravely.

It was Barcelona who brought us the bad news. He came running from the Secretariat, white as a ghost, scarcely able to speak. It took us some seconds to drag any sense out of him.'

'Tomorrow – at five o'clock – they're going to shoot him—'

A stunned silence fell upon us.

· 'Who?' I said, at last, although we all knew he meant Heinz.

'It's impossible!' cried Porta. 'They couldn't play a trick like that on him!'

'I've seen the papers,' said Barcelona. 'They're signed by a general. It's all fixed up for tomorrow morning.'

Again, that dreadful silence. We looked at each other, and there was horror on our faces.

'Poor sod,' murmured Alte. 'I just wish to God his old man had never written to him in the first place.'

'But he must have had the news from someone high up. He wouldn't be such a fool—'

'He thought he was going to be released tomorrow—'

'You wouldn't tell a person a thing like that unless you were sure—'

'Well, we're sure now all right. Who's going to break the news to him?'

'I will,' offered Little John, unexpectedly. 'I feel sort of – responsible for him. In an odd sort of way. I've never been able to stand that sort of officer, I've always loathed their ruddy guts. He's the first one I've ever come to terms with. I never thought the day would arrive when I actually felt sorry for one of the bastards.'

'He's only a kid,' said Porta.

I turned to look at Barcelona.

'Who's got to shoot him?' I asked, bluntly.

The reply was equally blunt; and brutal.

'Us,' said Barcelona.

'Christ!' Porta stared at him disbelievingly. 'They really pile on the agony, don't they?'

The Legionnaire held out a couple of cigarettes and handed them to Little John.

'Here. Give him these. A bit of opium won't do him any harm when the time comes. And I'll see what I can do about getting him a jab, as well.'

'I'll tell you something!' shouted Porta, suddenly, at the top of his voice. 'When the bloody revolution comes and it's our turn to shoot that lot I'm going to reprieve every last one of 'em and then change my mind again the day before they're due to be released. I'm going to make the sods suffer. I'm going to get them so screwed up—'

'All right, we heard you,' said Alte, wearily. 'No need to go on about it.'

Little John marched bravely off to see Heinz. The boy was reading a book, settled and happy for the first time since he had come to Torgau. He looked up and smiled as Little John opened the door of his cell.

'Hi, there! Come to let me out already?'

Silently, Little John shook his head. He held out a cigarette and Heinz laughed up at him.

'What's the matter with you? You look like a condemned man!'

He inhaled deeply on his cigarette and watched the smoke curling out of his nostrils.

162

'How soon do you reckon it'll be before I'm transferred to a disciplinary regiment? Straight away tomorrow, do you suppose?'

'No,' said Little John. 'I shouldn't think so.'

He turned his head and stared out of the small slit window high up in the wall. It was no use indulging in preliminary conversational skirmishing. He had a job to do, and the longer he left it the harder it would be, both for him and for Heinz. He turned back again, determined to break the news without any more ado. Heinz suddenly stood up and punched him amiably in the chest.

'You're a funny chap, you know, Little John! When I first came here I could hardly stand the sight of you. And now, believe it or not – though I'm anxious enough to go! – I think I'm actually going to miss you. God knows why, but there it is.'

'You won't miss me,' said Little John, roughly. 'I'm not worth missing. You'll be well out of it all, kid. Make no mistake about that.'

Berner's smile faded.

'What is it?' he demanded. 'What's eating you all of a sudden?'

'Sit down and I'll tell you.'

Little John's voice was harsh and grating, but his sympathy was obvious. Berner sank obediently on to his bed, his whole body tense with sudden alarm.

'What is it?'

'Simply this: they're not going to release you tomorrow. Or any other day.'

'What?'

Instinctively, Berner was back on his feet.

'You mean – they've turned down the appeal after all?'

'They never did anything else. It was a mix-up.'

'No! No, I can't believe it, you're lying! You're having me on!' Berner shook his head wildly from side to side. 'You've made a mistake, haven't you? Haven't you?'

'There's no mistake, Heinz. Someone had to break the news. I offered to do it.'

'You're mad!' yelled Heinz. 'I've got it here in black and

163

white!' He groped under his blankets and pulled out the letter from his father. 'See! Read what he says – "we've managed to get a reprieve and I'm arranging for your transfer to a disciplinary regiment". You don't think my father would write a thing like that if it weren't true, do you? He's a councillor, he knows what he's doing. It's you who's got it wrong! There must be someone else with the same name!'

'I'm sorry,' said Little John. 'You've just got to face it, Heinz. I don't know where your father got his facts from, but the execution order's come through and it's all fixed up for tomorrow. I hate having to do this to you, but—'

Berner heard no more than the first couple of sentences. Before Little John had finished speaking he had slipped unconscious to the floor.

A priest came to the cell before the boy had fully recovered himself. He was a young man with the rank of Oberleutnant. He wore a grey field uniform, with the German eagle and the swastika on his breast and a crucifix round his neck. He hesitated at the entrance to the cell, and his eyes met those of Little John. The message of scorn and hostility was unmistakable. The priest glanced for a moment at the prisoner, then bowed his head and left the two men alone. Berner grabbed hold of Little John's hand.

'When is it for?'

'Tomorrow morning. Five o'clock.'

'I see . . . Who's going to do it?'

'We are.'

Abruptly, Berner let him go. The boy crumpled up at his feet and flung his arms round Little John's legs.

'Help me! Help me, for God's sake! It's worse now than it was before. I can't stand it, you've got to help me!'

'Take my revolver,' said Little John, quietly. 'Bash me over the head with it and—' He made a gesture. 'It's quicker and simpler that way, believe me.'

Berner sat back on his heels.

'Shoot myself? I couldn't, I wouldn't have the courage. You do it for me, Little John. Put a bullet through me now. You can tell them I was trying to make a bolt for it.'

Little John shook his head.

'I'd have done it willingly when you first came here. But I can't shoot down a friend in cold blood. I shan't even fire on you tomorrow, and neither will Porta. We never do.'

'But what happens if none of the others do, either?'

'They will. They'll shoot straight and they won't miss. It'll be over before you know it . . . There wouldn't be any point the whole lot of us refusing to shoot. We'd just be sent before a firing squad ourselves and they'd get someone else to do the job . . . Look, why don't you have a word with Julius? He's scared stiff of authority, he'd shoot you down soon enough if you tried to make a bunk for it when he was here, Julius is a shit. He'd do anything to keep out of trouble. But don't ask me to do it. I couldn't . . . You understand? I just couldn't.'

Berner was crying, very quietly, his face hidden in his hands.

'I'll send the Old Man to see you. He'll talk to you. He'll do it better than me.'

Little John glanced round desperately, as if searching for help. His face suddenly cleared.

'Know what, Heinz? You might be a damn sight better off five minutes past five tomorrow morning than you are now. All these stories about heaven, they could be true. I mean, you don't know till you've tried, do you? A priest once told me you shouldn't fear death because you're always better off dead than alive. Well, it could be true.'

Heinz appeared not to hear these words of comfort. Little John tried a new approach.

'It's not death that's the trouble so much as the way you die. Take cancer, for example. Anyone'd be scared of that. Or paralysis. Or gas. Or things like that. But a firing squad!' He made an expansive gesture. 'Just a piece of pudding, me old mate! You won't feel a thing, I promise you. Like I said, Julius is a shit, but one thing I will give him: put a gun in his hand and he never misses.'

Again, the words had no visible effect. Little John pulled out his cigarettes and matches and tossed them on to the bed. It was an action that could earn him six months' hard labour if discovered.

'I've got to leave you, Heinz. I'm supposed to be on duty . . .

Smoke the fags, I would. There's a couple of opium sticks amongst that lot. Have a drag on them tomorrow morning, it'll help you get through ... Ring the bell if there's anything you specially want. One of us'll come ... O.K.?'

Berner said nothing, but continued silently weeping. Little John stood a moment regarding him, then left the cell. Out in the corridor he had an attack of sudden rage and aimed an almighty kick at a bucket full of water. There was pandemonium as the bucket clattered full speed ahead along the passage, crashing over the stone floor, bouncing off the walls. Then silence. Then Heide's voice, furious, from the floor below:

'What the bloody hell's going on up there?'

'Piss off and mind your own bleeding business!' roared Little John, by way of reply.

Heide prudently left it at that. It was asking for trouble to cross Little John when he was in that sort of mood.

After slouching about the prison in an aimless manner for some thirty minutes or so, Little John made his way to the guardroom and confronted Alte.

'You'll have to go and talk to Heinz. I promised him you would. I'm no good at explaining things, he needs someone like you.'

Alte looked steadily at Little John.

'What do you want me to tell him?'

'Oh, I don't know ... Whatever you think best. Something about Jesus and life after death and all that sort of crap.'

'Is he religious?' asked Barcelona, in astonishment. 'I never heard him ask for the Chaplain.'

'I don't know what he is, but he needs someone to talk to him,' persisted Little John.

'And just because you don't believe in it, it doesn't mean you mightn't want to hear all about it before you're due to go,' added Porta. 'In case it turns out to be true after all.'

Barcelona turned to the Legionnaire.

'Why don't you go and see him? You could tell him about Allah and his magic garden.'

The Legionnaire swung round on Barcelona, eyeing him with suspicion, evidently not sure whether he was serious or whether he was asking for a punch-up. Before he could reach any decision Alte was standing up and buckling on his belt. He reached out for his cap.

'All right, I'll go. I couldn't make a worse job of it than the priest. But I'll want a couple of you boys to keep a look out and make sure no one comes barging in.'

'Will do,' promised Porta.

Alte stayed three hours in the cell with the condemned boy. No one ever knew what he said to him, but certainly Heinz seemed more at peace with himself afterwards. Maybe he was just getting more accustomed to the idea of his own death, or maybe it was the Old Man's famous bedside manner, but all went well until the evening, and the visit of his parents.

They sat side by side, facing their son across a small table. On their right, standing by a pillar and doing his best to look like part of the stone work, was a prison warder. His presence was hardly noticeable, so well did he merge in with his forbidding surroundings. He listened, yet understood nothing.

Councillor Berner found it almost impossible to look his son in the eye. Frau Berner sat sobbing into her handkerchief.

'Heinz—' She stretched out a hand across the table. 'Heinz we must all try to be brave about this.'

The eyes of the stone warder flickered slightly as he followed the movement of the woman's hand: was she attempting to pass something to the prisoner?

'Heinz—' She whispered his name softly. 'Heinz, my poor boy—'

'You must speak loudly and clearly,' intoned the warder in mechanical tones.

'Father, is it true?' Heinz leaned over towards Herr Berner, his eyes burning with a last-minute hope. 'Are they really turning down the appeal?'

Slowly, his father nodded his head.

'It's true, Heinz ... As your mother says, we must all try to be brave. Remember one thing, my boy: some time, somewhere, we shall all be together again. Hang on to that. Never lose sight of it.'

'I'm so scared,' whimpered Heinz.

The councillor's lower lip trembled. He also was scared.

Heinz began suddenly to pour out a jumble of disconnected sentences, to which his parents listened in growing horror.

'The walk from the cell to the courtyard, that's the worst ... Julius is a shit, but give him a gun and he never misses – all be over before you know it ... It's not like cancer. You'd be scared of cancer ... or gas. It's a piece of pudding ... five past five tomorrow morning, I'll be better off, you'll see—'

'My God, his brain's gone,' thought the Councillor.

'Heinz,' said Frau Berner, gently, 'what are you talking about?'

Heinz looked at his mother with vacant bloodshot eyes.

'It's what they told me.'

'They? Who are they?'

'Friends of mine.'

'You mean – other prisoners?'

Heinz shook his head.

'No. The guards. Little John and the Old Man and all the rest of them.'

'They're your friends?'

'Yes.' A tear ran down the boy's face. 'And at dawn tomorrow they're going to shoot me.'

Frau Berner's face turned deathly pale. She swayed slightly, then quietly lost consciousness and slipped to the floor. Her husband, as he wrestled to get her back on the chair, wondered if the boy really were deranged. How could anyone call 'friends' those who were due to be his executioners?

The warder suddenly peeled himself away from the pillar.

'Time's up.'

Heinz and his father looked at each other. They stood up. The moment was impossible, there was nothing to be said. Heinz flung himself into Herr Berner's arms. For the first time in adult life, they embraced. The full horror of the final separation was upon them and it took two warders to pull them apart. The Councillor and his wife were flung into the corridor like sacks of flour. Heinz was led back to his cell. We collected him as soon as the coast was clear and smuggled him down to the guard room, where we filled him up with vodka and sent him back half doped to his cell.

Barcelona and I were on duty that night. The others went

down to the town and returned at midnight, filled to the ears with drink. Little John, as usual, was obstreperous and had a tendency to throw furniture about and stick his fist through window panes. Lt. Ohlsen came down from his quarters to tell him to shut up, but it turned out that he was not in much better case himself. He had evidently drunk almost as much as Little John, and it was left to Barcelona and me to deal with the situation.

Not far from the prison, in an inn called 'The Red Hussar', Herr Berner and his wife were spending the night. Neither of them slept, nor even attempted to do so. They sat side by side on the edge of the bed, staring ahead with vacant eyes, listening to the clock ticking away the last few hours of their son's life.

In his cell, Heinz Berner paced ceaselessly up and down, stopping now and again to bang his fists against the door and to let out a loud, echoing wail of despair, the cry of a drowning man in the middle of a deserted ocean.

They woke us at four – those of us who had slept. The Legionnaire was sent off to the arms depot. At four-thirty a major of the garrison came to check that we were all prepared for action. He paid the prisoner a last visit.

'Try to keep a grip on yourself. Remember your training as an officer. All men have to face death one day. As a soldier it's your duty to face it bravely, without flinching. Make sure you don't fail in that duty.'

With these words of encouragement he closed the cell door behind him, leaving Heinz Berner alone to await his fate.

Lt. Ohlsen appeared in the guard room looking haggard. His steel helmet was gleaming, his buttons and buckles flashed like diamonds, but the man himself had no sparkle. Alte approached him and saluted.

'All ready, sir.'

Lt. Ohlsen nodded, but said nothing. He turned and led the way along the corridor to Berner's cell. We all followed him. Heinz was waiting for us, lying on his bed and staring up at the ceiling. The Lieutenant laid a hand on his shoulder.

'It's time, Heinz. Try to have courage. We'll get it over as quickly as possible.'

Like a ghost, the boy sat up, swung his legs over the side of the bed, staggered to his feet.

'I have to tie your hands,' said Ohlsen, apologetically.

He held out a length of new white cord, and obediently, like a child having its gloves put on, Heinz placed his hands together and extended them towards us. His eyes were those of a man already dead. The Lieutenant looped the rope round his wrists, but before he could pull it tight the boy fainted. He fell so suddenly that it took us all by surprise. We stood stupidly, staring down at him, and I think every one of us had the same absurd hope in his mind:

'God, let it be a heart attack!'

Some men die easily, but Heinz Berner was not destined to be one of them. Lt. Ohlsen and Alte helped him to his feet. He recovered consciousness almost immediately. His mouth trembled. Suddenly he began to scream and shout, pleading with us, cursing us, begging us to spare him. There was nothing we could do. His control had snapped and not even Alte was able to get through to him. And what was there you could say to a boy of twenty about to face a firing squad? Particularly when you yourselves happened to be that firing squad.

We had to drag him bodily through the corridors and out to the courtyard. All the time he was crying and kicking. Porta's helmet was knocked off, Heide lost his rifle, I was punched in the ribs. For all of us, it was the final degradation of humanity.

From all sides we were assailed by loud cries of abuse. Men rattled their cell doors, whistled and shouted, stamped their feet, threw furniture about.

'Murderers!'

'Fascist swine!'

'Murderers!'

'Bloody murderers!'

Out in the courtyard it was a bright, crisp dawn. The air was sweet and fresh, the sky was clear. It was a day on which you were glad to be alive. I wondered whether it was easier to die on such a day, and I thought that for myself I should certainly prefer a brave show of weather for my send-off rather than the sad grey drizzle that had been Lindenberg's last view of the earth.

As we dragged him across the flagstones, Berner seemed to lose his last vestiges of sanity. His eyes rolled, foam specked his lips. It was a madman, now, who screamed and shouted. He was giving us a bad time, he was forcing us to live through a nightmare we should none of us be able to forget. But did one have the right to expect him to face such a death with any dignity?

With a desperate contortion of the body, our prisoner suddenly managed to slip his hands through the rope that bound them together. Before anyone could move, he had flung himself upon the Old Man, twining his arms and legs round him, clinging to him and screaming, screaming until I thought I should begin to join in.

'I don't want to die! I don't want to die! Help me, please help me, oh please help me!'

Lt. Ohlsen stood shocked and ashen-faced nearby. I had never seen him so visibly shaken. He was trembling, tears trickled unchecked down his face, he seemed in almost as bad a case as the prisoner himself. Alte was struggling with the boy, unable to detach him, unable to calm him. It needed four of us to prise him away, and in the middle of it all I suddenly vomited.

'You filthy bloody swine!' shouted Porta. 'Look what you've done to my bleeding boots!'

Little John, almost out of his senses, turned and clouted Porta on the side of the head. Porta promptly hit him back. It was a scene straight out of Bedlam.

On the far side of the courtyard appeared another firing party. Feldwebel Grün was in their midst, walking peaceably along between two guards, his roped hands held out before him. It was he who came to our rescue. He stopped in front of us and gravely regarded our prisoner.

'Don't be afraid,' he said. 'You're not the only one. We'll go out together in a blaze of glory, eh?'

I think it was surprise, more than anything else, that brought Berner to his senses. At any rate, he quietened down and for that we were all thankful.

We continued on our way across the courtyard. The Prison Chaplain now joined in the procession, walking behind us and solemnly asking the Lord to forgive us our trespasses.

The sun was up, filling the dim courtyard with a curious crimson light. Somewhere a blackbird was calling, and all about us were seagulls swooping and diving. It was a beautiful day to die.

Heide and the Legionnaire led Berner to the blood-spattered post, where so many other men had stood and waited for death. They attached the strap round his chest. Alte stepped forward.

'Shall I cover your eyes?'

'Just help me,' whispered Berner. 'Please help me. I don't want to die.'

Lt. Ohlsen bit his lip and turned away. I saw Little John put a hand up to his face. I stared past him and watched the seagulls, listened to their agonizing shrieks and wondered what they had come for, why they were not out at sea. When I looked back again, Alte had tied the scarf round the boy's eyes and stepped back into line.

Feldwebel Grün, attached to the second blood-spattered post, refused to be deprived of his last glimpse of the world. He stood upright and alert, watching the preparations for his own death.

'Please help me!' cried Berner.

It was the despairing cry of a child. A child who knew it was calling in vain, who had long since given up all hope, but who nevertheless went on trying, in the belief, perhaps, that people could not ignore it indefinitely. And now it was Lt. Ohlsen who cracked under the strain. He suddenly covered his mouth with his hand. made a curious choking sound and hurried back across the courtyard. We none of us blamed him. It would have been up to him to give the signal for firing. On the whole, we thought the more of him for being unable to do it.

His place was taken, after a few moments' delay, by a stranger, a lieutenant quite unknown to us, from one of the motorized regiments. His right sleeve was empty – we understood he had lost an arm at Stalingrad. He was not more than twenty-five at the very most, and his chest was ablaze with ribbons and stars. We hated him on sight. It seemed to us that he was intruding, that he had no right to be joining in the ritual slaughter. It was our pain, which we shared with the victim, and he could have no part in it.

The Lieutenant either forgot or deliberately neglected the traditional 'last cigarette'. Perhaps he was wise. It would have prolonged the agony by another ten minutes and could serve no useful purpose.

'First group, right turn!'

We executed the movement with automatic military precision. Alte surveyed us critically but could find no fault in the final result. We stood in a perfect straight line.

'Eyes front!'

Of their own accord, my eyes fixed themselves upon the spot that marked Heinz Berner's heart. I was ready to do my duty.

In a room of the 'Red Hussar' two other pairs of eyes were fixed upon the clock. One minute to five. One minute to go.

The Lieutenant looked steadily across to the clock on the prison tower. He missed the slight upward movement of Little John and Porta's rifles. Even had he seen them, he would have attributed it to an attack of nerves and unsteady hands. In any case, it scarcely mattered. There were ten other rifles trained on the target.

The clock struck five. The command rang out through the still air.

'Fire!'

Twelve shots merged together into one sound. A long cry gurgled into silence and blood. The body of Heinz Berner went limp.

That was the end of another execution, and all the seagulls flew back to sea.

It all ended up, of course, by our being moved from Torgau back into the front line. Porta and Little John were to blame; they and a condemned man who managed to escape.

During the course of the frenzied inquiry that followed, it was discovered that the prisoner had made use of tools which had undoubtedly been sent from the outside: a pair of scissors, a knife, the blade of a file. He had broken the lock on his cell door and made his way up to the roof. From the roof he had escaped over the outside wall with the help of a length of stout prison cord. It was only three days before he was due to be hanged.

Little John and Porta, who were on guard at the time – or supposed to be on guard – were immediately arrested and interrogated. They both remained obdurately stupid and at a complete loss to throw any light upon the incident. At the end of fourteen days the prisoner had still not been recaptured and the questioning was reluctantly abandoned.

We were all roundly abused by Colonel Vogel. An uncomfortable experience, even for war-hardened veterans like ourselves.

Before we were finally despatched from Torgau the Colonel came to bid us the customary farewell. He shook hands with only one person, and that was Little John. And Porta swore that as he turned away he was smiling.

CHAPTER TEN

TJESTNANOVNA. A small town near the Rumanian frontier and overlooking the Black Sea. Once it must have been full of people and traffic, the shops crowded out with goods for sale, the neat rows of whitewashed houses basking in the sunshine. Now it was deserted, abandoned by most of its former inhabitants, reduced virtually to rubble by repeated bombardments. At the start of the war it had been a railway junction, and the main road to Velkov had passed through the centre. Now it was a forgotten town; a place of no importance. Almost, it might never have existed.

We had occasion one day to go inside one of the empty houses, and we saw for ourselves with what frantic haste the occupants must have fled the town. Dirty cups and plates still lay in the sink; the kitchen table was still laid out as for a meal. Cupboard doors swung open, beds were unmade. In one room we found a single shoe, lying dismally by itself in the middle of the carpet. Half-way up the stairs we tripped over a yellow teddy bear. We stood staring at it for a while, each in his own way visualizing the scene of the family's departure.

'What a bloody war!' burst out Alte, suddenly. 'Can't even leave the bloody kids in peace!'

'Why should it?' said Little John, adopting cynicism as a way of covering his own emotions. 'What use was they to anyone? They can't fire a gun or drive a tank.'

With a contemptuous swing of the foot he sent the teddy bear flying up and over the banisters. It landed with a thump in the hall below.

'Who cares what happens to a bunch of lousy kids?'

It was the first time I had ever seen Alte lose control of himself. He swung round on Little John, his hand on the butt of his revolver.

'You shut your filthy mouth! I'm telling you now, if ever I catch you laying your hands on a child I'll kill you, so help me, I'll kill you!'

With this threat ringing in our ears, we watched the Old Man stamp down the stairs and go out through the front door. Little John turned to look at us, his eyes wide and puzzled.

'What's chewing him up, then?'

'I reckon you touched him on a soft spot,' muttered Porta.

'But he knows damn well I'd never lay a finger on a child!' roared Little John.

Porta shrugged, indifferently. We all of us had our moments of blind rage, or panic; the complete breakdown of self-control. It had happened to the rest of us, and now it had happened to Alte. Little John knew it as well as anyone, but nevertheless the incident had hurt.

'I'm the last person to hurt a kid ... YOU know that! How many times have I gone out of my way to save one of 'em? What about that kid at Lugansk? What about the transport at Majdanek? Who risked his life shooting at the guards, just so the little brats could make a break for it? And what,' he wound up, with relish, 'about that S.S. man I fed to the dogs?'

We all winced at the memory of the S.S. man.

'That was going too far,' objected Porta. 'I said so at the time, and I still say so now.'

That night in Poland was one we should never forget. In company with nine Polish partisans, we had come unexpectedly upon the transport – Jewish children, torn apart from their parents, dragged away from their homes, being taken God knew where for God knew what purpose. Little John had gone completely berserk, and one of the partisans, horrified by his behaviour, had made a futile attempt to calm him down. He informed us self-importantly that he was a Polish officer, and he pulled out a photograph of himself in uniform to prove the point. We informed him, without troubling ourselves with proof, that we were generals in the German Army. He almost certainly didn't believe it, but he hunched his shoulders and loped off into the woods, followed by six of his fellow partisans and those of the children who had managed to escape, and left us in peace to deal with the S.S. officer that Little John had shot. Two of the partisans remained behind. I'm not sure that it wasn't their idea to cut out the dead man's heart, but any rate they and Little John fell to with vigour while the rest of us stood watching, horrified and yet undeniably fascinated. When they had finished, they hanged the mutilated corpse by its ankles from the branch of a tree. Little John always claimed that the heart had been eaten by the local dogs, and possibly he was right.

In the deserted town of Tjestnanovna we found a deserted villa, and we took it over as our temporary barracks. It was splendid, perched high upon a hillside and looking out over the Black Sea. The first and second storeys were honeycombed with bedrooms, there must have been dozens of them, all done up in deep rose and pale blue, very frilly and feminine with deep looking-glasses whichever way you turned. We installed ourselves in the downstairs sitting-room, sprawling over the armchairs and sofas, our heavy army boots tramping across the fluffy rugs and leaving black marks on the pastel shades of the carpet.

'God bless Rumania!' shouted Little John, intoxicated by the faint, clinging odour of scents and lacy petticoats that filled the house. 'I shall spend the duration here!'

Porta swaggered across the room and flung open the french windows, which gave on to a terrace and overlooked the extraordinarily blue waters of the so-called Black Sea. Far beyond, in the distance, the war was still being waged; but for the moment it was none of our concern.

Later that same day, Little John, prowling about along the corridors of the first floor, came upon an enormous fat woman in the act of bundling clothes out of an airing cupboard. He was, on his own admittance, scared out of his wits, but he pulled himself together and bellowed to the rest of us to come to his aid. When we arrived, he and the woman were silently wrestling with each other. It was hard to judge which of them had the upper hand.

'What's going on here?' demanded Alte. 'Who is this? What does she want?'

Panting and blowing, the woman fetched Little John a sharp

kick on the shin. With a howl of rage, Little John closed his enormous hands round the woman's neck.

'Let her go!' ordered Alte, striding forward.

Reluctantly, Little John loosed his grip. The fat woman fell back into the airing cupboard, her multiplicity of bosoms heaving and trembling.

'Who are you?' repeated Alte. 'What do you want here?'

'I came to collect some things. I don't live here, but the house belongs to me. I need some more bed-linen ... my family has typhus.'

At the sound of the word, we all instinctively took a step backwards. The woman seized her opportunity. Muttering her apologies, she swept up a pile of sheets and blankets and waddled from the house. The Legionnaire followed her departure with thoughtful eyes.

'There's something odd about the walking lump of fat.'

'You reckon she's a whore?' asked Little John, eagerly.

'A whorekeeper, more like. I recognize the type ... Let's go take a closer look at her.'

The Legionnaire picked up his cap, armed himself with both revolver and knife, which he pushed down into his boot, and made for the door.

'Anyone coming with me?'

None of us was really very interested in the woman – only Little John, and wild horses wouldn't have dragged him out of the villa. During a solitary prowl about the town he had discovered a mass of provisions heaped up in the abandoned Kommandantur, and now his bedroom at the villa could have withstood a year's siege. Cigars were piled high on the bedside table. A whole regiment of bottles marched along the skirting boards, whisky, vodka, French cognac. He invited us inside to admire his handiwork, and, within reason, to help ourselves.

'What's this?' demanded Barcelona, picking up a large porcelain jug from the side of the bed.

'That's my pissing pot,' said Little John, jealously snatching it from him. 'Pink and blue flowers and golden cupids ... I think it's very suitable and I can empty it straight out of the window into the sea when it gets full.'

'Which it soon will,' murmured Barcelona, eyeing the array of bottles.

The Legionnaire soon arrived back, full of news and good humour. He installed himself in Little John's bedroom, sitting cross-legged on the bed with a bottle of cognac in one hand and a cigar in the other. He and Alte were the only two who liked cigars, but we were all determined to smoke at least one as a matter of principle. Heide had already been sick twice, but that was probably due to the bottle of vodka he had drunk rather than the cigars.

'Well?' we inquired, eagerly. 'What did you find out?'

The Legionnaire gave a triumphant laugh and poured half the cognac straight down his throat without flinching.

'Do you know what this place is?'

'No,' said Little John, sounding like a music hall comic. 'What is this place?'

'You'll be very pleased with me when you know,' said the Legionnaire, smugly.

'Come to the point!' urged Little John.

'Very well, then. To be brief – when business is normal, we have a red light burning outside our front door.' Those of us who were in the act of drinking nearly choked ourselves to an early death; those who were smoking turned blue in the face. Little John was simply too stunned to speak.

'You mean we're living in a brothel?' whispered Porta, hardly daring to believe the good news.

'Your actual brothel,' the Legionnaire assured him, with a slightly pitying smile.

The Legionnaire himself did not care overmuch for the delights of such places.

'But where are all the women?'

'The women!'

Little John suddenly gave a whoop of delight. Before our astonished eyes he did a quick striptease, retaining only his boots, his gun belt and his old bowler hat.

'I'm not going to need those a long, long time,' he announced, tossing his uniform trousers into a cupboard.

'What about your boots?' asked Alte, somewhat taken aback.

'Going without knickers is one thing. Walking about bare-footed is quite a different kettle of fish. Be prepared is my motto. Either way—' He waved a hand towards his apparel, or lack of it – 'I am now prepared for any eventuality.'

Porta, too, was busily preparing himself for coming events. His clothes followed Little John's into the cupboard and he pranced naked before us, yelling like a demon and stamping up and down with his boots on.

'Dressed up like a dog's dinner! Where are the whores? Where's the keeper of the brothel?'

'You've already met the lady,' said the Legionnaire, amused. 'She lives just down the road in a house that makes this place look like an air raid shelter. She herself is a stinking old sow who pours gallons of perfume over herself each day to cover the stench of her own sweat and save the trouble of washing. But I should say the establishment she used to run here would have been well worth a visit for those who like that sort of thing.'

Little John jerked his head.

'Would have? Whatdyamean, WOULD have?'

'That's your misfortune,' admitted the Legionnaire, with a sigh. 'According to the old sow, the girls all took fright when they thought Uncle Jo Stalin was coming ... They rushed off towards the west, and now, presumably, they're whoring some place where there's more demand for their services than here.'

Little John gave a loud shriek of despair and fell backwards on to the sofa.

'There isn't any place where there's more demand for their services than here!' declared Barcelona, wrathfully. 'I'm so randy I could have a go at anything!'

'What about the old sow?' wondered Porta. 'She'd be better than nothing—'

The Legionnaire shook his head.

'I don't advise it. I should say she's got one like a horse's collar ... once get lost inside it and you'd never find the way out.'

'The way in is all I care about at the moment!' snapped Porta.

'Suit yourself,' said the Legionnaire, hunching a shoulder.

'I shouldn't think she's got anything against the idea . . . She's called Olga,' he added, and he spoke the word with an air of the uttermost distaste.

'Olga,' said Little John, trying it out. 'I can't say I really fancy anyone called Olga—'

'I could fancy anything, from Olga to a milk bottle,' declared Barcelona. 'Why didn't you bring her with you, for God's sake?'

'Hang on a minute.' Porta turned solemnly to face us. 'You don't reckon the old bitch is trying to pull a fast one, do you?'

'How do you mean?'

'Well – telling us the girls have pissed off, simply because she doesn't like the look of us. We're not the smartest bunch of soldiers you ever saw.'

'I suppose it's a possibility. But where the blazes could she have hid them?'

'Wherever they are, I'll dig 'em out!' promised Little John. 'And if the old bird's been lying to us she'll live to regret it.'

'Don't do anything stupid,' begged Alte. 'A woman like that's bound to be well in with the police. You start bashing her about and you'll soon find yourselves in trouble.'

'Arsehole,' said Porta. He snatched up his trousers and threw himself into them. 'Come on! Let's go and knock her up.'

With the Legionnaire at our head, we swarmed down the road to Mme. Olga's. In his excitement and anxiety Little John had completely forgotten his lack of clothes. Nothing, now, would have prevented him from leaving the villa, abandoning his horde of cigars and alcohol, and marching off in pursuit of the elusive whores. He swung naked down the road, and we cheered him on.

'This is it.'

The Legionnaire turned in at the gate of a rambling snow-white villa, which seemed to float above the earth like a wedding cake resting on a cloud of flowers. Ignoring the notice on the front door, which requested one please to knock before entering, the Legionnaire led us boldly in. We marched six abreast across a vast entrance hall tiled in marble, straight through to a salon where Mme. Olga was seated at an elegant writing desk, her bosoms flowing across it like tidal waves. She turned apprehensively at the noise of our footsteps. We must have sounded like a whole army on the march in that great echoing hall.

'What do you want?' she said, and I could see the great beads of sweat breaking out like spots beneath her thick make-up.

'Momma mia!' breathed Porta, gazing awestruck upon the mounds of flesh, which seemed more plentiful than ever in these luxurious surroundings. 'That lot would feed a whole regiment for a month!'

Mme Olga was dressed in several layers of rouge, so you couldn't actually see her turn pale, but somehow you could feel it.

'I asked you,' she said, 'what it was you wanted?'

'The girls,' said Little John, tersely.

'Girls? What girls? If you mean my girls, then I'm afraid they're not here.'

She was plainly flustered. None of us believed a word she said.

'You wait till Ivan arrives,' said Little John, threateningly. 'He won't treat you nice and polite like this, you know. We're demanding, but he'll just go right ahead and take.'

'My dear young man, are you out of your senses? There's nothing here to BE taken—'

Little John advanced just one step towards her, his fist raised. Mme. Olga stumbled backwards and screamed.

'Any more lies out of you, you old shitbag—'

'Let her alone, Little John. I think she's ready to talk.'

The Legionnaire laid a restraining hand on Little John's arm, and Olga gave him a revolting smile, full of yellow teeth and ingratiating charm.

'Thank you so much, Obergefreiter. I feel that perhaps you and I—'

Mme. Olga broke off abruptly as there came the sound of doors slamming and more armies marching across the hall. She stood before us in a state of suspended horror. We turned to the door, ready to defend ourselves, but it was not necessary. The soldiers that burst into the room were Rumanians, and their interest lay not in us but in Olga. They made straight for her, shouting angrily, snatched her up and began tossing her back and forth amongst them. Up she went to the ceiling, her head crashing into the plaster; then down she fell to the floor, landing heavily on her vast behind in the fireplace. Her screams mingled harshly with the bellows of the Rumanians. Porta pulled out his flute and began dancing a jig on the edge of the scrum. Alte looked on, frowning, and the rest of us added to the pandemonium by giving a great cheer each time Olga hit the ceiling and letting out a concerted cry of 'Shame!' each time she hit the floor.

'That'll teach you a lesson, you old scrubber!' roared a Rumanian corporal, as they finally let her come to rest, in a flood of tears and a sea of black silk petticoats, in the middle of the carpet. 'I warned you we'd be back again!'

'What have you come for?' asked the Legionnaire, curiously.

'Same as you! What do you think?'

'I just wondered.'

'The Russians are on their way back. It's our duty to defend the place . . . but I'm buggered if I'll defend a brothel with no girls in it! Where are they, you disgusting old crab bag, you old whore, you old poxdrop?'

Once again, they turned on her. Little John had found a bearskin rug and was busily wrapping himself inside it. He hurled himself into the fray and began biting and snapping at the woman's ankles. Heide and Porta were quickly caught up in the mêlée. Pretty soon, Mme. Olga was being dragged about the house, upstairs and down, now by the hair, now by an arm, now by a leg. Little John cavorted wildly after the mob with the bearskin flapping round his waist. Furniture was overturned, china was broken, the rumpus could have been heard for miles around, and probably was, by the advancing Russians. When at last they tired of their fun and threw the unfortunate woman out of sight beneath a grand piano it seemed to me that she was more than likely dead. Not that I felt any pity for her, she was not the sort of woman who deserves pity; nevertheless, it did seem a trifle barbaric.

Little John had unearthed a huge barrel of beer from somewhere in the kitchen regions. He and a Rumanian private rolled it into the salon between them, cleared a table of its valuable collection of cut-glass vases by simply sweeping them to the floor, hoisted the barrel into position and turned on the tap.

'Just testing,' explained Little John, as a stream of liquid spurted out and spread in a brown stain over the carpet.

We drank it, out of flower vases and fruit bowls, but it was pronounced feeble stuff after the array of spirits in Little John's bedroom.

'Try a touch of this!' shouted one of the Rumanians, coming in to the room with his arms full of bottles.

Red and white wine, vodka, cognac and gin were poured into the beer and the whole mixture thoroughly shaken up. In the midst of our merrymaking, Mme. Olga foolishly recovered consciousness and came crawling out from the grand piano. Instantly, the pack turned on her again. A Rumanian sergeant fell down by her side on all fours and began to bark like a dog. Someone else gathered up a fistful of feathers from a burst cushion and tried to stuff them up her nose, only as fast as he pushed them up there she sneezed them out again. Heide emptied a vase of beer down the front of her dress and Little John sat on her legs in his bearskin rug and alternately growled and hiccuped.

'Where are the girls?' demanded the Rumanian sergeant, suddenly abandoning his role of the barking dog. 'Where are they, you rotten old knockerbag?'

Mme. Olga shook her battered bloodstained head.

'Have pity on me,' she whimpered. 'The girls aren't here. They're on their way to Sabina.'

'Sabina? What have they gone to Sabina for?'

'Because they were scared of you.'

The Rumanians exchanged glances amongst each other, evidently not sure whether to believe her. Porta had no such hesitation. He went charging across the room and stood menacingly astride her body, which still lay crumpled on the floor.

'Enough of your lies, old woman! Where have you hidden them?'

Mme. Olga began to weep. All her rolls of fat began rippling and heaving.

'They've gone to Constanza—'

184

'Oh? Constanza now, is it? I thought you said Sabina?'

'No, no. Constanza. They were ordered to go there. They had no choice.'

'Lying old bitch!' roared Porta, bringing his foot down within centimetres of her face. 'You'd better get them back here, and quickly!'

Little John pulled off his bearskin and began beating Mme. Olga about the shoulders with it. The Rumanians muttered mutinously. Heide snatched up the Legionnaire's knife and held it threateningly to the woman's throat.

'Listen, you miserable old bag, either you tell us where those girls are hidden or I'm going to cut your bleeding throat from ear to ear ... Now WHERE ARE THEY?'

If it had not been for the arrival of the two trucks, which chose that precise moment to draw up in one of the flower beds outside, it is likely that Heide would have carried out his threat. However, the sound of squeaking brakes and banging doors arested him, and he hurled himself after the rest of us, through the hall to the front door.

'I'm going mad!' shrieked Porta. He seized me round the waist and danced me about the hall. 'Can you see what I see? I'm going mad!'

'I can see it too!' I panted, trying to shake him off.

Little John was obviously yet another who could see the vision.

'It's the whores!' he shouted, at the very top of his voice. 'Two truckloads of 'em!'

The Rumanian sergeant waved his hand above his head and yelled something in his own language. With cries of delight, his men went charging after him, streaming down the path towards the trucks. Little John and Porta at once dashed after them, Little John having slight trouble with his bearskin. Alte sat down next to the Legionnaire on the window seat and began calmly to roll a cigarette.

'God keep the Russians from coming tonight,' he muttered. 'We'll fight them if we're drunk, we'll fight them if we're sober ... But who the hell's going to fight 'em if we're whoring?'

The Legionnaire hunched a shoulder.

'Who the hell cares?' he said. 'I shouldn't worry too much about it.'

From outside in the garden came the mingled sounds of shrieking girls and cursing Rumanians. Little John was galloping about on the outskirts of the crush, trying without success to lasso someone with his bearskin. It was Porta who led the mob inside. We watched in astonishment as the double doors burst open and Porta pranced through with his flute, like the Pied Piper of Hamelin. Only instead of children, it was whores. Dozen upon dozen of them. Some of them were fully clothed; others – whether by their own choice or because it had been forced upon them – were clad only in bra and pants. Little John had abandoned his bearskin as an unnecessary encumbrance and Porta seemed to have shed his trousers somewhere out amongst the flower beds. Barcelona performed a striptease act on the spot, which, for sheer speed, beat anything I've ever seen. Heide sent his pants flying through the open window, where they were caught by the wind and draped over the top of a flagpole. For a few seconds they billowed bravely in the breeze, cheek by jowl with the German flag, then slowly fluttered earthwards. A short while later they were discovered by a hungry pig, roaming the grounds in search of food. It devoured them completely, with every sign of enjoyment, but Heide was long since past the stage where one was concerned over a pair of pants.

Barcelona was sharing the sofa with two girls and a Rumanian soldier. They seemed to be one intermingled mass of arms and legs, not yet sorted out into two distinct couples. Someone yelled from upstairs that Steiner had fallen into a bath full of water. He was brought down to the scenes of merriment in the salon, soaking wet and half drowned, but he recovered quickly when half a bottle of vodka was placed in his hand, and seconds later he grimly set off in pursuit of a Greek girl. They both jumped out of the window, and that was the last we saw of Steiner for some time.

Mme. Olga had crawled into a corner and was sitting trembling on the edge of a chair. The Legionnaire went laughing up to her, full of happiness and goodwill.

'It really is so kind of you, Madame, to allow us the free run of your house in this manner. A perfect setting for revelry.'

He belched, quickly put a hand to his mouth and peered at her over the top of it.

'I do beg your pardon, Madame.'

Mme. Olga gave him a gracious smile.

'You, at least, are a gentleman, sir. A Frenchman, I don't doubt?'

'That is so, Madame. I am a corporal of the Foreign Legion ... caporal à la Légion étrangère. A votre service, Mme.'

'Get a load of that!' Little John dug Porta in the ribs and jerked his head towards the Legionnaire. 'This here is a very posh establishment what we're in—'

Porta showed no interest. He was too busy wrestling with a recalcitrant Jugoslav whore. Little John shrugged his shoulders, tightened the belt round his naked body and set off in pursuit of a toothsome blonde dressed in salmon coloured pants with green lace round the edges and a bright red suspender belt. She crashed headlong into a Rumanian corporal entering the room with a tray of glasses. The glasses and their contents flew into the air. The blonde fell giggling to the ground and Little John fell on top of her. The Rumanian swore vigorously.

One of the girls – Annie of Hanover, she said her name was – sidled up to me and I hooked an arm round her neck.

'I don't know who you boys are,' she murmured, 'but it certainly makes a change!'

'Think yourselves lucky the Russians didn't get here first,' I said.

Porta spun past with his Jugoslav. They did a full turn of the room and by the time they swam back into my field of vision the Jugoslav seemed not quite so recalcitrant as before. Porta was holding on to her, none too delicately, by the breasts. She showed no particular signs of disliking such treatment.

'Hi, Sven!' He dragged her to a halt in front of a group made up of Alte, myself, and Annie of Hanover. 'You still feel like writing your memoirs when the war's over? You'd never get anyone to believe this lot!' He turned to his girl and puffed out his chest. 'You want to hear some of the things we've done?' He checked them off on his fingers. 'We been across the Volga – we've swum in the Med. – we slid across the ice in the Bay of

Bothnia. We been everywhere and we done everything ...
Once we got so drunk it took weeks to get over the hangover ...
We can jump out of planes on the end of a parachute, we can
blow up bridges, we can drive tanks, we can drive trains, we can
rob and kill and spy and forge documents. You name it, we
done it ... I had a bath in champagne one time. What do you
think of that?'

'Not very much,' said Alte. 'Was I supposed to?'

'Piss off!' said Porta. 'I wasn't talking to you.'

He turned and yanked his girl towards the piano, where a
disgraced and demoted Rumanian lieutenant was playing the
music of his homeland. He played slowly and dreamily, no
doubt visualizing himself back in pre-war days, wearing his
lieutenant's uniform, in an elegant salon full of brother officers
and their ladies. His music conjured up the sound of horses'
hooves on gravel paths, the creak of leather and the jingle of
bits; the blowing of trumpets and bugles; a platoon of beautiful
blue Hussars galloping towards a lake ... Instead, the poor
man sat disillusioned in a wrecked salon, surrounded by tough
lower ranks whose thoughts were full of drink and sex.

Sadly, the ex-lieutenant began to sing. A lilting, mournful
song of love. Little John staggered up to the piano and emptied
a vase full of God knows what inside it.

'Hey, you!' He leaned forward and twisted his lips into a
horrible leer, his face only inches from the Rumanian's. 'You're
one of us, now, mate. You was a lieutenant, but not any more.
You're just one of us – and we don't give a monkey's cuss for
that trash you're playing. Give us something we can understand, can't you?'

The Lieutenant smiled, gentle and rather mocking.

'Something you can understand? I take it you mean breasts
and buttocks and that sort of thing?'

'That's more like it,' agreed Little John, eagerly.

The Lieutenant shook his head. Barcelona lurched up to him.
He was hideously drunk.

'My dear Lieutenant – my dear, very dear, Lieutenant – I
require you to shing – I require you to shing – a shong – about
death.'

He propped himself up against Little John and himself

played a few uncertain chords on the piano, then commenced to sing his song in a wailing tenor.

'The cannons are chanting their very last psalm,

Come, sweet death,

Take me in thy palm.'

He then threw back his head and gave a long, rattling, raucous laugh. For a moment he rolled an eye at the silvered sea, shot through with the ray of the sinking sun. A frown creased his forehead.

'Did you hear that?'

There was a brief silence in the room. In the distance, we heard the echoing rumbles of heavy gun fire.

'They're knocking at the door,' said Barcelona, solemnly. 'Boom-boom, let me in . . . And what do we care? I'll tell you: we don't give a tuppeny damn for any of 'em! Tomorrow we die! And in the meantime, I say fornicate and be merry!'

Barcelona collapsed in a heap on the floor. Little John calmly stepped across him, dunked his head in a large flower bowl full of beer and vodka, and drank deeply like a horse. He turned and spat in the direction of Mme. Olga, and when she had the effrontery to protest he grabbed a portrait of Adolf Hitler from the wall and brought it down over her head. It sat like a ruff round her shoulders.

'That,' declared Little John, 'is the right place for obscene paintings. Didn't you know there's a law against keeping pornography in the house?'

'She'll go to hell with the Führer and all the rest of the trash,' said Porta, dispassionately pouring half a bottle of cognac over the miserable woman's head.

'Wouldn't you like to come upstairs with me?' asked Mme. Olga, in honeyed tones. 'We could be private up there—'

'Who wants to be private with you, you fat old bag? You watch your tongue when you're talking to me.' Porta drew himself up straight. 'I, madam, am the backbone of this army, I'll have you know.'

He stalked away, leaving Mme. Olga sitting on the floor with Hitler round her neck.

'I can't stand the sight of you any more,' said Little John. 'There's too much light in this damn room.'

He reached up easily and yanked the bulb from its socket. With a howl of triumph he hurled it through the windows and on to the terrace. For a moment there was panic. Someone shouted that the Russians had come. The girls began screaming and running about in circles, one of the Rumanians pulled out his revolver and for no very good reason fired eight rounds into the floorboards. Little John roared with insane laughter. The Lieutenant played the piano, Barcelona lay on the floor singing about death. In the middle of the uproar, Mme. Olga discovered that her bearskin was missing. She wrenched Hitler from her neck, stumbled to her feet and began beating Little John on the chest with both fists.

'Where's my rug? My bearskin rug? What have you done with it, you thief? That rug was given to me by a Chinese soldier!'

'AND now it's being used for wiping the arse of a German soldier!' yelled Little John, hitting her hard on her fat backside. 'Shut up, you old cow, before I lock you away in a cupboard.'

Mme. Olga fell back, gnawing at her lips. She was indeed an old cow, but doubtless her predicament deserved some sympathy. She lived in fear of the girls becoming intoxicated and opening their mouths too wide. Mme. Olga had her guilty secrets, the same as any of us. And she can scarcely have failed to notice the black ribbon we wore on our left sleeves – the black ribbon with the two death's heads and the inscription 'Sonderabteilung'; the regiment of death. A regiment made up of ex-prisoners, thieves, assassins, revolutionaries, offenders against the state; desperate men, who had been offered the front line or the firing squad and had chosen the front line as being their only chance, albeit a slender one. We none of us cared overmuch for the conventions. Why should we, after the events we had lived through and the sights we had seen? We were amongst the best soldiers anywhere in the world, but we were an undisciplined mob: a band of ruffians who struck fear into the heart of the enemy and anyone else we came across.

Olga stood trembling, staring up at Little John. Was it possible that Little John was only a man as other men? Could one believe that the ugly grinning monster had ever had a family, a mother and a father? That he felt the same emotions as other human beings? Four times already this evening he had threatened to strangle her: if he ever found out her secret he would almost certainly carry out his threat. He could strangle an elephant with those vast hairy hands. Olga decided upon a policy of conciliation. She smiled sweetly, and Heide, passing by, stopped and looked again.

'Oh, how very charming!' he said.

Mme. Olga at once turned the smile upon him. Heide jerked at Little John's elbow.

'Wonder what the old bag would look like stark bollock naked? Let's get her clothes off and have a gander.'

A small, dark girl, sitting on top of a cupboard where Little John had parked her earlier on, overheard Heide's words.

'Wrap her in the bearskin, I should,' she advised. 'She's a hideous sight without her clothes on.'

Olga looked up at the girl and her lips twisted. Dear Nelly. Dear little Nelly from Belgium. She had been a fool to keep that one on. She should have been disposed of months ago. Olga flashed the girl a sickly smile.

'Don't shout like that, dear. No one's very interested in what you have to say.'

'You think not?' shrieked the girl. 'I wouldn't count on that!'

She sprang off the cupboard, ran up to Little John and whispered in his ear. Little John roared with delighted laughter.

'Is that so? Come on, old woman, get your knickers off! I've often wanted to see a bum like yours . . . Roll up, roll up! The fattest bum in the world is about to be put on display!'

The cry was taken up generally. People flocked from all four corners of the room to see the wonderful sight of Mme. Olga's naked bottom. Mme. Olga, forgetting her policy of conciliation, fought like a wild cat. You wouldn't have thought a fat old bag like that would have had so much spirit. She made a fair match for Little John. The Lieutenant played a series of excited chords on the piano and the crowd stood round alternately cheering and jeering. Quite suddenly, Mme. Olga flew into the air and came down on our heads. Someone gave a roar of rage, seized hold of her and threw her bodily through the crowd. She went across the room like a rocket, knocking over

Julius Heide, two of the girls and three chairs as she went. She finally fetched up against the piano, next to Barcelona, who smiled drunkenly at her. The Lieutenant, without a moment's hesitation, swung into a waltz.

The crowd gradually dispersed about its individual business. Little John and Annie of Hanover squatted on their haunches playing dice with a couple of the Rumanians. Annie was wearing a sailor's collar round her neck in place of a bra. For some time the Professor had been eyeing her rather nervously from the far side of the room. At last he plucked up courage and formally approached her, his pale face turning purple with the effort.

'Excuse me, I know I'm being rather forward, but would you care – would you like – that is, would you – I wondered if you—'

Little John glanced up at him.

'If you want her, take her. If you don't, fuck off.'

Annie swallowed half a glass of vodka and laughed in the Professor's face.

'Well?' she said.

The Professor turned and ran. We didn't see him again for several hours.

I sat in an armchair, a drunken and quiescent girl on my lap, surveying the scene and feeling pleasantly pissed. I watched Barcelona stagger across to the windows and vomit on to the terrace. I watched Porta touching up his Jugoslav. I noticed the little Belgian girl, Nelly, install herself on the couch between Alte and the Legionnaire. She seemed to have gone there not for sex but for conversation. Both men were listening intently to what she was saying, and the Legionnaire in particular showed a great interest. His eyes had narrowed and they were glittering in a manner that always bade ill for someone. Alte had lit up his pipe and was puffing furiously at it. I glanced across the room and saw Mme. Olga watching the trio with an air of disquiet. Evidently Nelly was being indiscreet – with the Legionnaire, of all people. He was a dangerous man to cross, and if she had succeeded in gaining his attention she must indeed have an interesting tale to tell, for the Legionnaire didn't care for women and he tended, as a rule, to ignore them.

Mme. Olga moved silently towards the door, but before she could reach it Porta had placed himself in front of her, blocking the way.

'Dear Madam Olga, you're surely not leaving us?'

He seized her by the arm and dragged her with him into the centre of the room. Little John gave a great cheer and a round of applause burst out from somewhere nearby.

'Ladies and gentlemen, gather round and see the greatest show on earth! Watch the fattest old sow in the world take off all her clothes! Keep your eyes skinned while she shows you the colour of her knickers!'

'Hooray!' shrieked Heide, standing very drunk behind him.

Mme. Olga cowered away, but her hour had come. The crowd was closing in again, laughing and clapping.

'Skirt!' cried Little John.

He tore it off her and sent it flying through the window to join Heide's pants on the flagpost.

'Titty holders!'

An enormous brassière flapped after the skirt.

'Gut squeezer!' yelled Heide, joyfully wrenching off the woman's corset and playing upon it as if it were a concertina. 'Genuine iron and steel gut squeezer!'

'Go on, take the whole lot off her and give the old devil what for!' shouted Nelly, from the sofa.

'Have patience,' murmured the Legionnaire, who was watching the scene with cold, unmoved eyes. 'Let them have their fun first. She'll get what's coming to her, don't you worry.'

At last the quivering bulk of Mme. Olga was revealed in its entirety, naked as a worm, fat as a maggot. The crowd drew in its breath, whether in horror or in admiration it was difficult to say. For myself, I was both impressed and repelled at the same time.

'Holy cow,' breathed Little John, clasping his hands together and holding his head at an angle. 'What a sight!'

'Where's the bearskin?' cried Porta, from his ringside seat.

The cry was taken up.

'Where's the bearskin? Get the bearskin!'

Within seconds we were surging about the room in search of

193

it. Tables and chairs were overturned. What remained of the glassware was joyfully smashed. Cushions were ripped open, curtains were pulled down. One of the Rumanians came staggering in with a dustbin, which was promptly tipped upside down in the middle of the carpet.

'Where's the bearskin?'

'Find the bearskin!'

'Find the bearskin!' echoed Barcelona, crawling on hands and knees about the floor.

Suddenly, three shots rang out. Everyone jumped round in the direction from which they had come. It was Porta. Crouched behind an overturned armchair, firing his rifle at the top of a cupboard.

'It's up there!' he told us.

Little John dragged Barcelona across the room by the scruff of his neck, climbed on to his back and peered over the top of the cupboard.

'It's that damned bear! I'll make sure of it this time!'

He pulled out his knife and made several wild slashes in the air. Mme. Olga screamed. The bearskin suddenly slid over the edge of the cupboard and fell over Barcelona's head, blinding him completely. He began to crawl in circles, yelling for someone to save him from the bear.

When at last a semblance of order had been re-established, when Mme. Olga was wrapped sullenly inside her ruined bearskin and Barcelona had been propped against the mantelpiece, the Legionnaire went into action. With his cap pushed to the back of his head, a cigarette stuck to his lower lip, he slouched arrogantly across the room to Mme. Olga.

'Something we ought to talk about, you and me.'

She looked up at him, her eyes wide and terrified. Behind the Legionnaire stood Alte and the girl Nelly. Mme. Olga would evidently have served herself a better turn had she fled the town with the rest of the inhabitants and left the girls behind to fend for themselves. Greed had kept her on. First there was the Rumanian Army, then the German Army; almost certainly there would very soon be the Russian Army. Business had promised to be good. Unfortunately for her, it had proved a little too good.

'Olga,' said the Legionnaire, softly, 'how do you get on with the Gestapo?'

'Gestapo?' babbled Olga. 'What do I know about the Gestapo? I don't know anything about them. I've never had anything to do with them.'

'Really?' murmured the Legionnaire. He fingered his knife, thoughtfully. 'You see this, Olga? You see this knife? I had it with me all the time I was with the Legion.' He laughed, as if at some private remembrance. 'I've lost count of the number of people I've had cause to use it on.'

Olga made one last, defiant stand. She stood up straight, lost her bearskin but attempted a show of dignity.

'Why tell me?' she said. 'It's no concern of mine how many people you've killed.'

'It might be, soon,' suggested the Legionnaire. 'When you're the next one on the list.'

'Stop talking and get on with it!' urged Nelly. 'She deserves all that's coming to her.'

'And more!' cried another girl.

She pushed her way through the gathering crowd and turned to face us.

'You know how she got to be the owner of this place? The Gestapo put her in here! And this isn't the only one, either. She's got places in Bucharest and Sarajevo, as well.'

'And how do you think we got here?' demanded Nelly. 'You think we're just whores, born and bred? Well, we're not. We were dragged here by the Gestapo. We weren't give any choice in the matter.'

'Not unless we were Jews,' added the other girl, bitterly. 'If we were Jews we were allowed to choose between a brothel or the gas chamber.'

'And that fat cow standing there was put here to keep an eye on us. Make sure we didn't talk.'

Accusations began to pour in from all quarters.

'Only last month she sent five of the girls to Ravensbrück because one of them complained to an officer who came here—'

'What about Desa? She strangled Desa with her own hands—'

'She's hand in glove with the Gestapo. She had Haupt-strumfuhrer Nehri to dinner here every night for a month—'

With a sudden howl of rage Porta flung himself at Mme. Olga's throat. The Rumanian lieutenant began a furious crescendo of sound on the piano. Somehow, Mme. Olga managed to break free from Porta's grip. She ducked under his arm, evaded the howling mob of girls with desperate agility, gave a wide berth to the Legionnaire, who was watching the scene with a sardonic smile, and went running naked towards Alte. He was the oldest of us; also the sanest and the most humane. He was probably the one person in the room who might have mercy on her, and Olga had immediately sensed it. She threw herself at his feet, babbling and pleading incoherently. So long as Alte was prepared to listen to her, the rest of us stayed our hand. The Old Man stood gravely looking down at her. He brought out his pipe, filled it, lit it, slowly shook his head; then turned and left the room. It looked as if Mme. Olga's fate was sealed.

We closed round her in a threatening circle, men and girls together. It was a strange sight. Most of us were half naked, yet still clutching revolvers. The Legionnaire was the only one who had kept his clothes on, and perhaps for that reason he looked stranger than any of us.

'Kill her!' shrieked Nelly. 'Kill her like she killed Desa!'

'And Margaret Rose! She had her shot by the Gestapo!'

Once again, the accusations came pouring in. Yvonne and Ilse had been sent to a concentration camp. They had died on the barbed wire, trying to escape. Mme. Olga had several times threatened the other girls with the same fate. Then there was Silva. Silva had told a visiting lieutenant how she had come to be in the brothel, and for that she had been whipped to a pulp and left in the cellars to rot.

'She took all our money off us. Every penny we had.'

'She used to strip us naked every day and examine us.'

'She used—'

The Legionnaire held up a hand.

'O.K. I think we've heard enough now. But we've got to do

the thing properly – hold a court of inquiry, weigh the evidence, decide on a fitting sentence.'

He picked up a broken chair and set it with a bang in the centre of the circle.

'That's for Yvonne,' he said. 'And that's for Ilse – and that's for Desa – and Margaret Rose and Silva. And this one—'

'That's for Lone!' cried one of the girls. 'She was hanged at Tichilesti.'

'Right.' The Legionnaire set up another chair. 'That's for Lone, who was hanged at Tichilesti.'

Porta held out a chair.

'Here you are. This one's Gerda. She was shot out in the garden there for throwing a bottle at the old hag.'

'And don't forget Monica—'

'And Sonia—'

'O.K. That'll be enough.' The Legionnaire waved a hand towards the chairs. 'The nine members of our jury. In theory there should be twelve, but—'

Before he could finish speaking another flood of names had poured in. Alice, Cecilia, Gola—

'Fair enough,' said the Legionnaire. 'That makes up the twelve. Twelve chairs, twelve dead girls. Now then—' He beckoned to Nelly – 'you're to be the judge. I'm the prosecuting counsel. No need for a defence, she hasn't got a leg to stand on.'

'I want to be a judge, too,' announced Little John.

The Legionnaire hunched a shoulder.

'Just as you wish. Come on, Sorka, you can be the third one.'

He beckoned to Porta's Jugoslav, who took her place beside Nelly and Little John with a hard smile on her lips. She had passed through nine state brothels in her time, and she plainly had no pity left for anyone.

'Take this.' Little John handed her his revolver. 'You can use it as a hammer if people start kicking up too much of a racket. We'll need a bit of peace and quiet to deal with this case.'

'O.K.' Sorka thumped on the floor with the butt of the revolver. 'Silence in court! Bring the prisoner in!'

Olga was helped forward with the sharp end of Porta's bayonet in one of her naked buttocks.

'You've no right to judge me. I haven't done anything. The Government makes the laws, not me. I just do what I'm told. I'm no more to blame than anyone else.'

'Shut up!' said the Legionnaire. 'The jury will tell you whether or not you're to blame.'

'Well, of course she is!' burst out Little John, who was drinking vodka in court.

'What are you accusing her of?' asked Nelly.

The Legionnaire turned to face the twelve empty chairs.

'Ladies of the jury, in the name of the people I accuse Olga Geiss of the following: murder; slavery; torture; and treason.'

Little John looked severely towards the prisoner.

'Did you hear that? What have you got to say for yourself? Guilty or not guilty?'

'Not guilty,' said Olga, faintly.

Sorka banged with her revolver.

'The accused can sit down. What is the jury's verdict?'

Again, the Legionnaire turned towards the row of chairs.

'Ladies of the jury, do you find the accused Olga Geiss guilty or not guilty of the aforesaid crimes?'

He listened a moment, then turned back to the three judges.

'The jury return a verdict of guilty.'

'Of course she's guilty!' said Little John, for the second time. 'All we've got to do is pass sentence. For myself I think she ought to suffer death by slow hanging ... with a lighted candle stuck up her backside.'

Olga gave a loud scream and threw herself to the ground. At the same moment, a harsh voice addressed us from the far side of the room, from the double doors that led into the main hall.

'What's going on in here?'

We had been so engrossed in our court of inquiry that none of us had heard the sound of footsteps on the marble tiles. Three men of the local police force were standing in the doorway. It was an Oberfeldwebel who had spoken. As we turned in a body to face them, he suddenly opened fire into the crowd. There was a scream; then Annie of Hanover, her eyes wide with astonishment, slid slowly to the ground and the blood began gushing from her mouth.

'Save me!' shrieked Olga, from the back of the crowd. 'They're going to torture me!'

'Quiet,' said the Oberfeldwebel. 'Leave this to us. We know what we're doing.'

He took a step forward. As he did so, there was a flash of steel past his right shoulder then the Legionnaire's knife embedded itself in one of his companions. The Oberfeldwebel spun round. The wounded man stared up at him with disbelieving eyes, the knife lodged in his chest, then very slowly he slithered to the ground and lay still. He ended up by the side of Barcelona, who had been incapably drunk for the past half hour, and his right hand fell across Barcelona's face. There was a thud as his revolver rolled out of his grasp. Barcelona, acting on nothing more than a drunken instinct, at once picked it up and levelled it – more or less – at our friends across the room. He plainly had no idea who they were, much less what he was doing or why he was doing it, but in that second Heide had thrown himself upon the Oberfeldwebel and brought him crashing earthwards. Calmly, the Legionnaire retrieved his knife and wiped it clean on the front of his battledress. The Rumanian lieutenant wandered back to his piano and began playing what sounded like a death march.

'Before continuing with the inquest,' said the Legionnaire, 'I think it might be better if we closed the doors. Sven, would you mind?'

By the time I arrived back, it seemed that the inquest was already over. Mme. Olga, her smile of triumph wiped off her face, was weeping and wringing her hands together.

'In the name of the people,' intoned Sorka, pitilessly, 'you, Olga Geiss, are to suffer death by hanging. One of the judges has demanded that you should also suffer torture and your body be thrown to the dogs.'

'That was me,' explained Little John, as if we couldn't have guessed. 'It's the least she deserves.'

'Very likely,' agreed the Legionnaire. He turned to Mme. Olga. 'Did you hear that, old woman? Have you anything to say before the sentence is carried out?'

Whether she had or not, she was given no chance. Porta tore down some velvet curtains and ripped off the heavy cord which operated them. Little John snatched up a discarded pair of stockings and tied a gag round the victim's mouth. One of the Rumanians bound her hands together with a red silk brassière. Mme. Olga did not give in without a fight. She wriggled and twisted, bit, kicked and elbowed, but the girls closed in upon her and it was a miracle she was not torn to death before we got her to the gallows.

One end of the curtain cord was attached high up on the flagstaff. The other was formed into a loop with a slip knot. Still heaving and kicking, the mountainous body was then carried by many willing hands up to a window on the top floor. The loop was placed round Mme. Olga's neck.

'Jump,' ordered Little John.

Mme. Olga balanced precariously on the edge of the window sill, all her fat white flesh quivering and threatening to unbalance her.

'Jump!' roared Little John, for the second time.

She jumped at last; or fell; or was pushed. Her body wrapped itself round the flagpole, hanging at the end of the cord. Her double chins seemed to swell up like so many balloons, and then her neck stretched out very long and thin.

A silence fell in the upstairs room. Some of us turned away. Some of us leaned out of the window and stared with globulous eyes, hypnotized by the horror of that fat white body swaying to and fro at the end of the cord.

'The bitch,' said Nelly. 'She got off lightly if you ask me.'

Silently we returned downstairs, pushing the two policemen before us. The Rumanian lieutenant was still gently playing his death march. Barcelona had vomited on the floor and seemed slightly less drunk than he had been.

'O.K.' The Legionnaire turned to the Oberfeldwebel and his companion. 'Which of you two killed the girl?'

We stared down at Annie of Hanover, lying on the floor in a pool of her own blood. The Oberfeldwebel turned crimson.

'I – I suppose I must have done. My – finger – that is, I pulled the trigger by mistake. I never meant to hit anyone.'

'I'm sure you didn't,' agreed the Legionnaire, soothingly. 'Nevertheless, you're a damn sight too dangerous to leave lying around. Anyone could come across you – and get shot by mistake.' He jerked his head at Heide. 'Take him outside and get rid of him.'

'Willingly!' said Heide, his eyes gleaming.

They disappeared. We heard their footsteps echoing across the marble hall, we heard the front door open and close. Then there was silence, and we all stood listening. The Lieutenant let his fingers rest quietly on the piano keys. The girls stood watching from the windows. There was a tense air of expectancy in the room, and even Little John and Porta were silent. And then came the sound we were waiting for: the chatter and rattle of a machine gun, followed by a single shot from a P.38.

'That's it,' said Porta.

The Legionnaire picked up a bottle of cognac and solemnly raised it to his lips.

'Let's get on with the celebrations,' he suggested.

No one was averse to the idea.

CHAPTER ELEVEN

THE merrymaking and drinking went on. We had almost forgotten the war that was still being fought somewhere to the north-west, and it came as an unpleasant shock when the first of the retreating armies began to make their appearance. It seemed that the Russians were breaking through everywhere, that the entire front line had collapsed, that our troops were in a state of panic and disorder. So much we learned from those who could spare the time to stop and enlighten us on their maddened flight away from the front and towards the passes of Kunduk. There were men from all regiments, rushing pell-mell from the scenes of battle. Gunners, engineers, members of the tank corps, all intent on putting as much distance as possible between themselves and the swiftly advancing Russians. Someone yelled that the enemy had broken through at every available spot and were only half a mile from the village. Someone else passed on the information that over the river several divisions of our troops had been cut off by the Russians. It appeared that everyone who could was running, even those who had been brought up as reserves, fresh and eager to fight, only days before.

We ourselves were now attached to the Third Rumanian Army, and orders came through that we were to stand firm and hold our position. All of us, the Rumanians and ourselves, even the girls, saw the folly of the situation: a whole army, eight divisions of fighting men, was in flight, and we, a small group of mixed nationalities, were expected to hold out against the enemy. We looked out of the window at the retreating hordes and we had a bloody good laugh. There was nothing much else we could do.

How had the mass panic begun in the first place? In a sadly familiar fashion. It appeared that initially a small number of

T.34s, to restore the morale of the flagging Russian troops, had been sent ahead in the hope of breaking through the German front lines. These were taken by surprise and the tanks had crashed through with comparative ease, firing to right and to left and leaving behind them a state of hysteria and confusion. Some fool had lost his head and sent an urgent message to the effect that they were surrounded, that the Russians were forging ahead and retreat was the only answer. The cry was taken up, parrot fashion, and was soon echoing through the ranks. The panic had begun. One thought only was uppermost in men's minds: get the hell out of it before the tanks had completely encircled them and they were trapped.

The news that filtered through grew ever more alarming. The small number of T.34s became, in the fevered imagination of the fleeing soldiers, a whole battalion, an entire regiment, several divisions. A captain solemnly assured us that the entire Russian Fifth Army had broken through and was on its way towards us – a piece of information we knew for a certainty to be false, since the majority of the armoured divisions were licking their wounds on the other side of Kertz. It was this same captain, however, who gave orders for all secret documents to be burnt and for all vehicles – except one, which he appropriated for his own use – to be destroyed to keep them from falling into the hands of the advancing Fifth Army.

Some years later, this same captain wrote an account of the strategic withdrawal from Tabar Bunary. The account is now one of the standard textbooks on the subject and is in current use in military training schools. The captain was decorated for his brilliant handling of the withdrawal and has since been elevated to the rank of colonel.

The T.34s that had caused the fiasco could hardly have believed their luck. They stuck nose to tail along the main road, driving scores of half-demented soldiers westwards before them. Those few who tried to keep their wits about them and hang on to their military sang-froid were soon submerged in the general sea of panic. One elderly major general, going under for the third time, gallantly fought his way back to the surface and found himself at the tail-end of the retreat amongst the sick and the wounded. The major screamed and shouted and threatened, but the main body of the army swept boldly past him and out of sight. He remained with the stragglers, tears of shame and humiliation pouring down his cheeks. Unfortunately, tears alone were not enough to stop the advance of the Russian tanks, which slowly crept up on the rearguard. Salvoes of shots from the heavy guns ploughed up the road before, behind and on either side of them. The major could have run. Instead, he wrenched off his stiff collar and the shining cross at his throat, snatched up a handful of grenades and made a dash with them towards the nearest of the approaching tanks. He was only a few yards away when he tripped and fell. The grenades rolled harmlessly into a ditch at the side of the road. For a moment the major hesitated. He lay in the road where he had fallen and the leading T34 was almost upon him. In reaching up in search of a handhold the major came into contact with one of the exhaust pipes, from which the flames were leaping. His hand was burnt to a cinder before his brain had a chance to react. The edge of his cape was caught by one of the caterpillars and the major's body was swiftly wound up and crushed against the wheels. They heard his cry inside the tank A lieutenant glanced out of the slit and laughed as he saw an arm sticking up in a parody of a salute. The Major's body was swiftly sliced to ribbons. The little that remained was mashed to a pulp by the other oncoming tanks, and soon all that could be seen was a trail of blood and a hovering swarm of flies.

It was three months later, in Germany, that the Major's widow heard of her husband's death: he had fallen in battle, when leading his troops in an attack on heavily fortified Russian positions. No one ever fell during a retreat. There were no such things as retreats in the German Army.

At Kita, on the other side of the frontier, a court martial was being held in the town hall. No one had yet thought to inform them of the situation in the outside world, and meanwhile they were having the time of their lives: they had as many deserters on their hands as any court martial could have wished, and they were condemning them to death right and left without batting an eyelid. At the very moment when the line of T.34s was entering the eastern gate of Kita, the court martial were condemning out of hand a young private who had thrown down his arms in the face of the enemy. The presiding colonel was in his element. He knew his law down to the last letter; to the last comma, the last semi-colon. He lost himself in a sea of verbosity, the long legal sentences ebbing and flowing about the court. Inevitably, the outcome was death. It was the Colonel's dearest hope and belief that on the signing of his two-hundredth death sentence he would be promoted to general and recalled to Berlin, there to serve on the Judicial Council of the Reich. At present he was only on his one hundredth and thirty-seventh, but a few more days like today and he would soon fulfil his quota. And with any luck he would reach the two hundred mark without ever having witnessed an execution. The Colonel abhorred violence. For him, his one hundred and thirty-seven victims were not human beings so much as material for the judicial machine, passed to him for preparation, passed on afterwards for processing. If he thought about them at all, it was only to reflect that war demands its sacrifices if the final victory is to be gained.

He drew himself up and regarded his latest victim, the young private who was about to be condemned to death as an example to others. A military policeman tapped the boy on the shoulder.

'Come on, lad. Time we were leaving. It's all up with you now.'

The boy had listened impassively to the Colonel's final summing up. He had made no move when the sentence of death had been passed. But the simple words, 'It's all up with you now', seemed suddenly to strike through to his heart. He turned to the court and flung out his arms wide, screaming and protesting. The M.P. dropped his paternal air and gave the boy a sharp clip round the ear. Next moment he was heaving him bodily out of the courtroom with a knee in the small of his back.

As the doors swung open, the sudden sounds of a bombardment were heard. A second before there had been silence; now the air was full of noise, the thudding of heavy guns, the whine of bullets, the explosions of shells and the staccato chattering of machine guns. The courtroom stood shuddering a moment, then a fine plaster dust rained down from the ceiling.

'What the devil's going on?' demanded the Colonel, brushing the sleeve of his immaculate pearl grey uniform.

One of the judges, a Captain Laub of the Seventh Motorized Regiment, left his chair and walked across to the window. He glanced out, casually, then turned back with his face ashen.

'It's the Russians!'

'Hell's bells, the Russians are nowhere near here! Get a grip on yourself, man! Are you attempting to spread false rumours?'

'No, sir.' The Captain stiffened. 'Perhaps you'd care to take a look for yourself?'

Before the Colonel could reach the windows, Major Blank, the prosecutor, had joined Captain Laub and confirmed the news.

'I'm afraid he's right, sir. It is the Russians.'

'How the hell did they get this far?'

'God knows, but they did.'

The M.P. had automatically released his hold on the prisoner. They stood close together, as if for protection, covered in the fine powder that was still gently raining down on them. Quite suddenly, the condemned soldier turned and ran. He crashed through the deserted corridors of the building and out into the street, straight into the arms of a leather-jacketed, fur-capped giant who was on his way up the steps into the town hall. The giant grabbed hold of the soldier and shouted out in Russian. The soldier, too petrified to speak, twisted out of his grasp and promptly received two bullets through his skull. At that short range, they blew off most of his head.

'See,' Dr. Goebbels would have said, 'even those whom we have condemned to death are still willing to stand up and fight for the Reich!'

But Dr. Goebbels himself could not have said what became of that particular soldier. The body lay for a short while on the steps of the town hall, until a Russian tank commander, taking the corpse to be a live soldier feigning death and probably only waiting his chance to throw a couple of hand grenades into the oncoming troops, hurled an explosive and blew off the arms and the legs. What remained was crushed to a pulp beneath enemy tanks. The pulp was no doubt discovered and disposed of by some starving dog or cat, of which there were many roaming the streets, and that was the last of Private Wulff. For a long time he was posted as missing, treated as a deserter. His relatives and friends in Germany were subjected to long hours of intensive questioning; his mother was arrested on a charge of harbouring her son. No one ever knew the truth.

The fur-capped giant shouted out an order and half a dozen brown-clad Siberians rushed up the steps and into the town hall. The Colonel looked up from his desk and regarded them with an air of grave surprise. Captain Laub pulled out his revolver, but before he could use it he had received a shower of machine gun bullets in his stomach. He sank slowly to the floor, his eyes full of puzzlement. The Colonel turned in protest to the Russian corporal who seemed to be in charge of the raiding party.

'I object to this brutality! Calm yourself, for heaven's sake, and act like a trained soldier!'

Corporal Balama spat on the floor and raised his machine gun. The Colonel stepped back a pace.

'We offer no resistance. Fighting is obviously useless. As far as we are concerned, our destinies are in your hands ... Put down that gun, man!'

The other soldiers laughed.

'Stoi!'

The Corporal turned round and for good measure gave the M.P., still crouched in a corner, a hard jab in the belly with the butt of his gun. The man let out a shriek, more of fear than of pain, scuttled across the floor and fell babbling at the Colonel's feet, seizing him round the knees. The Colonel kicked out, but was unable to extricate himself. A smell of unwashed humanity rose up, rank and rancid, and almost suffocated him. It was one of the worst moments of the entire war.

'Dawaï, dawaï!' commanded the Corporal.

Again, his soldiers fell about laughing. They began repeating it, 'Dawaï, dawaï!' and herding the members of the court martial together in one corner of the room. The artillery feldwebel who had acted as chief witness against one of the accused received a bayonet in the back of the neck. The clerk of the court left behind three children and a widow, but the widow had two lovers to keep her occupied and for her, at any rate, her husband's death was probably a happy release.

A Russian commissar came into the hall and let loose a new string of orders. He sounded curt and evil-tempered. The survivors of court martial number 4/6 306 were at once marched outside and crowded together in the back of a T.34, which had run out of ammunition and was returning to base with a cargo of prisoners.

Little John and Barcelona Blum, who were hiding behind a ridge of trees, heard the approaching tank when it was still some way off. The driver was pushing ahead at a speed which hardly seemed warranted, in the circumstances, but he was an old hand at the game and his instinct no doubt warned him of hidden danger. The Commissar, too, seemed ill at ease. He cursed incessantly and for no apparent reason, and he directed a stream of abuse at the driver whenever the motor coughed or spluttered.

Little John stretched out on his stomach, his chin supported on his hands, moodily watching the T.34 as it toiled up the road towards them.

'That cretin down there's asking for trouble,' he observed. He turned to Barcelona. 'You feeling like a bit of fun and games? Cover me while I go down and have a bash at it.'

'Let 'em pass,' said Barcelona, carelessly.

'What d'you mean, let 'em pass?' Little John sounded indignant. 'We're supposed to be guarding the whorehouse, ain't we? Keeping out the Ruskies? And you say sit up here on your great fat arse and watch a sitting duck go by without lifting a little finger to—'

'Belt up, for Chrissakes, you give me a headache ... What the blazes can one solitary tank do? It can't leave the road on account of there's marshes on either side. If they make one little move in that direction they've had it, and you know it as well as I do.'

'So? We're still letting 'em get off scot free, ain't we?'

'Don't be so bleeding thick! Where d'you think they're going to get to, coming along here? It doesn't lead anywhere, except to the sea, so sooner or later they'll have to come back this way.

And when they do, we'll have laid out a nice little bed of mines to greet 'em.'

'I reckon the silly buggers must've lost their way or something . . .'

Little John turned back to the road and watched the tank go past. He suddenly sat up and pointed.

'Hey, look at that! It's full of our own chaps—'

'Wounded heroes going back to Moscow, more like.'

'Take a bet?'

At that moment, the motor cut out. The tank lumbered to an ungraceful halt. There were several vain attempts to start her up again, then the sound of angry voices reached the two hidden watchers. Little John grinned. He picked up his M.G. and rammed it against his shoulder, pushed his hat to the back of his head and took aim.

'Don't be such a bleeding idiot!' snapped Barcelona. 'We're not here for that. The Old Man didn't tell us to sit up here and take pot shots at people.'

'Get stuffed,' said Little John, equably.

The first to die was the Commissar. In his fury he had leapt out of the tank and was threatening the driver from the road.

'You know what you'll get for this, don't you? This is an outrage, it's a flagrant breach of—'

What? Discipline? The driver never knew, and probably never cared. There was a crack, and the Commissar suddenly folded up in mid-sentence and fell neatly to the ground.

'What's going on?' yelled a voice from inside the tank.

Silence. No sound but the wind rustling through the tree tops, the branches sighing and creaking. No indication at all where the sniper was hidden. And then the frogs in the marshes began an anxious croaking, as if making a comment on the event that had just taken place, and this was a signal for the prisoners cowering in the back of the tank to lift up their heads and begin whispering amongst themselves.

'What was it? One of ours?'

'Search me.'

'Must have been one of ours.'

'I suppose so.'

'Who else would be firing on us?'

'Dunno.'

'Where'd it come from, then?'

No one answered, because no one knew. The dead Commissar lay in the road where he had fallen, his arms flung out before him, his head turned sideways in a pool of blood. The blanketing silence returned. The gunner suddenly jumped out of the turret and ran round to the front of the tank, anxiously scanning the road on either side. He was followed, reluctantly and nervously, by his two companions, huddled together for greater safety.

Up in the thicket of trees, Little John laughed silently to himself. Once more he took aim. Once more his finger curled itself round the trigger.

'Look, give it a rest, will you?' Barcelona jabbed angrily at him. 'We're not here to play games, we've got other things to do that are more important.'

'What's more important than killing off the enemy?' demanded Little John. 'It ain't every day of the week you find people damn fool enough to get out of a T.34 and go waltzing about in the middle of the road ... Now let me alone before I get really mad.'

The shots rapped out, one after another, in quick and accurate succession. The frogs stopped croaking and leaped silently away into the heart of the marshlands. One of the German prisoners suddenly stood up and began waving his arms in the air.

'Tovaritch! Tovaritch! I am your friend – do not shoot!'

Little John stared down at him in amazement.

'Look at that turd down there—'

'What an exhibition!' Barcelona spat disgustedly. 'Look at 'em, cuddling up together like a flock of bleeding sheep ... It's a wonder Ivan didn't shoot 'em outright. I would, in his place. What'd they want with a bunch like that in Moscow?'

'What'll we do with 'em?'

'Dunno ... Take 'em back with us, I suppose.'

Barcelona raised himself on one knee and waved down to the German prisoners. Slowly and apprehensively they began climbing down from the tank and making their way up towards the thicket, follow-my-leader along a narrow path of twigs and brushwood that had been laid across the marshes. They found themselves met by a couple of common soldiers, both filthy dirty and unpleasant to look upon.

'What the devil—' began the Colonel, as Barcelona unceremoniously seized him by the arm and dragged him under cover.

'Not so loud!' hissed Barcelona, rather irritably. 'We're at war, in case you didn't know it. You want your head shot off?'

The Colonel drew himself up straight.

'I must advise you—'

'Put a sock in it!' snarled Little John, placing a vast grimy paw over the Colonel's mouth.

At that moment a salvo of shots was fired from somewhere behind them.

'What's that?' demanded Major Blank, slipping into the marshy ground in his sudden haste to reach cover. 'Who's firing on us?'

'Who do you think?' said Barcelona, watching with a sneer as the immaculate Major paddled on to dry land with mud right up to his crutch.

'The Russians? Where are they?'

Barcelona jerked his head indifferently.

'Somewhere over there ... I suggest we get going while there's still time. Just follow me and keep your mouths buttoned up.'

'May I ask—'

'No.' Little John prodded the Colonel in the behind with the butt of his M.G. 'Get going and keep your mouth buttoned up like he said. First man who talks gets a round of this straight through his belly.'

They carried on, through the thicket, across another area of marshland, into the shelter of a thickly wooded hillside. Barcelona called a halt and conferred with Little John.

'What d'you reckon? Do we press right on or lie up here until it gets dark?'

Little John scowled.

'We didn't have all this trouble on the way out. Ivan left us pretty well alone then It's only because we've carted this load of shit along with us—'

'We'll lie up for a bit.'

'Suits me.'

Little John threw his M.G. to the ground and himself after it. Barcelona waved a hand towards his small band of followers, who were huddled together in the middle of a clearing.

'O.K., you lot, you can take it easy. We're going to rest up here for a while.'

The Colonel scraped his throat. He made another effort to assert his authority.

'I consider it would be better policy to push ahead without any delay.'

'Certainly. Why not?'

Barcelona dropped down beside Little John, pulled out a battered tin of tobacco and began rolling a couple of cigarettes.

'I'm not stopping you. Go right ahead.'

Major Blank drew in a sharp breath. He waited for the Colonel to say something, to do something. The two common soldiers, seated side by side on the damp ground at the foot of a tree, stared insolently up, their eyes gleaming out of unshaven faces encrusted with the dirt of several days. A new salvo of shots made the ground shake beneath their feet. The Colonel flung himself down on to the wet earth and covered his head.

'No need to carry on like that,' said Barcelona, kindly. 'You'll get used to it. They don't mean any harm, they're just letting us know that they're here.'

'Well, I don't like it!' snapped Major Blank, helping the Colonel to his feet. 'I grant you,' he said, as a face saver, 'that you are more aware of local conditions than I am, but it seems to me pure folly to hang about here in range of their guns—'

'Look,' said Barcelona, with the air of one trying to speak reasonably to a retarded child, 'if you want to get yourself killed, you just go walking off for another ten metres or so and you'll find it dead easy. Dead being the operative word . . . There's a ridge of high ground over that way. It's littered with the bodies of men who thought they could go over the top in daylight and get away with it. The only chance of getting back to the whorehouse in one piece is to wait a couple of hours until it's dusk.'

The Major opened his mouth, then closed it again. It was the Colonel who finally asked the question.

'Back to the – back to where, did you say?'

'The whorehouse.'

'You mean – your base?'

'That's right.'

'Why do you – why is it—'

The Colonel waved a hand, and Little John came kindly to his rescue.

'It's your actual pukka brothel,' he informed the outraged officer. 'Tarts and all. We're just as anxious to get there as you are, but the way I see it there's no point in risking your neck. Not even for a whore. We're safe in here. Out there—' He jerked a thumb behind him – 'the fighting's still going on. Get your head blown off in a couple of shakes. Just not worth it.'

Barcelona handed him a cigarette. The two common soldiers leaned back against their tree trunk in a cloud of evil-smelling smoke. The Colonel shuddered and withdrew some distance.

'Filthy swine,' he muttered.

For about half an hour there was comparative peace in the little wood. And then, somewhere to the south-west, the conductor raised his bâton and the full orchestra came crashing in with the opening bars of war. The little wood trembled and shook as the sounds reverberated through the hills and lifted high across the marshes. And this time Little John and Barcelona were the first to fling themselves headlong to the ground. This was no ordinary skirmish. It sounded as if the entire front were exploding. The immaculate Major grovelled in the mud, digging and shovelling with his hands as if trying to tunnel his way in to safety. The Colonel was lifted bodily in to the air by the first blast. He came to rest on top of Little John, and he lay clutching him for the remainder of the bombardment, not noticing the undeniable stench of unwashed feet and armpits that clung to Little John like a second skin. Little John, on the other hand, twitched his nostrils at the faint perfume that came from the Colonel's well-groomed head of white hair. He raised his head, about to remark on the smell, but his eyes met the Colonel's, and they were the faded blue eyes of an old man, an old man terrified half out of his wits, and for once in his life Little John found the strength to remain silent.

The hills and marshes were blazing infernos for miles around. Men, horses, vehicles, heavy guns spouted like geysers high into air, propelled by the force of the explosions. An entire infantry battalion was wiped out in less than ten minutes. An ammunition dump went upwards in a roaring mass of flames and smoke. The sky was bright red with a thousand fires and filled with a whirling mass of shrapnel.

They saw none of this in the wood. They lay flat on their stomachs with their faces pressed hard into the ground, covered in mud from head to foot. Barcelona was the first to rise.

'So much for bloody Goebbels and his tales about Ivan being out of the bloody war,' he remarked, sourly.

Little John pushed the Colonel away from him, sat up and spat out a mouthful of mud and leaves. He looked about him at the members of the court martial still on all fours. Two of them were dead. The other three lay trembling.

'Good dogs!' he shouted, encouragingly. 'Seek him out, seek him out!'

Major Blank raised a cautious head.

'Come on, you bleeding heroes!' roared Barcelona, prodding the nearest body. 'The war's still on!'

The Major rose with tattered dignity to his feet. He removed a wet leaf from the end of his nose, smoothed the lapels of his sodden uniform. He fixed Barcelona with an icy eye.

'As soon as we reach your unit I shall speak to your C.O. about you.'

Barcelona hunched a careless shoulder.

'If you think he'll really be interested.'

'I shall make sure that he's interested.' The Major shot out a quivering finger and pointed it dramatically at Barcelona and Little John. 'I'm having you both put on a charge the minute we get back! I'll have you court martialled, I'll have you up before the firing squad!'

'Just as you like,' said Barcelona, smoothly.

Major Blank turned apoplectic purple. He reached for his

gun and remembered, too late, that the Russians had taken it from him. Barcelona and Little John exchanged pitying glances.

'Shall we get going?' suggested Little John.

They left the wood and crossed once more over the marshland. The path of branches and twigs was narrower than the other had been and it swayed and rolled beneath their feet like a skiff in the midst of high seas. Little John went at the head, Barcelona brought up the rear. Both had their eyes and ears open, their guns at the ready, prepared to shoot at anything that moved.

The Colonel was too old for such games. He had grown used to a life of ease and plenty and the hardships of war were to him an unknown quantity. He slithered and slipped on the moving pathway, resorting now and again to travelling on creaking all fours. His thatch of silvery hair was plastered in black mud. His high collar flapped loose over one shoulder, his riding breeches were torn the length of the leg. Sweating with the unaccustomed exertion, panting with fright, the Colonel hobbled along in a nightmare. He thought of soft mattresses and silk sheets, of fragrant scents and silver rose bowls; he saw nothing but stinking marshland, mud-covered soldiers and unnaturally red skies full of the noise of death.

Half-way across the marsh, the Colonel lost his footing and fell heavily into the sucking black ooze of the bog, which lay in wait like a live thing greedy for victims. The entire party came to a halt.

'What's up?' said Little John, looking round.

'What have we stopped for?' demanded Barcelona, peering impatiently up the line.

They saw the old man struggling in the mud, and they stood impassively watching as Major Blank knelt at the edge of the path and held out arms that were not quite long enough towards the Colonel. The M.P. pulled off his jacket and flung it across the marsh. The Colonel caught hold of the sleeve. They pulled, without success.

'If I were you,' advised Little John, calmly lighting a cigarette, 'I wouldn't thrash about quite so much. You'll go down slower that way.'

216

He and Barcelona stood side by side and stared dispassionately.

'Five minutes?' suggested Little John.

'About that. Could be a bit longer if he stops jumping about.'

Major Blank looked round at them.

'Come and give me a hand . . . That's an order.'

Little John grinned. Neither he nor Barcelona moved. They knew the Colonel's reputation. They knew about the one hundred and thirty-seven victims. They stood their ground.

Slowly, Major Blank rose to his feet. He cast about for a large branch, found one, armed himself with it and approached grimly down the path towards the two common soldiers. Little John raised his gun. The Major ignored the warning. A second later the gun cracked and the Major threw up both arms and joined his colonel in the bog. The M.P., with a wild yell, began zig-zagging away from them down the narrow path. Barcelona coldly took aim and pulled the trigger. The last surviving member of the court martial had gone.

'That,' observed Barcelona, with an air of deep satisfaction, 'was a good day's work. A bloody good day's work. It gives me more pleasure to get rid of three scum like that than any number of Russians.'

Little John was already at work on the victims' mouths with the pliers he always carried with him.

'How about that?'

He dropped three gold teeth into his bag of booty.

'That makes six altogether. Not bad, eh?' He fished one out and fitted it into a gap in his own mouth. 'Reckon it'd fit me?'

Barcelona shook his head.

'Asking for trouble if you do that. You forgotten Porta's making a collection of 'em, too?'

'He's a fellow collector, not a rival,' said Little John, indignantly.

Barcelona gave a sarcastic laugh.

'I wouldn't be too sure of that! Sooner you take the risk than me, anyhow.'

They continued on their way, alert for the least sign of

danger. Dusk had come and gone by the time they arrived back at base, and the sky was pitch black apart from one persistent rosy glow away to the south-west. With the help of vodka and hot sausages they made their report. Alte listened gravely to their story.

'There's no doubt about it,' he said, when they came to an end, 'we're surrounded ... Cut off. Julius and Sven report heavy troop movement behind us, you report Russian tanks and infantry in front of us.' He turned to Porta. 'How about the beach? Any signs of life down there?'

'Plenty. The place is lousy with snipers.'

'Mm.'

Alte drew deeply on his pipe. He placed the thumb and index finger of his left hand high on the bridge of his nose and gently kneaded the skin up and down.

'Now how the hell are we going to get out of this mess?'

'Get out?' screamed one of the girls, who was dressed up in bright green pants and bra and playing at dice with a Rumanian corporal. 'Why do you want to get out? Are the Russians coming?'

The Old Man ignored her. He spread out a map and beckoned to the Legionnaire to join him.

'What do you reckon?'

The Legionnaire pored over the map for a while, and after much studying and much frowning he stabbed a finger on to it and traced the path of a long green line that wavered across the page.

'Here. We might just be able to get through that way.'

'Marshland,' commented Alte.

'It's all bloody marshland round here.'

'Marshland and dense forest ... Sixty kilometres of it.'

'It's either that or stay here and be shot. I can't see any other way out.'

'True enough.'

'Hey!' shouted Little John, suddenly surfacing from his bottle of vodka. 'Let's have a tune ... Where's the pianist gone?'

'Yeah, fetch the pianist!' agreed Barcelona, waving a half

eaten sausage in the air. 'Why don't we have some music?'

'Because the pianist is bleeding dead, that's why not,' said Heide, in his usual pleasant way.

'Dead? How?'

'Shot himself through the head, didn't he?'

Little John leaped to his feet.

'Where's the body?'

'Sit down and save yourself the bother,' said Porta, pushing Little John back again. 'I've already been there.'

He held up one gleaming gold tooth. Little John made a jealous dive for it, but at that moment Alte came to a decision.

'Get ready to leave immediately. Ivan could arrive at any second. I'd just as soon take my chance out in the open as be butchered indoors . . . Heide, have a scout round and see if you can pick up enough revolvers to give the girls one each.'

'Right-oh.'

The girl in the green pants turned round and screamed again. 'Revolvers? I couldn't! I don't know how to use them!'

'You'll soon learn,' said Alte, dryly.

We were out of the house within fifteen minutes and making for the marshes, with Little John and Porta at the head of the column. We moved at a pretty good speed and were under cover of the trees before we heard the first sounds of a bombardment.

'That's Ivan,' said Porta. 'Looks like we just got out in time.'

'Let's not stop to gloat,' suggested Alte. 'Just keep going.'

We moved in single file through the trees. We must have been a curious sight. There was Little John at the head – well, Little John was a curiosity in himself – followed by two of the girls wearing an odd mixture of female civilian and male military garments and holding revolvers at a decidedly awkward angle, followed by Porta, followed by four Rumanians, whose khaki uniforms could easily have been taken for Russian, followed by a gaggle of girls followed by the rest of us. At one point we had to cross a bridge guarded by three Russians. We dealt with them easily: I think they were too stunned by the sight of us to fire immediately, and by then it was too late, we were upon them. Three of the girls at once appropriated the Russian greatcoats and peacocked over the bridge in them.

'Bleeding women,' muttered the Legionnaire. 'If we get caught with them dressed up like that we'll be shot as spies before you can so much as blink.'

'Probably be shot anyway,' I said, morosely.

When the Russian tanks entered the little Rumanian village that we had so hastily vacated, the first sight to meet their eyes was the body of Olga hanging from the flagstaff, with the large notice containing the one word, TRAITOR, slung round her neck. For almost twenty minutes the Russians directed their shells at the deserted villa, and then came to the conclusion that perhaps there was no one at home. There was a long discussion on the possible identity of the hanged woman, and the conclusion was reached that she must have been a partisan, a heroine, killed by a band of fascist pigs. Her body – or what was left of it after the intensive shelling of the villa – was first of all photographed hanging from the flagstaff then cut down and buried with full military honours.

Her grave may be seen today. On the headstone are the words:

'Here lies Olga Geiss. She fell in the cause of liberty.'

It must have been round about the same time as the funeral was taking place that Porta and Little John, crouching side by side on the ground to fulfil the requirements of nature, had a rather basic discussion on life and death and things in general.

'Hitler,' remarked Little John, regarding a photograph on the page he was busy ripping from a newspaper.

Porta grunted. After a bit, he also ripped out a page.

'Hm . . . I've got Stalin,' he commented.

There was a moment of silence.

'Not bad quality, this newspaper.' Porta stood up and adjusted his trousers. 'Quite soft and smooth. Almost as good as a real bog roll.'

They folded up the rest of the pages and put them in their pockets for future use. Together they strolled back on to the road.

'I wonder?' said Little John, thoughtfully. 'D'you reckon it could be called high treason to wipe your bum with a picture of Adolf?'

Porta took his time, weighed the question in the balance, sifted the pros and the cons.

'Probably,' he agreed, after much deliberation.

Little John nodded.

'I thought so . . . Pity it was only a picture.'